About the

Richard now lives in Milford, CT, where he writes fiction full-time. He worked for DEC, the minicomputer company, as writer and Internet Evangelist. He graduated from Yale, with a major in English, went to Yale grad school in Comparative Literature, and earned an MA in Comparative Literature from the U. of Mass. at Amherst. At Yale, he had creative writing courses with Robert Penn Warren and Joseph Heller.

His published works include: *Parallel Lives* (published by All Things That Matter Press), *The Name of Hero* (historical novel), *Ethiopia Through Russian Eyes* (translation from Russian), *The Lizard of Oz* (satiric fantasy), and pioneering books about Internet business. His web site is seltzerbooks.com

Made in the USA
Monee, IL
02 August 2020

Beyond the Fourth Door

Richard Seltzer

Beyond the Fourth Door

ISBN 13: 9781734685558
Library of Congress Control Number: 2020943318

Cover Photos: victor-freitas-B0zAPSrEcFw-unsplash and mr-xerty-c61jSfa3ong-unsplash.

Cover design © by All Things That Matter Press
Published in 2020 by All Things That Matter Press

To my wife Barbara (1950-2012)

Acknowledgments

This book had several lives. It began more than fifty years ago as *Restless*, a story fragment that wanted to become a novel. Later it grew to *Say Uncle* and still later to *Sandcastles*, incorporating short movie scripts that I had never filmed as well as a couple of short stories, but it had no ending. The old drafts and notes gathered dust for nearly forty years, then suddenly the characters came alive and started talking to me in my sleep and told me the new beginning, told me to throw away the second half and gave me a new ending, with a new concept of what may lie beyond death or instead of death.

I want to thank:

Robert Penn Warren who commented on *Restless* fifty years ago

Ed Trobec and Rex Sexton who knew it as *Say Uncle*.

My Uncle Paul who saw it as *Sandcastles*.

Jean Otis Freeman and my grandparents Leona Daly Seltzer and Warren Ray Seltzer who provided inspiration.

Rochelle Cohen, Rex's widow, who provided frequent helpful feedback and encouragement on the final version.

Gabi Coatsworth for her monthly Writers' Rendezvous meetup sessions and advice, which led me to find my terrific publisher, All Things That Matter Press.

My son Bob for his continuing support.

Epigraphs

"I was immediately overcome by that sense of the world's strangeness which visits children as intensely as if they were accustomed to be somewhere else ... "
"I wished one could live slowly as one can play music slowly ... "
"'If we were to be given life,' stammered Rosamund,' we should have been given it forever.'"
> The Real Night by Rebecca West

Part One ~ Where Did the Years Go?

1 ~ Rude Awakening

May 2018, Boston, Massachusetts

Frank wakes up in a hospital room. He has no idea why he's there.

A young man in green scrubs asks, "What's your name, sir?

"*Sir*? Why do you call me *sir*? Nobody has ever called me *sir*.""

"Force of habit, sir. Now can you please tell me your name? I need to make sure you're matched with the right records."

"Uhland. Frank Uhland."

"Very good, sir. Thank you."

"And why am I here? What happened?"

"You had a routine colonoscopy, sir. The doctor can go over the details with you. I need to check a few facts. You're seventy, right?"

"No. I'm in the class of '71, not '70."

"No, sir. I mean your age."

"What? I'm a sophomore at Yale. I can't afford to miss class. I have papers due. What do I have to do to sign myself out of here?"

"You seem confused, sir. That's natural after anesthesia."

"For God's sake, you don't think I know how old I am?"

"Just look in the mirror, sir. Behind you on the wall. That will help you get oriented and back to your old self."

Frank turns to look. "Are you kidding?" he exclaims. "Is this some kind of joke? Is that a trick mirror? That's an old man over there. That isn't me."

"You're seventy years old, sir. It says so right here on your records and on the photocopy of your driver's license."

"That's impossible. Nobody wakes up fifty years older than when they went to sleep."

"That's you in the mirror, sir. What you see in the mirror is the same as what I see looking straight at you."

"What year is this?"

"2018."

"Good God! Who stole my life?"

"I'm sorry, sir. Nothing unusual has happened to you. It was a routine procedure."

"Tell me—who is my next of kin? You must have that on your records."

"Paul Uhland and Brenda Grossman, your son and daughter."

He slaps himself, then slaps himself again. Nothing changes. He is still in a hospital bed, still wearing a johnny. This guy in green scrubs is still standing beside the bed.

The orderly continues, "Brenda is in the waiting room. She can come in now or you can go out to her when you feel up to it."

He stands quickly, feeling light-headed. He grabs hold of the bed railing to steady himself and then asks, "How do I get to the waiting room?"

"I'll show you, sir. Come with me."

In the hallway, as they pass an open office door, Frank spots an old woman sitting at her desk and staring back at him, wide-eyed, as if in shock. She has red and green hair, but she looks familiar. He might have seen her when entering the hospital. He could never forget someone with hair like that.

A dozen people are sitting in the waiting room. He doesn't recognize any of them. Then a woman, about forty, closes the book she's been reading, stands, and walks toward him. Her face is expressionless.

"Let's get you dressed and out of here," she says to him. "I have to pick up the kids at school."

"Are you Brenda?"

"Of course I'm Brenda. And I was Brenda yesterday. And I'll be Brenda tomorrow. Pull it together, Dad. Okay?"

"You're my daughter?"

"Come on, Dad. We don't have time for practical jokes."

"Am I sick? Did I have an operation?"

"Come on. It was just a colonoscopy. No big deal. I'm sure the anesthesia will wear off soon. Let's get the hell out of here. I have to pick up the kids, get you home, then get on with my life."

"I'll help you, sir," offers the orderly. "Right this way."

After he's dressed and they're walking to the car, Frank asks, "Do I live with you?"

"No way, Dad. You've been living alone since Mom died six years ago."

"And who is *Mom*?"

"Your wife of 39 years. My mother."

"And what was her name?"

"You've got to be putting me on."

"Seriously. Who did I marry?"

"Jesus. I should march you back in there and get you tested. You've lost it. But I have to pick up the kids."

"There's nothing wrong with my mind," he protests. "When you wake up and fifty years of your life have disappeared, it's natural to be disoriented. I'd have to be crazy not to be." He stares at Brenda, opens his eyes wide and exclaims, "Marge! You must be Marge. No, you must be Marge's mother. You're the image of her, only twenty years older."

"Thanks, Dad. That makes my day. You think I look old enough to be my mother's mother. And you don't even remember your wife's name, my mother's name. She was *Evelyn*, Dad. The love of your life was named *Evelyn*."

"Well, the only woman I ever thought of marrying was named Marge, and she was twenty when I last saw her. How old are you, Brenda?"

"You know damn well how old I am. You were in the delivery room when I was born. You saw me pop out. You've told that story dozens of times. You don't know how old I am? Do the fucking math. And Mom's dead. Evelyn's dead. Do you hear me? Six years dead. You're weirding me out, Dad."

"Evelyn? Who the hell is Evelyn?"

"Okay, Dad. So you've forgotten Mom, and you're having fantasies about some old college flame named Marge. Cut it out, please. I don't want to hear it. You're not old enough to be that far gone. I don't know why you're doing this, and I don't have time to find out. Just stop the crap and get in the car."

"Evelyn? That's a complete blank. My whole life from the last fifty years is a complete blank."

"Okay. We've got to get going. I don't have time to help you piece it all together. Get in the car. Let's get out of here. By the time we get to your apartment, the anesthesia will have worn off, and once you sit down at your computer with all your photos and files, you'll snap out of this."

"Computer? I have a computer? And I know how to use it?"

"Good God!"

When they're on the road, Frank starts chuckling.

"What now, Dad?"

"I just got an idea for a novel."

"So now you're a novelist?" she asks in disbelief.

"You mean I'm not? I thought I would be. Maybe the real me is a writer, and I'm writing this scene that we're in and all that stuff I don't remember is just background and doesn't really matter."

"Thanks, Dad. That makes me feel great. Your marriage, your kids, your career, the part of your life that involved me—that was all nothing. You're glad to be done with it. Thanks."

"No, honey, I didn't mean that."

"Don't *honey* me. You don't even know who I am."

"Okay, stranger, sweet understanding patient stranger, I just had another silly idea I'd like to share with you. Call it 'Living Backwards'. This guy wakes up in a nursing home. Nobody knows who he is or how he got there. The admin staff run paperwork on him as an indigent with Alzheimer's. No ID. No known family. No known friends. They check him in and get Medicare and state insurance to pay his fees. He's healthy. His short-term memory is sharp. But he can't remember anything from the past. They figure he's about 80. Ten years later he looks 70. And ten years after that he looks 60. It turns out that he was born an old man and is living backwards, getting younger all the time. I was chuckling to think that maybe I was just born as an old man, and now I'm going to get younger."

"Fat chance, Dad. You're not getting any younger, nor am I, nor is anyone else."

"If anyone could, it would be Charlie."

"What?"

"My uncle, who was young enough to be my brother. Charlie. You must know Charlie."

"You used to talk about him. But I never met him. He and his wife Irene disappeared about five years ago. If he doesn't show up soon, he'll be missing, presumed dead. That's what you told me."

"Well, Charlie would be the one. He would find the Fountain of Youth. He would dream the impossible dream and make it real. Over breakfast, he'd figure out the meaning of life. Then over lunch, he'd deal with more important matters."

2 ~ A Penny for Your Thoughts

"Why did that man stare at me like that?" she thinks. "Who does he think he is? Who does he think I am? Who am I?"

She draws a blank. She has no idea who she is.

She tries not to panic. There's probably a simple explanation. A senior moment. A premature senior moment. She's young. She can't remember how young exactly. But she knows she's in college. She knows she has a psychology paper due on Monday. She just had a nightmare about that. She often has nightmares about papers that are coming due and sometimes such a dream gives her the inspiration she needs to write well and fast. That's what just happened. She now knows exactly how to skewer B. F. Skinner and his behaviorist nonsense. Her mind is laser-focused, not confused. She is in full command of her faculties. She's in peak paper-writing form. She just can't remember who she is.

She sees a mirror hanging on the wall to her right. She stands. Her body feels different. Her balance is off. The dull persistent pain in her neck and back is gone. She looks in the mirror and sees an old lady with bright red and green hair. She screams.

A nurse who was passing in the hall rushes to her door. "Penny? Are you okay, Penny? Can I help?"

"I'm fine. Really, I'm fine. I just found out something personal that's disturbing. It was a surprise. I over-reacted."

"Earl? Was it Earl? He's such an ass. You should have dumped him long ago."

"Yes, Earl. That's it. You know me well. And, rest assured, I'm dumping him."

As soon as the unknown friend leaves, she shuts and locks her office door.

She thinks she has a good grasp on reality. She has language. She can understand what is said to her and can speak intelligibly. She automatically forms thoughts in the English language. The ability to speak must be controlled by a different part of the brain than that which stores specific language-based memories. She can't remember, but she can think; and because she can think, she is. And even if nothing triggers her memory, she should be able to reconstruct the essentials and move forward.

The nameplate on her desk reads "M. Penelope Franklin, M.S., Ph.D." A blue square of paper attached to the nameplate announces in red marker, "Call me Penny." The nurse called her *Penny* and considered it natural to find her in this office. So this is her office, and that is her name. First problem solved.

Beside the nameplate stands a candy jar. Instead of tootsie rolls, M&Ms, lollipops, or gum drops, it's filled with pennies. Another blue square of paper announces, "A penny for your thoughts."

Other colored squares of paper with writing on them are stuck to the desk.

Framed diplomas on the wall show that she has a Ph.D. in Chemistry and Chemical Biology from Northeastern University. She also has an M.S. in Psychology from Tufts. And she earned that master's degree more than twenty years after her doctorate.

Taped to the wall, without frames, other certificates indicate that she's a psychotherapist and that her specialty is treatment for memory loss. Ironic, she notes.

In another frame, she sees an "Alzheimer's Bill of Rights." One item is highlighted: "Everyone has the right to live in a world of his or her own." Taped to the wall beside that is a newspaper clipping of an obituary from fifty years ago, for Bernard Callahan, a victim of Alzheimer's. She guesses that was her grandfather and that because of him she's afraid of getting Alzheimer's herself. That would explain the squares of paper on her desk and on the bookcase —with the kind of information that most people would easily remember. Most people would keep that kind of information private rather than display it—her address and phone number and social security number and to-do lists. Apparently, she was obsessed about memory loss long before this current incident.

When she reads the reminder notes, she senses no familiarity. Nothing triggers memories or give her the slightest twitch of recognition.

Walking back to her chair, she notices the elephant in the room —a keyboard and an upright flat rectangular surface. She has no idea what those are for. The keys on the keyboard appear to be arranged in the QWERTY format, like a typewriter. It doesn't surprise her that there isn't a real typewriter in the office. A secretary must do her typing for her. But what is this gadget, and why is it in the prime position on her desk, right in front of her chair?

A desk calendar indicates that today is Wednesday, May 2, 2018. The year looks odd. Years should begin with nineteen, not twenty. She last remembers herself as she was in college. Apparently, that was fifty years ago. Technology may have advanced in that time. To cope here and now, she'll need lessons fast, from someone who knows what's going on. If she doesn't cope here and now, her colleagues will realize that she has major memory loss. She could be institutionalized, warehoused with Alzheimer's cases.

She won't give up. She can and will cope.

She picks up a telephone receiver from an odd-shaped box with buttons instead of a dial. She hears a dial tone. She presses zero and connects to a hospital operator. She says she's having a problem with technology in her office and asks if a technical repairman can come. She doesn't need anything fixed. This isn't a screwdriver kind of thing. She needs somebody who can explain things to her, somebody who can help her figure out what she can do with the technology and how to do it. No, she doesn't want to search online, whatever that is. She needs to talk to a human being.

While she waits for the tech guy to arrive, she takes a deep breath and leans back in her chair. Her mind isn't empty. She's aware of a whirl of images and sounds and tastes and smells and tactile sensations, but no orderly word-based thoughts, just raw sensations. She remembers images that she guesses are of herself seen in a mirror as a child, as a young girl, as a teenager, in college. But she remembers nothing since that. She has the ability to organize and process thoughts. But she doesn't remember thoughts she had in the past. Maybe this isn't Alzheimer's. Maybe she didn't have a stroke. It feels like a rogue wave came up on the beach and knocked out all the structures of reason, all the sandcastles she had built; and now the wave has ebbed, and she can and should build new structures.

Her pocketbook is on the floor near her feet. She picks it up and empties the contents onto her desk. She sees herself in a makeup mirror.

This time she laughs at the red and green hair. That hair makes her memorable. What's the point of a life that isn't memorable?

Employee ID card. This is Tufts New England Hospital in downtown Boston. Driver's license—same name as nameplate. Street address in Andover, Massachusetts. Same red and green hair. So this isn't a passing fad. This is her normal mode. Maybe people do such crazy things all the time in 2018.

Fifty-two dollars in cash. Half a dozen plastic cards. A rectangle of metal and plastic about the size and shape of a 3X5 card. A key ring with what looks like a house key and a weird-shaped key with a plastic thing attached. Car key? She asks herself. And maybe now cars are high-tech. After fifty years they should be. A flash memory of the Jetsons cartoon show. By now, cars should be obsolete. That could be a key to a flying machine.

She wouldn't have a clue how to handle a vehicle like that. And if she can't drive, how the hell is she going to get home to Andover? A taxi ride would cost far more than she has in cash, especially considering the probable inflation. Her fifty-two dollars today might be worth no more than ten dollars was fifty years ago. And she doesn't know how to get more cash.

She thinks, What's my bank? Where's my bank? And how do people bank now? The world outside this office is teeming with challenges and risks.

Until she remembers or learns enough to cope, she has to stay put.

The tech guy arrives. She points at her desk and says, "This thing doesn't work."

He sits down, pushes a button in the lower right corner, and the flat rectangular surface lights up.

"Is that all?" he asks, dumbfounded.

"It's new," she improvises. "I just got it, and nothing seems to be where it should be. To me, it's from a different world."

"Oh," he laughs. "You must be an Apple person, and this is a Windows machine. You should sign up for training. It's quite a switch. Even the simplest stuff can be a challenge."

"Exactly. A challenge. Especially for me. I'm not the least bit technical. And I have signed up for training. But it'll be a week before that starts.

And I need to do stuff now. Could you please give me a beginner's lesson?"

He smiles and takes hold of a small plastic gadget beside the keyboard.

"What's that?" she dares to ask.

"That's a mouse. A Mac has a finger pad on the keyboard to do the same kinds of things. But you must have seen and heard about computer mice?"

"Of course," she quickly reassures him. "But I've never had to use one myself. And yes, a computer, a complete computer on a desk."

"Yes," he confirms. "The wonders of technology. When I was in college in the eighties, something with the power of this would have been as big as your desk."

"And when I was in college in the sixties, it would have been as big as this room."

"And this desktop All-in-One is no more powerful than a laptop."

"Laptop," she echoes trying hard not to mask her perplexity and anxiety.

"And that iPhone you have there is almost as powerful."

She tips him thirty dollars and asks him to explain everything from scratch, not just about the computer but also about the iPhone, which she says is new to her as well. She says she wants him to presume that she knows nothing. She doesn't want him to take anything for granted. If he can get her started and point her in the right direction, she'll be able to learn on her own and get a lot of work done before the official training starts.

He's surprised to discover that the computer is fully populated with files. She explains that her boyfriend, Earl, set it up for her. He transferred files from her old machine. And now Earl cheated on her. Normally, she would have asked him for help. But now there's no way she'll ever speak to him again. It's high time she became self-sufficient and took charge of her life.

The tech says, "You sound like my mother, after her second divorce."

First, he accesses her account on the hospital calendar. Her password for that is on a square of paper beside her keyboard. He lectures her on the importance of not writing passwords down, and certainly not leaving them in plain view. Then he clears her schedule for the rest of the day. After three hours, she feels confident with both the computer and the iPhone, and she can find her way around the Internet. She's ready to explore on her own.

In keeping with her obsession with memory loss, she has a folder called *memory clusters* where, in addition to her resume, important documents, and family photos, she has lists organized by topic with names of old teachers and friends and favorite movie stars and sports figures and trivia of all kinds to help her recover a name by association if and when it slipped her mind. She also has notes that would be helpful in writing an autobiography if she should ever feel the urge to do so.

Reading this material and viewing the photos in slide-show mode, Penny hopes that some random image or snippet of information or turn of phrase will trigger a rush of memories.

No such luck. She feels she's reading about a stranger, someone who's divorced and has kids. She has a hard time paying attention to all these photos when she doesn't know who the people are or how they are connected to her. She gets drowsy from boredom.

She's been sitting motionless for too long. She feels lightheaded and nearly falls, leaning against her desk and shaking her legs until they wake up and can support her weight.

Once again, she sees herself in the mirror. The old lady is wearing a pants suit, with a tight-fitting blouse. She herself, her real self, in her real body would never dress that way. She remembers wearing bulky sweaters and loose-fitting sweatshirts. It's not just the difference between college and business dress. Something is wrong about this look and style. She wonders, What happened to my prominent bust? Does old age do that to a woman? Am I shriveled and sagging inside my brassiere? Did I have breast cancer and go through a double mastectomy?

She sits down at her computer again and looks for medical records. She checks to see if she has any of the ills that often come with age—heart problems, high blood pressure, diabetes. She seems to be in good health now. But she learns that years ago, she had chiropractor visits for chronic back and neck pain, which got worse over time. The weight of her breasts was affecting her posture, and, over time, that was damaging her spine. Her doctor and her chiropractor had recommended breast reduction surgery. Her husband didn't want her to do it. When he complimented her and flirted with her, he always mentioned her breasts. And when they made love, he got wound up and ready by seeing them and touching them. Soon after the divorce, she had the surgery as part of her declaration of independence.

She ventures out to eat dinner in the hospital cafeteria, then gets a large take-out coffee and goes back to her office. Fortunately, there are signs pointing the way to the cafeteria and the offices are numbered.

She begins again. Her resume gives her a framework and after reading the autobiographical snippets two or three times, the pieces start to fall into place.

Her father was over fifty when she was born. He was diagnosed with Alzheimer's when he was seventy and she was in college. The obituary on the wall is his.

She wanted to find a cure or treatment for conditions like Alzheimer's based on a hunch that there's a connection between memory and sexual stimulation. In particular, she was interested in the chemical components of memory and how they are affected by hormones like oxytocin "the commitment or love hormone". While her friends partied, dated, married, and had kids, she studied and earned a Ph.D. in Chemistry.

She couldn't get a research and teaching position at a major university, so she went to work in industry and wound up dealing with perfumes, hair color, cosmetics, and deodorants, paying her dues in hopes of getting an opportunity to pursue her own research. After ten years of long hours and total dedication to her work and with no sign that she'd ever get a chance to do what she wanted to do, she got married and became a stay-at-home mom with two kids. Her husband was a workaholic like she had been, working for the same consumer products company she had worked for.

After twenty years, when the kids were both in college, she and her husband were financially well off, and they could start a new life together. But he continued to work long hours. He had no mission in life. More money in the bank and a better title wouldn't make a difference in their lives. He worked hard out of habit, and he couldn't or wouldn't stop.

She divorced him and went back to school to get an M.S. in Psychology. If she couldn't do the basic research necessary to decipher the nature of memory, at least she could help people with memory-loss problems. But once on the job, she found her role was mostly dispensing pills. And since she wasn't a doctor, she had to refer her patients to an M.D. who actually wrote the prescriptions. All she could do was recommend changes in diet, lifestyle, and exercise. Now she was retirement age and looking forward to getting off the workaday treadmill. A reminder note tells her that her retirement form is in the bottom right desk drawer. It's already filled out and signed. She just needs to add the date and turn it in.

Out of curiosity, she takes a blank piece of paper, signs her name, and compares that with the signature on the retirement form. The signatures match.

Her parents had named her Margaret, Marge for shot. After her divorce, she did a remake of herself. She changed her name to M. Penelope Franklin. Not her maiden name *Callahan*, and not her married name *Jansen*. She doesn't know where the *Franklin* came from. But she had chosen that new name as a declaration of independence—along with coloring her hair red and green.

She lives alone in a one-bedroom apartment in Andover, north of Boston.

In the recycle bin of her computer, she sees a folder and half a dozen documents with the name *Earl*. Earl doesn't appear in her contacts list, nor is he a friend on Facebook.

She falls asleep with her head on her desk until dawn, when she resumes her research.

3 ~ Rip Van Winkle

Leaving Tufts New England Medical Center, the traffic is bumper-to-bumper. Brenda says the congestion in downtown Boston is as bad now as it ever was, despite the expenditure of billions of dollars on the *Big Dig*. At this pace, it could take two hours or more to get home.

She uses her iPhone to call her husband and ask him to pick up the kids and leave them with the O'Gradys.

"Who was that?" Frank asks.

"Lou, of course. My husband Lou, who you've known for fifteen years."

"And where does he work? What does he do?"

"People's Bank. He's an identity-theft specialist."

"In this world, people can steal your identity? Maybe that's what happened to me. Somebody stole my identity."

"Stop with the nonsense. Please. It's bad enough driving in this mess. Identity theft has to do with the Internet."

"What's the Internet?"

"Enough. Please."

"And what's that gadget you used to call him?"

"A cellphone, of course. You have one in your pocket."

He checks. He does. He stares at it, mystified.

"Don't you know anything? I can't do everything for you. I gave you a ride to the hospital because you were getting a colonoscopy. You needed someone to drive you, because of the anesthesia. You do it for me. I do it for you. But I've got a job. I can't afford to get caught in traffic like this."

"You have a job?"

"Yes, in this world, women have jobs. We don't just do housework. I work online at home, for pay."

"*Online*? What does that mean?"

"Look, Dad. There's no point in my explaining the universe to you. You have to snap out of this."

"And what do I do?"

"You worked for one computer company after another. Now you're retired. Enough already."

"But, please, Brenda, while we're stuck in traffic, please indulge me. Something you say may trigger my memory."

She takes a deep breath. From the movement of her lips, she's counting to ten, slowly. Then she explains the high-tech features of the car—the GPS, the entertainment system. the buttons to remotely unlock the doors. the button on her electronic key that sets off a beeping noise to help her find her car in a parking lot. She says there are cars powered by electricity and self-driving cars should be available soon.

Frank is surprised that Brenda's car works the same as his old rusted Falcon. He'd have no trouble driving a car like this, despite its extra bells and whistles.

He's also surprised there are gas-powered cars still on the road. Last he remembers, supplies of petroleum were dwindling. Experts thought the world would run out of it in fifty years.

Frank is overwhelmed by what Brenda tells him about cellphones, computers, the Internet, ATMs, online banking.

He asks, "How many people live on Mars now? And are other planets habitable?"

Brenda laughs.

Frank protests, "I know very well that people walked on the moon long ago."

"And that was the end of it. We haven't gone back. There are no men on the moon, much less on Mars, though now there's talk again of doing such things."

"And robots? Are some of those people on the sidewalk robots?"

"No way. Aside from toys, robots today are machines that look like machines—factory equipment on assembly lines."

"So, this isn't like sci-fi?"

She laughs. "Sure, we have new electronic gadgets. But the basics are the same. We haven't been invaded by aliens, and nobody has laser pistols. Life expectancy has gone up a little, but not much. Most of the changes have been social and political."

"What about war?" he asks. "Did the Vietnam War end?"

"Long ago."

"Did I fight there?"

"No. Thank God. You lucked out. Your senior year they started doing the draft by lottery, and you got a high number."

"And that was the last war?"

"No way. There have been wars since, far too many of them. It's hard to keep track of them all."

When the car comes to a halt, gridlocked, Brenda demonstrates features on their iPhones. She calls him and texts him and shows him the Internet and how to Google. He catches on quickly, and when the traffic speeds to a slow crawl, he continues to use his iPhone to search the Internet. He finds it easy to think about two or three things at once.

Eventually, Brenda picks up Barry, who's twelve, and Denise, seven, and takes Frank to his apartment in West Roxbury, a part of Boston near the western suburbs. On the way, they pass the house where the family lived for thirty years—where she grew up, where her mother died. He doesn't recognize either the house or the neighborhood. Nor does he recognize his one-bedroom apartment a few blocks away, which has floor-to-ceiling bookcases on all the walls.

He checks the books which are all strange, except a shelf of dog-eared Modern Library Classics near the floor. He picks up a paperback entitled *Future Shock* and considers it a good name for what he is going through.

He sits down on a well-worn reclining armchair, shuts his eyes, leans back, then opens his eyes. No change. He's sure he has never seen this place before.

His right hand discovers switches on the arm of the chair. He tries them. The overhead lights flash, then dim. Music starts.

He smiles. "I wonder if I wired that myself."

"Yes," affirms Brenda. "You were proud that you were able to do that. Then, with each upgrade in music tech you upgraded it."

"What?"

"From 33 rpm records to cassette tape to CDs and now digital files streaming over the Internet. You kept buying the same music over and over—folk music from the sixties and seventies. Technology moved on, but your taste stayed the same."

She finds his laptop on the floor by his bed and turns it on for him.

Guided by Brenda, Frank explores the folders and files on his computer while Barry hooks up his PlayStation 4 to the flatscreen TV and plays videogames. Denise sits on a cushion in the corner and video chats with friends on her iPad.

Brenda opens a folder with photos of his wedding. He recognizes many of the people he sees, but not his bride, Evelyn, or her bride's maids. Brenda shows him photos of her birth and infancy and childhood: birthday pictures, Christmas and Easter and Thanksgiving pictures, summer vacations, Brenda's marriage, George's marriage, their kids as infants, and growing up.

The pictures of him long ago look like him. And in photos from the missing years, he sees himself morph into what he looks like now. But, in his gut, he doesn't feel the reality of anything after college. It's like seeing photos of someone else — of an identical twin who he was separated from at birth.

They find folders with thousands of unorganized photos, with numbers and letters as titles, in dozens of subfolders. Brenda copies them into a single folder and starts a slide show. While Frank watches, Brenda obsessively cleans his apartment. She says she doesn't understand how he can live this way, in such filth.

At first, Frank stares at each photo for a minute. There are some from college and from before that that feel familiar to him. But there are thousands of shots of people and places he doesn't know. He increases the speed, then increases it again and again, until the images appear and disappear so fast that the effect is like looking at a movie, the eye connecting one to the next in a colorful blur of motion. This isn't getting him anywhere.

He asks Brenda to take him back to the hospital. He needs help with his memory problem, which isn't going away. She calls the hospital. Better go to the same place in case they screwed up. It could be a side effect of the anesthesia. If so, it's their responsibility to fix it. There's a psychotherapist on staff who specializes in memory. Central scheduling gives him an appointment for the morning. Dropping him off won't take her far out of her way. In his state, she knows he couldn't get there on his own.

Frank shuts his laptop and watches Barry play an action-packed videogame with movie-quality graphics. Barry's character battles one monster after another. Barry, his thumbs flashing, adroitly deals with each challenge. Then, suddenly, his character appears in a different world with different enemies and new challenges.

"What happened?" asks Frank.

"I found the door."

"What door?"

"The door to the next level. It's no big deal. I've been here before. These games always have levels. In different games you have to do different things to go from one level to the next. In the old days, reaching a new level would mean the enemies moved faster or it took more hits to damage and kill them. Now sometimes you go to a different place, like playing a new game."

"How do you know all this?"

"I've been playing these games since I was three. When you've been doing this stuff long enough it's no big deal. You own a ton of retro games. I've seen you play them for hours. I can hook one up for you if you want. The old Atari 2600 with Pacman and Space Invaders and Pitfall or the Atari 800 with adventure games, or the NES with Tetris"

"What are adventure games?"

"Those are stories. In the old days the stories were told with text and still pictures. You had to solve puzzles to get to the next level and to win. The idea isn't much different from what I'm doing now, except for the graphics. They had multiple levels, multiple worlds. It was like life, man."

"Like life?"

"You've seen the movies about parallel worlds, haven't you? Some scientists say that's the way things really are. Science inspires game designers, and game designers inspire scientists. And lots of scientific experiments nowadays are computer simulations that look like videogames."

"How do you know all this?"

"It's on the Internet. Everything's on the Internet."

Barry sets up the NES for Frank and plugs in the Tetris cartridge, which he says is Frank's favorite. It takes Frank a while to get used to the controller and to get into the flow of the game, which is a matter of maneuvering falling shapes. But Frank is soon addicted.

Brenda takes the kids home, then comes back and sleeps on the sofa. She doesn't want to leave her Dad alone in this state of mind.

Frank stays up all night playing Tetris. Then at dawn, drunk with sleeplessness, he scrambles to find pen and paper and starts writing, automatically, watching with surprise as the words and sentences take shape, and turn into a story. Maybe he's a writer. He's elated, and he doesn't want to risk losing that mood by exposing his story to Brenda's cynicism. He puts the story in his pocket. Maybe he'll be able to share it with the therapist. Maybe it holds a clue to what happened to him and how to reverse it.

4~ Love at Second Sight

Frank knocks on the door of the office of M. Penelope Franklin.

No answer. Through the frosted glass, he can tell that someone is sitting at the desk.

He knocks again. No answer.

He tries the door. It's locked.

He says loudly, "Please, Dr. Franklin, I have an appointment with you for ten o'clock, and it's ten o'clock now."

The door opens and there stands the lady with red and green hair who he noticed yesterday.

"You're mistaken, sir. I have no appointments."

"But I made the appointment yesterday. Please check your scheduling system."

"The scheduling system is wrong. I have no appointments today and will have no appointments tomorrow or ever. I'm retiring. I just turned in the paperwork."

She goes back to her desk, then flourishes a copy of the document.

"Will there be a replacement?"

"I have no idea. I'm out of here. Period."

"But I have a serious problem. I suddenly lost my memory of everything from the last fifty years."

"That's extraordinary."

"I don't think it's amnesia or dementia."

"You seem to know it all. You don't need me."

"I mean I have no trouble dealing with new information. I can memorize. I can reason. I know what happened yesterday and today. And I can remember what happened in college and before that. But nothing—not my own children and grandchildren, not photos, not objects I've had for years—can trigger any memory of what happened over the last fifty years. Have you ever heard of such a thing?"

"Unfortunately, I have."

"You say *unfortunately*. What do you mean by that? Is there a cure?"

"I certainly wish there were. But I know of none. I can't help you. I'm sorry. I have problems of my own to deal with and I'm out of here."

"Well, if you can't take me on as a patient, can you please listen to me for a few minutes. I think I'm a writer. My daughter says I'm not. But I wrote this story as soon as I woke up this morning. It wrote itself, like it came straight from my unconscious. I think it might help solve this mystery."

She hesitated, but before she could object, he started reading aloud.

***

"Title: Love at Second Sight."

A seventy-year-old man is on a transatlantic flight. The plane is full. The seats are small, with little leg room. He's elbow-to-elbow with a stranger, a woman of comparable age, in the window-seat beside him.

He's tired and lonely. He's a recent widower who went on a trip to Paris alone and saw nothing, met no one—just ate, slept, and wandered through the streets in a fog. Now he wants to sleep. The sooner the flight is over, the better. He's relieved that this woman beside him hasn't started a conversation.

He drifts off and has a memory dream of when he was seventeen on a flight back from Paris where he had spent the summer on a student exchange program. A girl his age was in the window-seat beside him.

Short, maybe five-two or five-three, with jet black hair and a Botticelli face. She was wearing a bulky white sweater and a red and green plaid skirt. Her blue-green eyes were concentrating on *L'Etranger* by Camus, which she was reading in French without a dictionary. He presumed that she, like him, was returning home. He wondered if she, too, lived near Philadelphia, or if this was just the first leg of her journey. He wanted to strike up a conversation but didn't know how to start. It would have been easy when he first sat down, but he had let that moment pass, and he didn't want to get off to a bad start interrupting her reading when she was deeply involved. He would wait. Eventually she would put the book down or a stewardess would stop by to offer food and drinks. He pulled a book out of his backpack, *Introduction a la Méthode to Leonardo da Vinci* by Paul Valéry. That should impress her if she noticed. He didn't take out his French-English dictionary, even though he would need it. He looked intently at the pages. He was so self-conscious that he couldn't make sense of the words on the page, but he turned the pages as if he were reading. Then he realized that he was turning the pages too fast to be credible. He hoped she hadn't noticed. He didn't want her to think he was a phony trying to impress her. He slowed down, turning pages at the same pace that she turned hers. Otherwise, he sat stock still, maintaining what he imagined was a sophisticated, intelligent look, until he drifted off to sleep.

When he woke up, the plane was dark, except for foot-level lights in the aisle. It took a while for him to orient himself, to remember that he was on a plane. Then he felt a strange sensation in his left hand. As his eyes adjusted to the dark, he realized that the girl's hand was resting on his. Apparently, she was asleep. Her book was open, upside down, draped across her lap. Her skirt was scrunched up, revealing her right thigh, nearly to her underpants. Her hand probably fell into his by accident when she drifted off to sleep. Since her eyes were closed, he felt free to look at her closely. She was gorgeous. Her pouty lips, her cleft chin, the bit of hair above her nose between her eyebrows—every detail of her looks became to him an indicator of beauty, even though he had never thought of those features that way before. And her hand in his hand, their fingertips barely brushing, gave him an erotic sensation unlike anything he had ever experienced, far more intimate than a kiss, even a French kiss with his girlfriend back home. Dreamlike images passed through his mind—them talking together and the two of them falling for one another, and, despite all odds, finding ways to meet each other again. They went to the same college, and later married, and had kids and grandkids. Their whole future life together flashed through his mind, and it was a wonderful life. The first step would be to speak to her. But he was paralyzed.

He didn't dare move his hand, much less speak. What would she think of him if she woke to find that this stranger beside her was holding her hand? And he didn't want to move his hand. He didn't want this intense sensation, this magic moment to end.

He was hungry and thirsty. He needed to urinate. But he couldn't move.

He felt an electric tingle through his fingertips, coming from her fingertips. She might be awake, just pretending to sleep. She might feel drawn to him, just as he was to her. This might be a moment of mutual ecstasy, more than just chance, the two of them fated to meet like this.

Then, unprompted by his conscious mind, his hand squeezed her hand.

He felt a shock of fear, mingled with hope. He would never have done that deliberately. This moment, this possible future life might now be over, ending in embarrassment and shame—that he would dare to take the hand of a girl he had never spoken to, a stranger on a plane. But having squeezed, he couldn't help but hope for a miracle, and the miracle happened. She squeezed back.

He had to urinate badly, but he didn't dare break the contact, losing his only connection with her, his only hope.

He studied her face. There was not the least sign of recognition or consciousness. She was probably dreaming, imagining that his hand was someone else's hand. By chance, he had become a placeholder in her dream, a substitute for the person she wished she were with.

He felt like an intruder. He didn't deserve her tender fingertip caresses, her gentle squeezes, her light sensory passion. But he welcomed any contact with her. If her feelings were already fixed on someone else, he had no chance with her, and this accidental contact with her was all he could hope for. He would savor it while he could and cherish this moment in his dreams for the rest of his life.

Then he wakes up. Yes, he is on a plane. Yes, he remembers he is on his way home from Paris. But he's seventy, not seventeen.

A woman's hand is in his hand, but it's not the hand of a teenage girl. It's the hand of a mature woman, about the same age he is.

She's asleep, like the girl in the dream.

Black hair with gray roots. Pouty lips. Cleft chin. A bit of hair between her brows.

Her hand squeezes his hand, and he has an electric shock of recognition.

'Hello,' she says. 'It's been ages since we did this before. Maybe this time we'll get it right.'"

***

"What do you think of that?" asks Frank. "Could that be a clue?"

The therapist glares at him, impatient. "Nonsense. Total nonsense. I don't teach creative writing. Get out of here. Now."

He stares at this seventy-year-old woman with red and green hair—the colors of the plaid skirt in the story. She has blue-green eyes.

"Marge?" he asks.

Her face is blank. She says nothing.

He sticks out his tongue and touches the tip of his nose with it.

Her eyes flash recognition. "Frank?" she asks softly touching his cheek with her fingers. Then she pulls back and shouts, "What the hell are you doing here? I hate your guts."

"And I hate you, too," he says, and leans forward as if to kiss her, but stops short.

"This is crazy. I'm a twenty-year-old in the body of a seventy-year-old. I can see hints of who you were in your eyes. But I can't kiss you. The way you look, it would be like kissing my grandmother."

She slaps him hard, then puts her arms around his neck, pulls him close, and kisses him. He shuts his eyes and kisses back. She slaps him again. He opens his eyes. She kisses him again, and this time they maintain eye contact.

They hug each other like they're standing on a ledge on the side of a cliff and the cliff is spinning out of control.

The hug lingers until it feels awkward, and they pull apart, trying to orient themselves in this new emotional space—strangers who were lovers a few months ago, and who now feel like strangers not just to each other but to themselves.

Frank stares at her, silently, still looking for traces of the Marge he used to know in this old lady standing in front of him. When he finally thinks of something to say, his tongue is so dry he finds it difficult to form words. Eventually, he mumbles, "I saw you yesterday, here in this office, sitting in that chair. I walked by in the hall. I had never seen hair like that. It looked as if you were as surprised to see me as I was to see you."

She answers, "I was surprised to see anything at all. I was surprised to be in this world. I had no idea who I was or where I was or how I got here. My memory was a blank. I had and I have the same condition as you."

"Maybe it's contagious," he chuckles.

"And maybe we're both really twenty years old, and this is a room in your grandmother's house. We just think we're old. The old folks we see when we look at one another and when we look in the mirror are illusions."

"Keep dreaming that, sweetheart, and I'll try to dream it, too," suggests Frank. "That's better than jumping from being twenty to being seventy in an instant, like we stepped out of our bodies into limbo and other people lived our lives, and fifty years later, after what was just a minute to us, we stepped back in."

"Or maybe that fifty years didn't happen," she offers. "Maybe what other people remember is an illusion. Maybe reality is discontinuous. Maybe jumps like this happen all the time, only they're usually short, and our minds fill in the gaps, like when we watch a movie; only this time, for us, the jump was huge."

"You're scaring me now."

Marge pulls away from him, sits in the desk chair, and stares at him, "So maybe what I remember from fifty years ago didn't happen. Maybe you didn't act like a bastard and betray me."

He shoots back, "And maybe you didn't dump me and play around with Charlie."

"I hate your guts," she repeats, but this time she smiles as she says it, realizing how silly this sounds.

He smiles back, then asks, "Are you married?"

"What?"

"I don't see a ring."

"I'm divorced. And I just dumped a boyfriend. I stayed up all night checking stuff on my computer. That was as exciting as reading a phone book or reading a stranger's to-do list or reading resumes from job applicants."

"I'm widowed," Frank replies. "The woman I was married to for nearly forty years, the mother of my two kids, died six years ago. You should have seen the look on my daughter's face when she realized that I didn't know her name or her mother's name or anything about either of them."

"I've been divorced for decades," says Marge. "I have two kids who are both married with kids, in California. I haven't spoken to them since this happened. They have no idea that I don't know who they are. I've been faking it here. I'm sure my co-workers must have noticed I'm acting peculiar. But you're the only person who knows how lost I am."

"Well, look on the bright side. If we happen to fall in love again, we won't be cheating on anybody."

"Enough," she spits back at him. "This is no time for flirtation. I've forgotten everything, absolutely everything, and I suspect you have, too. Not just personal memories. I don't know where my car is, and if I did find it, I wouldn't know how to unlock it or start it. I know my street address, but I don't know how to get from here to there. I've spent all the cash in my pocketbook, and I don't know if I have any money in the bank, or what bank, or how to get my money. For God's sake, I'm helpless and clueless. Since I woke up here yesterday, I've stayed in this office except for eating in the cafeteria. I slept here on the floor with the door locked, not knowing what else to do. A technical guy told me how to use my computer and cellphone. But everything else in this wacky world is a mystery to me."

"Well, I learned a few things from my daughter, and I think I can help you," Frank replied. "The car and the banking stuff shouldn't be a problem. Your keys and your cards are here. I bet those papers stuck to your desk have the passwords and codes you need. And your car can tell you, literally tell you, how to get where you want to go. So where do you want to go?"

"Nowhere," says Marge.

"But you said you're retiring, today, right now. Aren't you moving out of your office and going home?"

"Honestly, I don't know what I'm doing."

"Well, you can't stay here. Let me help you."

"I don't need help."

"Baloney. Gather up your personal stuff. Make a copy of your computer files. I'll check at the information desk in the lobby and get boxes."

"You expect me to get into a car with a total stranger?"

"Face it, lady – to us, everybody's a stranger. We've known each other for a few minutes, and we know one another better than anyone else in this world."

"I can't make decisions."

"First things first. You have to go home. For all you know, you may have a cat or a dog, or some elderly relative who depends on you. And you need to rummage through your stuff. There's no telling what might trigger your memory."

He doesn't wait for her to answer. He leaves to get boxes.

On the way, Frank calls Brenda and tells her he doesn't need to be picked up. By an amazing coincidence, the therapist turned out to be an old friend of his from college. They're catching up on old times. Maybe their talk will bring back his memory. She'll drive him home. He hesitates to mention that the therapist is Marge, the Marge he told her was more memorable to him than her mother Evelyn. He sees no reason to upset Brenda with that.

5 ~ Sandcastles Revisited

"Too fast. Too fast," Marge repeats silently, reminding herself to be skeptical and cautious, while smiling sweetly and letting Frank decide everything.

She feels like she just woke up and found herself alone on a desert island, then discovered a man was there as well, just one, and she knew him from before, and she had broken up with him before. If someone had asked her who was the last person she wanted to be marooned with, this is the guy. Yes, she's elated that she isn't alone, and together they might figure out a way to survive. But Frank? Why, oh why is he the one?

Her feelings are a jumble. She feels a residue of attraction for a man she, not that long ago, may have loved. That is mixed with anger and hatred for a man who was reckless about her well-being and betrayed her. And mixed with that, she feels physical repulsion for a man who looks old enough to be her grandfather—as old to her as she appears to him.

She's disoriented. She has no idea what happened to her memory, and hence she distrusts her reason and judgment. It feels like their breakup just happened. She still feels the pain in her gut that she felt back then. This is the same guy, she reminds herself, though he looks much older. This is Frank. She can't simply fall into his arms. She can't let herself fall on the rebound for the very man she's rebounding from.

She's amazed at her docility, her lack of will power. She should take charge. At the very least, she should drive her own car. But her mind is in neutral, or rather her minds, because she's experiencing multiple streams of thought at the same time. She doesn't feel in control.

She retreats within herself, watching and waiting. She's content to sit in the passenger's seat and stare at this strange world with its new models of cars, with its billboards advertising companies and products she never heard of.

Meanwhile another part of her mind listens to Frank as he rambles on about what he learned over the last day.

Still another channel of thought tries to figure out who Frank is now and who he was before, and how far she can trust him.

In the middle of Frank explaining online banking, Marge asks, "Are we dead?"

"Does that matter?" he replies. "Wherever we are, we have to learn to deal with the practical matters we're faced with. We have to cope. We don't have to understand." He continues describing what he's learned, firming up and organizing his knowledge and insights while explaining them to her.

For all his talk of practicality, Frank doesn't seem to take their situation seriously. He seems to relate to what's happening as if it's a story. He's wrapped up in the plot and puzzle of it like a reader or a game-player, rather than being shocked and scared to the limits of reason, which any sane person would be.

There are no surprises at Marge's apartment in Andover. There are no pets, no signs of dependents. Frank copies the backup he made from her work computer to her personal laptop. He insists that she pack a couple of suitcases with clothes. He says they don't know where they will spend that night or the next. They need flexibility to figure out what has happened to them and what they can do to fix their memories and build new lives. She carries out his wishes, zombie-like, while the multiple tracks of her consciousness race to make sense of the multitudes of unknowns she encounters.

On the drive to West Roxbury, in Marge's red Toyota Camry, she drifts off to sleep while Frank maneuvers through heavy traffic on Route 128.

***

She's sitting on a sofa. The skin of the hands on her lap is spotted. The veins are pronounced. The joints of the fingers are gnarled. She feels pain in the joints of her hips. She's sitting next to an old man who is holding what she now recognizes is a laptop computer. She has woken up in that same nightmare world. This is his apartment, with bookcases on every wall.

He's reading to her.

She interrupts him, "I'm sorry. I don't understand a word that you're saying."

"Okay. It's probably better that we read separately and silently at our own pace. I'll put a copy on your laptop."

"A copy of what?"

"*Sandcastles*, of course. Haven't you heard a word I've said?"

"Patience. Please. Tell me again."

"This is a novel I wrote based on what happened to us and my family and Charlie and Irene. I started it when we were in college. I remember writing the first few chapters back then, when I called it *Restless*. I must have continued writing it during the time we don't remember. From what I see here, I believe I finished it about 30 years ago."

"Is this a record of what happened?"

"The best I can tell, it's fiction based on what happened. The names are real. And it resonates with what I remember."

"The title *Restless* sounds familiar."

"Yes. It should. There's a chapter that tells about the first time you came to see me at Yale. I was trying to impress you, so I told you I was writing a novel, and you asked me to tell you about it. I made up that title on the spot."

"You mean you weren't writing a novel?"

"Not then, when I said that I was. I hadn't written a thing yet. I was trying to impress you."

"You lied to me."

"Yes. But that's not the point. This is a complete account, more or less true, of our life back then. Reading this could trigger memories, not just facts, but sensations of what we lived through."

"So, I'm a character in this story you want me to read. That feels weird. Even if I know those events happened, I won't have seen them the way you did. And you probably made stuff up to fill in the gaps when you didn't know what happened or what people were thinking. And you made changes to make it a better story. You weren't trying to record what happened. You were writing a novel, for God's sake. You want me to read a pack of lies? And you think that's going to cure my memory loss?"

"Come on, Marge. Give it a try. And the same folder has files with background notes and copies of letters, with other versions of what happened."

"Letters?" she objected. "You expect truth from letters? Whoever wrote them was trying to convince or persuade. That's just lies packaged another way."

"Enough with the negativity. Give it a read."

She does read, but the experience is painful, like looking at the world through dirty glasses. What she reads triggers parallel thoughts—judging what may be fact and what fiction and imagining other variants. To her, going into the manuscript of *Sandcastles* is like falling down a rabbit hole into Wonderland.

While reading, she finds the song "Memory" on her computer and plays it. Frank doesn't object. He's so immersed in his reading that he doesn't notice. This is the first time Marge has ever heard that song. It was written for *Cats* in 1981, during the gap in her memory. She sets it to continuously replay, and a channel of her mind gently meditates on the lines "I can smile at the old days/ I was beautiful then/ I remember/ The time I knew what happiness was/ Let the memory live again."

She opens another window on her laptop and looks up *memory problems* and finds a description of the movie *50 First Dates* where Drew Barrymore is a woman who has to jot notes each night to remind her in the morning who she is and who she loves and what's she's doing.

She looks up Alzheimer's and confirms that the first symptom is failure of short-term memory.

She looks up *pi* and finds a page listing the first million digits of that number. She copies the first fifty digits into a new document and stares intently at them. She creates a new document and types as many digits as she can remember. She's able to reproduce thirty-five without error. Amazing. Far better than she would have expected. There's nothing wrong with her short-term memory. That's a relief.

She hasn't had any trouble finding the word she wants when she wants it. She even remembers the word for such a problem: aphasia.

Her computer has Rosetta Stone language learning software. Greek, Italian, Japanese, Russian.

She reviews the notes in her Memory Cluster folder. She has been obsessed about memory for decades, not just as a profession, but for herself personally, ever since her father was diagnosed with Alzheimer's. She's been teaching herself languages as a mental exercise. She opens the

Greek version of Rosetta Stone. She recognizes the alphabet. She knows many of the answers in the drills. That kind of memory didn't go away when personal memories did.

The brain seems to process different kinds of memory in different ways. She and Frank are retaining what they learned yesterday. But they've lost primary memories, what they lived through and directly experienced for decades, all the way back to the time when they were in college.

From the way she's analyzing their condition, she seems to have retained some of her professional training — her patterns of thought, how she approaches problems. And Frank has retained a proclivity toward writing fiction.

She finds a note of hers about Carl Sagan's *Dragons of Eden*. It confirms the need to transfer data from short-term to long-term memory, the connection of sleep and dreaming to the transfer process. All that's missing from her old theory, the theory that motivated her study of chemistry and biology is the sexual link and the possibility that the release of sex-related hormones is essential for the transfer process. Chances are good that her theory was right. People don't need year-round sexual stimulation for reproduction. They need it for memory.

She sees her notes about "oxytocin, the commitment hormone". She does a Google search. Its release is sexually triggered. But there's no sign of research linking it to memory. Not yet.

Meanwhile, she's reading *Sandcastles*, the manuscript that Frank wrote, and it's getting more interesting, demanding more of her attention. Irene, Charlie's German wife, tries to live her life as if it were performance art. Irene enjoys playing pranks and tricking people into believing made-up stories. She's a puppeteer. Beware of Irene, she tells herself. Don't trust anything Irene says. And what about Charlie? Can she trust him?

What she reads doesn't align with what she remembers. And what she remembers may have been manipulated by Irene. How do you tell the dancer from the dance? How do you tell the liar from the lie? Do you remember what happened or do you remember what you and others said about what happened? How can you know what's true? Are we alive or dead? she wonders. And does that matter?

Maybe what you believe is what matters because that's what motivates you. The story matters more than the truth, and the truth is unknowable. Frank would like that idea—putting fiction over science.

Part Two ~ Sandcastles

6 ~ Mansions and Ghosts

August 1940, Silver Spring, Maryland

"Sarah, you did write the boys, didn't you?"

"Yes, Carl. Of course." Sarah poured him a cup of coffee. The kitchen seemed larger than before. She had to stretch to reach the breakfast dishes in the cabinet and to put them in their proper places at the table. "You know I write every day."

Carl gulped his coffee. "Wyoming isn't on the other side of the world. How long could it take for a letter to get there? They should have started home when Sue first turned sick." His voice dropped. "Now she's been dead a week ... Where in God's creation are they?"

Sarah stopped. She didn't need to put a plate at Sue's place. "Yes. Of course. In God's creation."

Carl looked up at his wife in surprise—a delayed reaction to the bitter taste of unsweetened coffee. At that moment he realized her voice had changed. It was strange, but familiar, like the voice of some older relative.

He looked at her closely as she returned the extra plate to the cabinet, then adjusted her own plate, fork, and spoon. A few streaks of gray in her black hair framed her face and gave it definition. If nature hadn't provided those streaks, a hairstylist might have. Hers wasn't the fragile beauty of youth that faded with a shift of mood, or the beauty of middle age that changed with fashions. She knew who she was and was pleased with her life. But today her self-confidence was shaken. Her mouth was set in a thin expressionless line and her eyes, which seemed darker than before, avoided contact with his. She had changed, and he had, too. This last month had been hell for both of them. "Sarah," he said gently, "I was talking about Sue."

"Yes, Carl. Sue. Where in God's creation? And where's the sugar?" She stood up. "Nothing seems to be where it should be." She groped among the canisters and jars of preserves on the counter.

"It seems you spend your whole life straightening and cleaning," he said.

"The house is getting too big to handle," she admitted. Then she turned and looked him straight in the eye. "How does a house grow, Carl?"

"If houses really grew, I'd be out of business."

"In *John* 14 it says, 'In my father's house there are many mansions.'"

"I thought the word was 'rooms.'"

"'Rooms' in the Standard Revised. 'Mansions' in the King James. I always wondered how a house could have mansions instead of rooms. But that's how this place feels to me now. The rooms seem huge."

"If a customer told me that, I'd take it as a compliment, but from you ... "

"I love this house. You know I do. There's nothing like it in the world. I could sit for days curled with a book on that bench in the alcove by the fireplace."

Carl slowly stroked his mustache. "Maybe it's time to think of building another smaller place that would be easier to care for," he suggested. "After all, Russ will be leaving for college next month, and then Fred. Then there'll be just the two of us in this big old place. It's time to move on."

"Don't talk of moving," she said quietly, but firmly.

They heard footsteps on the walkway, and both grew tense with expectation. At this time of the morning, it could be either Rem Jones the mailman or the Reverend Schumacher. If it was Rem, there could be another letter from their sons.

Their ten-year-old daughter, Sue, had died suddenly of pneumonia while her two teenage brothers were away at their Uncle Harry's ranch in Wyoming. The boys wrote home often, with messages intended for Sue.

There was no telephone at Uncle Harry's ranch, so Carl and Sarah couldn't call and tell them that Sue had died. And Sarah had insisted that a telegram would be too cold and cruel. She had written them a letter, but couldn't bring herself to mail it, though she let Carl believe she had sent one letter after another. Instead, she added to the first unsent letter each day, and her guilt at not sending it grew as Carl became more impatient with the boys for not coming home.

Two days ago, Carl, who was normally cool-headed and practical, threw a screaming fit when another letter from the boys arrived. The unintended irony of their references to Sue pained him, and he lashed out at them.

Sarah found some consolation in that same letter. As long as the boys didn't know what had happened, Sue was still alive to them.

The footsteps on the walkway had the light, quick pace of the young Reverend Schumacher.

Carl took a deep breath and sipped his bitter coffee. "Why did I let them take the car?" he asked rhetorically.

"It's the only way to get there. You said so yourself. The train would leave them a hundred miles from the ranch."

"Then they simply shouldn't have gone."

"It was time they grew up and learned to go off on their own and rough it. That's what you said."

"And what's the point of their seeing Harry? I know he's your last living uncle, and we can't expect him to live forever. But he'll just fill their heads with war stories—as if they don't get enough of that from the books he sends them every Christmas and birthday, and the papers are full of news of that new war in Europe. To hear Harry talk, you'd think that war was a great opportunity—a chance to see the world and be a man among men. The less we hear from him the better."

At the outbreak of World War I, Harry had left behind his wife and volunteered to join the American Expeditionary Force under General Pershing. He had received a field commission and, by the end of the war, rose to the rank of captain. After the war, he traveled for two years in Russia, the Middle East, and North Africa, purportedly on military-diplomatic missions. He loved to talk about those times and exotic places and to show off the coins, postcards, photos, and artifacts he had collected. But to any question about what he did there, he replied with a wink, "I'm not at liberty to divulge that."

Now Harry lived with his second wife, Martha, and their three-year-old daughter Matilda, on a ranch in Wyoming. He called the ranch *Cairo*, and in addition to cattle, he raised camels, which he sometimes sold to circuses and zoos, but mostly kept for his own amusement—holding endurance races across the barren plains.

"Harry's harmless," said Sarah.

"Harmless? The man's a dream-maker, and there's nothing in this world more dangerous than that. If it hadn't been for my grandfather and his sandcastles, I'd have never ended up a builder."

"And do you regret it?"

"No, but that's not my point."

***

The Reverend Schumacher, a Lutheran minister, was twenty-five and unmarried. At first, Sarah had found it difficult to turn for solace to a minister half her age, who had hardly known Sue. But he was so sincere and ardent, she couldn't turn him away. Since the funeral, the Reverend came by nearly every morning to sit with her in Sue's old room, often in silence, but sometimes reading passages from the *Bible* and then talking about them.

Sarah admired his erudition, his familiarity with foreign languages, and his faith that the words of the *Bible* are the words of God Himself. It was refreshing to see a young man who felt he had an important mission in life. She hoped he'd be able to keep that faith for many years.

Sarah's son Russ was planning to go into the ministry. He'd be starting at Gettysburg College next month, in pre-seminary. Sarah wondered if Russ would ever be this ardent and well-informed. How could her little ragamuffin ever become a *man of God*? To her, regardless of his height, and he towered over her, he was still a little boy — wrestling with his brother Fred in the backyard and teasing his sister Sue.

The morning sunshine streamed through the window in Sue's room, surrounding the Reverend Schumacher's light brown hair with a halo-like glow. Sarah sat and stared at the miniature horses Sue had arranged on the windowsill, while the Reverend Schumacher considered the possible meanings of familiar gospel passages in the original Greek.

Sue had loved horses. She had nearly a hundred miniatures and dozens of pictures of horses, clipped from magazines, adorned the walls. One picture, drawn by Uncle Harry, was a pen-and-ink sketch with a horse's skull large in the foreground, lying on a desert plain, and with the Rocky Mountains and a herd of cattle in the distance. Sarah had had it framed for Sue just before the boys went on their trip. Sue had been angry that she, who loved horses, wasn't being allowed to go on this amazing trip to Harry's wild west.

Today, Sarah surprised the Reverend with a passage she had selected. "What does the word 'mansions' mean in the King James version of *John* 14:2, 'There are many mansions in my Father's house'? How can there be mansions in a house? A house is small. A mansion is big. It makes no sense. Why would one translator say *rooms* and another *mansions*? What did Christ really say?"

The Reverend Schumacher was delighted that Sarah had asked him. "Christ is speaking to his disciples at the Last Supper. He is telling them about life after death. He is reassuring them that there will be room enough for them in heaven, his Father's house. Perhaps it's meant as an echo of the Christmas story — in heaven there will be room in the inn. But it suggests more than just space in which to live.

"The King James translation just anglicized the Latin, even though *mansion* has a different meaning in English. The Latin is *mansio, mansionis*, which means a stay or a sojourn, and, by extension, a halting place, a stage of a journey. Perhaps the passage means that life after death is a stage of a journey; that there are many such stages and that the journey through the house of God is a long one, requiring many rest stops. Perhaps our life here on Earth is just one such stage."

"And what are the words in the original Greek?" she inquired, expecting that the words of Christ would have magic power.

The Reverend consulted the pocket-sized Greek *New Testament* he carried with him. "*En te oixia tou patros mou monai pollai eisin.*"

"And what part of that means many rooms or mansions?"

"*Monai pollai.*"

"You mean like *monopoly*?" she asked.

"That word has different roots, but the Lord works in mysterious ways. Far be it from me to discount the suggestiveness of our living language."

"And the key word is *monai*?"

"Yes, in the singular, *mone*. The letters are *mu omicron nu eta*. It's pronounced like the impressionist painter *Monet*, or like the French word for loose change—*monnaie*. It's an unusual word. Its meaning is very similar to the Latin *mansio*. But, to the best of my knowledge, it has no derivatives in English. *Money, monopoly,* and *monastery* all come from different roots. You might say it's a word that died without offspring."

"I often think of my father's house," Sarah said as she stared up at her Uncle Harry's drawing of a horse's skull. "The house was connected to the barn so you wouldn't have to go out in the snow to get to your horse and buggy. It's still standing—painted blue now instead of white, and the new owners have turned part of the barn into a garage. We lived in the few steam-heated rooms in the center of the house. But in the summer, I spent lots of time in the many rooms of the attic, the barn, and the basement, and in the *secret passage.* That was what we called the crawlspace under the peak of the roof that led from the barn to the house. I hope that God's house has rooms like that—rooms where you can go off and be alone, rooms where you can cuddle with a good book, big empty rooms you can fill with your imagination.

"These last few nights I've dreamt that there's a secret room where I stored my most precious things—things that have been lost for years: a rusty iron ring a boy gave me in grammar school, a notebook of poems I wrote, and photos of Sam my brother who ran away from home. And there were doors from there to other rooms. Last night, I dreamt that Sam and Sue weren't really dead. They had been playing a game of hide-and-seek with me. To find them, I just had to open the right door."

***

Russ and Fred drove up Georgia Avenue, down Blair Road, and past all their friends' houses before parking the olive-green 1938 Nash two blocks from home. They were savoring their final hours of freedom and working out the last details of their grand entrance. They were bringing home a horse's skull, the very one Uncle Harry had drawn, as a present for Sue.

"What if she's over at Nancy's?" asked Fred.

"No chance," answered Russ. "Sue and her friends all sleep late on Saturdays."

"I'd better check those trenches she dug in the woods. That's where she goes on hot summer days to curl up with a book."

"Wake up, Fred. How many times do we have to go over this? It's early in the morning. She's in the house. There's nowhere else she could be. Believe me."

"You're sounding like a preacher already."

"Okay, buddy," said Russ, slapping his brother on the back of the head and parrying a counter slap.

"What if Dad sees me first?"

"Dad's probably on his way to a building site. If not, he's doing paperwork in the study. Mom's the one to watch for. She'll probably be cleaning up in the kitchen, but she could be anywhere in the house. Your job is to find Sue without letting Mom see you."

"Okay. Okay. Enough is enough."

"You know everything, right? So what are you going to do once you find her?"

"I'll tell her our coming back early is a secret, that we're going to surprise Mom and Dad. I'll bring her out the side door by the driveway. And you'll be hiding in the bushes with the horse's skull."

"Brilliant. Now go to it, buster."

Fred slipped quietly in the back door and crawled under the dining room table. Shielded by the long white tablecloth, he could see and hear without being seen.

He heard his father's footsteps going from the kitchen to the study and then back from study to kitchen, pausing, then going back again. Fred had never known his father to pace like that. And where was his mother? She was the one he'd expect to be moving about. Normally, she was never still for a moment, always cleaning and straightening, even while reading a book or talking to a friend. Something felt wrong.

Fred took a deep breath, waited until the footsteps returned to the study, then got up and tip-toed to the alcove by the fireplace. He could hear his father's heavy pacing even louder now.

Carefully, he leaned his head out of the alcove and looked around the living room. Something was missing.

The two spinning wheels, the baby grand piano, the sofa bed, the two stuffed armchairs, and the rocking chair were all in place, as before. But on the wall above the sofa, where once there had hung a dozen small family photos, now he saw one large photo of Sue. He recognized the pose. It was a formal professional shot, taken last Christmas. But this was an extremely large print—maybe three feet by two feet. The matting and the frame were black.

Fred quietly walked over and knelt on the sofa to get a better look. Inside the glass, against the photo itself, were several newspaper clippings. The headlines were cut off, except on the smallest one, which was from the Washington Post. They were death notices.

Fred heard his own scream before he realized that he was screaming. And then he couldn't stop screaming, running across the room, through the hall, tripping over his father, and bursting out the side door by the driveway, still screaming.

***

Sarah was upstairs in Sue's room, with the Reverend Schumacher. She had heard footsteps in the driveway and once again had tensed, expecting Rem Jones, the mailman. Smiling and pretending to pay close attention to what the Reverend was saying, she counted to herself. If there was another letter from the boys with no sign that they knew about Sue, she could expect that Carl would once again roar with anger.

Instead, she heard a shrill unearthly scream, then the sound of running and the side door slamming.

She and the Reverend raced down the stairs and bumped into Carl, who was getting back on his feet and moving toward the door.

Just then, they heard a second scream, almost as loud as the first, and a horse's skull loomed in the window, casting a dark shadow into the hall.

***

Frightened by Fred, Russ had let the skull fall on his own head. It stuck, blocking his vision; and when he tried to pull it off, the bone dug into his temples and ripped at his ears. He staggered around the driveway in pain, while Fred bellowed incoherently.

Meanwhile, Carl, Sarah, the Reverend Schumacher and Rem Jones watched in shock.

7 ~ Castles and Other Dreams

Russ kept asking, "What were the odds?" He, who had never shown any interest in math, became absorbed in statistics and probability. He found comfort in calculating the odds of Sue dying, the odds that all twelve letters their mother had written would get lost, and then that he and Fred would decide to come home unexpectedly. The likelihood of three such unlikely events happening in sequence was many times greater than the number of atoms in the known universe.

When Russ told the Reverend Schumacher about these calculations, the Reverend said, "The ways of God are indeed mysterious." Russ didn't find that answer satisfying. His mind needed something to work on, something to do, some way to assert control. If he had been told to say "Hail Mary" a million times, he would have done that. But being a Lutheran, not a Catholic, he sought salvation in working with numbers. As a freshman at college that fall, Russ found it difficult to focus on any course except statistics.

Meanwhile, at home, Fred took advantage of his new status as the only child in the house. He repainted the room he and Russ had shared and rearranged the furniture the way he wanted it. He ate what he wanted, stayed up as late as he wanted, and nobody hassled him about chores or homework. But after a few weeks of what felt like total freedom and self-indulgence, he felt restless and dissatisfied.

Before, Fred had always wanted to do things differently than his older brother but had buckled under to him when pressured. Now, there was no one for Fred to react to and define himself against.

One sleepless night, he moved to Sue's old bed and slept more soundly than before. Then he started visiting the Reverend Schumacher and spent time alone in the fields, staring at the sky and the horizon.

For years, Fred had been determined to go to a different college than Russ and pursue a different career. Now, to his surprise, he felt a growing bond of solidarity with his older brother. The following fall, he joined Russ at Gettysburg, intending, like him, to become a Lutheran minister.

***

Pearl Harbor and America's precipitous entry into the war came near the end of Fred's first semester—a time when Russ was close to failing several of his courses.

The war news stirred up memories of Uncle Harry's tales of the Great War and his travels afterwards in Paris and Istanbul and Cairo. Russ tried to join the Army but couldn't pass the physical because of flat feet. Fred, who was miffed that his brother had taken that step alone, tried too, and was rejected because of a dislocated shoulder—an old basketball injury.

Russ wrote to Uncle Harry about their problems, and Harry let them know that people were getting into the service who were in far worse shape than they were. He gave them advice on how to get around the bureaucracy.

Sarah and Carl had taken comfort in the knowledge that physical imperfection was likely to save their sons from the war. They were outraged at Uncle Harry's intervention.

Around the same time that Russ and Fred left for basic training, Sarah found out that she, at nearly fifty, was five months pregnant. She had gone to her doctor several times, and he had insisted that the discomfort and weight gain she was experiencing were due to change of life. Now, having heard the baby's heartbeat, he embarrassedly changed his diagnosis.

Carl rejoiced—it was a blessing from heaven. Sarah considered it an unaccountable burden.

During the last months of her pregnancy, she reread the *Old Testament*, lingering on the story of Sarah and Abraham as well as *Job* and *Ecclesiastes*. She also kept a journal, where she obsessively recorded everything she could remember about Sue, as if memory could resurrect her. On the fly-leaf of that diary she wrote: "Sue died while I was watching. Suddenly, her body was there, but she wasn't. She, whatever *she* was, left her body, like going from one room into another, only we couldn't see that other room and the door that leads there.

"I often dream of houses—huge old houses with secret passages leading to hidden rooms.

"I don't believe in reincarnation. But I do believe there is something else, somewhere else, a hereafter.

"It's as if Sue lived in a vast house, but she spent all her time in one little room, the size of a closet. And the door was shut. She didn't even know there was a door until it opened, and she passed from one room into another."

When Charlie was born, he looked so much like Sue that it was painful for Sarah to look at him. Even though money was scarce, they hired a neighbor to help take care of him for the first few years of his life.

Meanwhile, the private construction market dried up as the war made building materials scarce and drove up prices. Carl reluctantly gave up his independence and took a job as a foreman on a government project. Around that same time, he found out he had diabetes and had to carefully watch his diet, which added to his growing depression.

For two years, the only good news was the bored and boring letters they got from Russ and Fred who were stuck at Army camps in the swamps of Georgia and Louisiana. Fortunately, they were never shipped overseas. When they came home on leave, they looked at little Charlie as an unwelcome intruder, to be ignored, at best.

Charlie learned to talk late—no one was listening closely enough to him to recognize and reinforce sounds that came close to *mama* and *dada*.

When he was three, Charlie often tagged along with his father to building sites. His father tolerated him there as long as he didn't touch anything. Charlie stood patiently and watched all day as workers dug the foundations, poured the concrete, and raised the framework.

Carl was both puzzled and pleased by Charlie's quiet, intense interest. Neither of his other sons had showed interest in his work. "I wonder what he day-dreams about when he's standing there like that," Carl said to Sarah. "What kind of a mansion is he building in that mind of his?"

When the war ended and gas rationing stopped, Carl drove Charlie around Washington for the pleasure of seeing his wide-eyed reactions to the sights.

Sarah mocked Carl, "You're old enough to be Charlie's grandfather. That's what you're doing, you know. You're not treating him like a son.

You're just enjoying him like a grandson. Lord only knows how he's going to learn discipline and values, the way you spoil him."

That rebuke tickled Carl's fancy and encouraged him to take Charlie on more excursions, especially to the beach in the summer.

When Carl was a child, his grandfather had taken him to the beach at least once each summer. They'd go by train, from Lancaster to Philadelphia and Philadelphia to Ocean City, New Jersey.

Grandfather Uhland couldn't swim. The beach, for him, was a place for castles and dreams, and his were not ordinary sandcastles. He was a craftsman, a cabinetmaker. He made wooden pull-toys: crocodiles and bears and elephants that opened their mouths and wiggled their ears and tails when you pulled them. And he made elaborate castles out of sand and wood on the beach.

All winter long, Grandfather Uhland made drawings of historic castles in Ireland, Wales, and Germany, countries where his ancestors had lived. Then he carved and warped pieces of wood until they were the right size and shape and prepared all the materials he'd need to create those castles, in exquisite detail, on the beach.

He didn't want to attract crowds. He'd look for an empty stretch of beach.

He built his castles close to the water, at low tide, and watched with glee when the sea came in and battered those magnificent towers and leveled them just as it leveled the crude structures that three-year-olds made. For him, that was the point of building on the beach—to watch the waves come and wreck the elaborate castles. When the waves knocked down a castle, Grandfather and Carl would retrieve the wood. Then once again, they'd build the same castle or a new one—at least one for each tide, for as long as they were at the beach.

As long as they had their dreams and their drawings, they could build a new one, as good as or better than all the ones that had gone before. And the sea was doing them a service by erasing them. In washing the old ones away, the sea was preparing the surface for more castles.

8 ~ Aunt Rachel and the Wizard of Oz

In July of 1946, Russ, recently discharged from the Army, arrived home from Georgia with his new bride, seventeen-year-old Rachel.

He had the cab stop at the corner and left their luggage under a bush. Then he paused to admire Rachel.

When she was disoriented, as she was now, she looked very young, naïve, and vulnerable. But alone in bed at night, she could turn bold and provocative. He enjoyed comforting her, then shocking her, to watch her switch from one extreme to the other. He was fascinated by her fluctuating, lustful innocence.

He took hold of Rachel's hand and pulled her along, as he slid quickly and quietly toward the house. They hid behind hedges, then behind a large oak tree, then dashed to the front door.

"Remember," he told her, "they don't know you exist. Stay right here by the door. I'll go around to the side. It ought to take me five to ten minutes to set them up. Then I'll get Mom to open the front door, and you'll say ... "

"Hello, Mom, I'm your new daughter."

"Right. You've got it. It'll be unforgettable. Just stay put and wait for your cue."

Russ crept back the way he came and picked up the suitcases. Then he strolled up the driveway to the side door. He tried hard to maintain a poker face, but, inside, he was laughing at this surprise he had prepared for his parents.

He knew they would love Rachel. They would be as delighted as he was that he had met her and won her. It was as if he had won a million dollars, and he wanted to spring the news on them with dramatic flair.

He also had a surprise in store for Rachel. He had never told her he had a baby brother. The way she loved kids she'd go wild over little Charlie.

"Mom. Dad. I'm home," he hollered as he opened the door.

No answer.

"Mom? Dad?" He put the suitcases down and ran to the living room. It was empty.

He hollered even louder, "Mom, Dad," and rushed into the hall and up the stairs. Still no answer.

He ran back down again, and, out of breath and disappointed, opened the front door for Rachel.

"Hello, Mom ... " she blurted out, then broke into laughter.

"Hush," Russ put a hand over her mouth. "They aren't here. They must be visiting with a neighbor. We'll still surprise them, just a different way. Come on in. I'll show you around. Then I'll hunt them down and set them up. Believe me, this will work great. I can't wait to see the look on their faces."

"God," she exclaimed as she walked in the door.

"Watch your language. How many times do I have to tell you —my parents are very touchy about things like that. Never, and I mean never, use the name of God in vain in this house."

"All right, already. But this place is wild. It's just the way you described it." She went straight to the fireplace, walked into the alcove, and curled up on the bench. "Come over here," she hiked up her skirt above her garter belt and started unbuttoning her blouse. "You know how I've been looking forward to this."

"Not now. They could walk in the door any minute."

"But we're married," she coaxed. "Remember, anything goes when you're married."

"But not in my parents' house. Besides, there'll be time enough for that later."

"Russ, you are unbelievable. But I love you anyway." She nuzzled her head against his shoulder. When she stood up straight, her forehead was even with his chin.

He slowly ran his hand through her long, straight black hair, and caressed her ears, adorned with gold-plated loop earrings he had given her. He held her close. "Okay, you Delilah. We both know you can get your way with me whenever you want. But please don't tempt me now. Come on, I want to show you the house."

He led her upstairs, then had her wait in the hall while he scampered up a pull-down staircase to the attic and came back with the horse's skull.

"You mean that really happened?" Rachel asked. "That whole wild episode?"

"Of course. And come in here. This was Sue's room. There's the drawing Uncle Harry did of this same skull. See, it's a good likeness." He put the skull on the floor in front of the picture. "And over there," he pointed to the other wall, "is that blow-up photo of Sue that spooked Fred when he saw it in the living room."

"God," she started to say, then corrected herself. "Gosh. This room looks like a young girl still lives here."

"Mom's left everything the same, like she expects Sue to come back. From what Dad says in his letters, Mom's gotten superstitious. Every year, on Sue's birthday, she bakes a cake, and sets it up with the right number of candles, as if Sue were still alive and getting a year older each year. According to Dad, Mom claims she has seen the shadow of a young girl, in this very room, by that very window."

"Oh, I'm scared of ghosts," Rachel murmured, nuzzling up to him again. "I need a big strong man to protect me." She turned her head to the side so their lips could touch.

He laughed and pushed her back, "Not now."

"But we've never kissed in a haunted house before."

"And you know I couldn't stop with just kissing you. Wait here. I'll find my parents and bring them back. Then I'll come up and tell you my new plan."

"Why not just tell me now."

"Believe me, if I knew it, I'd tell you. I'll figure it out as I go along."

He threw her a kiss from the door.

***

When Russ first came barging into the house, little Charlie, age four, was playing with tin soldiers in his parents' room. Frightened by the shouting and the loud steps, he crawled under the bed and hid. Then he heard soft voices coming from Sue's room. Then loud footsteps rushed downstairs again.

Slowly, cautiously, Charlie crept out and inched his way toward Sue's room.

Now, standing in the doorway, he saw Sue herself, sitting in her old room, with light streaming through the window behind her. Her face was in shadow, but even from the doorway he could feel the warmth of her love, a warmth he had never felt before.

She was playing with her miniature horses on the windowsill. He'd never seen a grownup play make-believe before. Her hands slid from one figure to the next as her attention moved. Then she tossed her head back and shook her hair as if she, too, were a horse.

He walked up to her, slowly, without saying a word. He knew without a doubt who she was and presumed that she knew him — after all, he was her brother. Even a ghost would have to know that much. He wondered why it had taken her so long to appear to him.

Charlie tripped over the horse's skull on the floor. The girl turned toward Charlie. Sue had disappeared, and in her place stood another girl, about the same age — a pretty girl, with long black hair. Charlie screamed an unworldly scream, and the girl ran up to him, picked him up, and hugged him tight to comfort him.

"Where did she go?" asked Charlie in confusion. "What did you do with her? Where did you hide her?"

"Who?" asked Rachel.

"Sue. My sister Sue. She was just here. You made her go away. Tell her you won't hurt her. Please call her back."

***

Meanwhile, Sarah, walking back to the house from the end of the driveway, saw the shadow of a young girl at Sue's window. She stopped, shut her eyes, turned away, then looked again, and the shadow was still there. She took her glasses out of her pocketbook, wiped them clean on her blouse, and looked again. The shadow was still there.

With trembling voice, she began to repeat the Lord's Prayer, "Our Father ... "

Then the shadow moved, and an unworldly scream broke loose — Charlie's scream.

Sarah ran up the driveway, stubbed her toe on the doorstep, banged her knee on the door, tripped up the stairs, and found this strange girl with a wild frightened look, holding Charlie.

The girl hesitated in confusion, then blurted out, "Hello, Mom, I'm your new daughter."

Sarah grabbed a broom from the corner and waved it at Rachel, shouting wildly, "Out, you madwoman, you imposter, you demon."

Rachel clutched Charlie and ran through the upstairs hall, down the stairs, and out the side door to the driveway.

Sarah came racing after her, waving her broom, and shouting, "Unhand my son, you, you ... "

Rachel cowered, helpless, with her back to the wall. "Your son?" she asked. "But your sons are in the Army or were in the Army. You're—"

"Old enough to be his grandmother? Yes, indeed, but he's mine." She reached out her arms to him. He hesitated a moment, then pulled away from Rachel and ran to his mother. She picked him up and hugged him warmly. Then she shifted her attention back to the intruder. "And who are you to be playing Goldilocks, wandering into other people's houses?"

"As I tried to explain—"

"Don't explain anything. Just tell me who you are!"

Rachel hesitated, then answered, "My name is Mrs. Uhland."

"What?"

"Mrs. Rachel Uhland. Mrs. Russell P. Uhland. Your son's wife."

"Impossible. You're just a girl, no older than—"

"Than your daughter Sue would have been? Russ told me about her many times."

Stunned, Sarah stared and held Charlie even tighter.

"Russ wanted to surprise you. I thought we should invite the whole family to the wedding, or wait and have the wedding here, or at least tell you what we were doing. But Russ insisted. He's a big kid the way he loves surprises, and I love him for that. He had this whole script worked up with what he was going to say to you and Mr. Uhland, and how he'd get you to open the front door and there I'd be standing. But nobody was home when we got here. Nobody except the little one."

"Charlie."

"Yes, Charlie. That must have been another of Russ's surprises—not telling me he had a little brother. That rascal. If I didn't love him so much, I'd hate him," Rachel laughed.

Sarah stepped forward to take a closer look at this girl. Confused and innocent, wearing a plaid skirt and white blouse and saddle shoes with green socks, Rachel looked like a ninth grader just home from school.

Russ emerged from the backyard, walking with his father. "Oh," he stopped short. "I guess you've met already."

"This little girl says she's your wife."

"She most certainly is." He ran up and lifted Rachel with one arm under her knees and another under her back.

"Is this some kind of joke?" asked Sarah. "She's not old enough to be married."

"She's seventeen, Mom. In Georgia, that's nearly an old maid. Besides, you were sixteen when you married Dad."

Rachel craned her neck upwards toward Russ, perhaps to kiss him or perhaps to bite him, in anger at the humiliation he was putting her through.

"Seventeen?" repeated Sarah. "Why, Judy Garland— "

"What, Mom?" asked Russ.

"Judy Garland was seventeen when she played Dorothy in *The Wizard of Oz*. Who could ever imagine Dorothy as a married woman?"

"Oh, that's a wonderful movie!" Rachel nuzzled Russ's neck, all sweetness now. She kissed him behind the ear. "I saw in the paper that it's playing again. When it first came out, I saw it three times and loved it more each time."

Sarah stared at her, unaccustomed to seeing signs of affection in public. She held Charlie tighter. She was still trying to absorb the shock that Russ was married. "Sue was ten when I took her to it. I haven't been to another movie since then. Come to think of it," she added distractedly, "Charlie has never been to a movie at all."

"Oh, but he must go. He simply must," insisted Rachel. "That's the most magical movie of all time, and movies are the most magical experience on earth. Please let me take him, Mrs. Uhland, please."

Sarah turned to Russ, then to Carl. She had no idea what to do or say, and she could tell that Russ and Carl were equally confused. Her son had married a puzzling and perhaps wicked little girl. That was an incredible mistake that could throw all their lives in disorder. But the question at hand was whether to take Charlie to the movies. Sarah felt dizzy. On impulse, she responded, "We'll both take him."

"Great idea," Russ confirmed, with a sigh of relief. "I'll check the times in the paper. That'll give you two a chance to get acquainted while Dad and I catch up and take care of the yard."

"The lawn could certainly use a mowing," added Carl, with a smile.

Sarah smiled too, put Charlie down, and gave him a pat on the behind. "Run upstairs, wash up, and put on your best Sunday clothes. And don't forget to wash behind your ears and under your nails. Let's make an occasion of this. It's not every day you see your first movie."

***

Charlie was confused, but he did what he was told. It was bad enough having to get dressed up and go to *God's house* every Sunday. Now he had to get dressed up on a Saturday to go to some new kind of place. Rachel said that there would be lots of people. Mom said he'd have to behave and stay still and keep quiet. He hoped this wasn't something he'd have to do again and again, like going to church. He'd rather stay home with Dad and Russ and play and work in the yard. But he knew there was no arguing with Mom.

The building was as big as a church, but instead of wooden benches, there were grownup seats with arm rests. Mom wanted to sit in the back and Rachel up front. They sat in the back. Then Charlie stood on his seat to see over people, and Mom picked him up, and they moved to the front row.

He was just getting comfortable in his big soft seat when the lights went out. It was darker than nighttime. With one hand he grabbed his mother's arm, and with the other he found Rachel's hand. He held his breath and squeezed tight.

Then the curtain opened, and he was almost knocked over by the light, the color, the music. Creatures appeared that were many times bigger than anything he had ever seen before. He wanted to ask, "Which one is God?" But he figured he was supposed to know without asking, and Mom might get upset that he hadn't paid attention in Sunday School.

Rachel gave him a hug, and whispered to him, "They look alive, but it's just a trick. Look up. See that beam of light? That's where the pictures come from. They're just light on a screen. Nothing to be afraid of."

"Oh, I'm not afraid," he answered, then quickly looked over at Mom to see if she was mad at him and Rachel for talking. But Mom was just staring at the screen and smiling.

Cartoons switched to news reels, to previews, to a Tarzan serial, to the feature. To Charlie, it was all one long sequence of pictures, one surprise after another, average looking people and things mixed together with storybook characters and things, like in a dream.

Rachel leaned over and whispered. "I used to live in Kansas. But I never saw a tornado," she added.

"What's a tornado?"

"That is," she said, pointing to the screen, where wind was blowing things every which way.

When the movie switched from black-and-white to full color, Charlie jumped like he had when light first hit the screen.

Afterward, Charlie remembered Rachel's words more clearly than the words of the movie. And the pictures he remembered best were the ones that she named and described as he watched. Years later, he'd say that her voice had controlled a camera shutter in his mind. "Ruby shoes, Munchkins, Scarecrow, Tin Woodman, Lion." One snapshot after the other, held forever in memory.

When the Great Oz first spoke, Charlie leaned toward Rachel and whispered, "Is he God?" But she didn't answer.

The cackling laugh of the Wicked Witch of the West cut into him. The Witch scared him so much it hurt. He shut his eyes and tried to think of other things.

He slept through the rest of the movie, his scary dreams mixing with sounds and images from the movie.

He was glad when it was over, and they were safely out on the sidewalk again.

Then Rachel started singing the rainbow song, and Mom joined in. Rachel took one hand of his and Mom the other, and they started dancing and skipping up the street, chanting, "Lions, and tigers, and bears! Oh, my!" It was like they were kids with him, or he was a grownup with them. He laughed like he'd never laughed before and hugged them both with abandon. And they hugged back like he was the most important person in the world and they both wanted him all to themselves.

***

That day, and every day for a week, Charlie kept talking about the movie and asking questions. Rachel read the book to him. Then they went to see the movie again the next Saturday, and the Saturday after. Gradually, he began to see the story, instead of just pieces. He was fascinated with it, and he loved the grownup attention he got when he talked about it.

"Is our house like that, Mom?" Charlie asked at bedtime. "Can it take us to some other world?"

"Charlie, don't be silly. That's just a story, like a dream."

"You mean dreams aren't real?"

"I suppose they're real in their own way. But things aren't what they seem in dreams. One thing stands for another."

He didn't know what that meant so he asked, "Do you dream, Mom?"

"Of course," she answered. "We all do. That's part of being human — like remembering and building things and talking and reading."

"What do you dream, Mom?"

"Lots of times I dream of houses," she admitted.

"Ones that fly and fall on wicked witches?" he asked.

"No, I dream of the house I grew up in. Sometimes the house has extra rooms like attics on top of attics, and passageways leading to new passageways. Some are empty, and some are storage areas, like at our summer house, with trunks and boxes stacked high. I go wandering through those rooms, from one to another, opening boxes looking for a lost recipe as if the world depended on my finding it. Or I walk into a room that's furnished like a living room, well-kept and dusted, with a warm cup of tea sitting on the table, waiting for the owner, whoever she may be, to come back. Or I wake up in a strange bed in one of those rooms and can't find the passage that will get me out again. Sometimes I think I catch a glimpse of your sister Sue, playing hide-and-seek in those rooms."

"Have you ever seen me there?" he asked.

"No, I haven't seen you or Rachel in my dreams, not yet. But I will someday. I'm sure of it. That's the way dreams are."

After that, Charlie made a habit of asking his mother about her dreams when he went to bed at night. Even when she was busy and, in a hurry, she'd linger a few minutes to answer his questions. And his own dreams, instead of jumping from here to there to everywhere, like they had before, began to resemble the dreams she told him — often dealing with huge old houses with unexplored rooms. He was no longer afraid of falling asleep.

9 ~ Charlie's Coming of Age

Sarah Daly was born in 1892 in Plymouth, New Hampshire, the small town where Daniel Webster lost his first court case, in a one-room schoolhouse that was now the town library. Nathaniel Hawthorne died there at the Pemigewasset House—a large white frame hotel, just a block from the Daly house.

The Dalys were a typical Victorian family—many children and few survivors. Sarah was the youngest. Sam, the sibling closest to her in age, ran away at twelve. He took ship in Boston, as a cabin boy, and was lost at sea, presumed dead. Her sister Margaret became hysterical in her late teens and was put away in an insane asylum, where she died ten years later. Another brother died of pneumonia. Two others died as infants.

When Sarah was six, her father and her brother Harry headed west to see if the prospects there were as good as newspapers and magazines claimed. They spent a year wandering and doing odd jobs on ranches in Colorado and Wyoming.

Harry loved the land and the life. But Sarah's father gave up and returned east to his family to spend the rest of his days working in a shoe-tree factory in Plymouth.

Sarah met Carl Uhland, her husband-to-be, at the Pemigewasset House. She was doing maid's work there during summer vacation from high school, and he had come north for the mountain air, on his doctor's recommendation. In late August and September, he suffered badly from hay fever, everywhere but at sea or in the mountains.

Aside from his allergies, Carl was muscular and tough—a successful builder, who had begun as a construction hand. He was the only son of a Pennsylvania Dutch farmer and the grandson of a cabinetmaker. Carl wasn't interested in farming. From the day when his grandfather first showed him how to make sandcastles using boards for support, Carl had dreamt of building houses, one after the other, whole neighborhoods of houses, teeming with children. After finishing high school, he hiked to Washington, D. C., where he found work in the flourishing building trade.

When Carl and Sarah married, he was twenty-one and she sixteen. He built a house for them in Silver Spring, Maryland. He also built a summer cottage at Colonial Beach on the Potomac in Virginia.

The cottage was near a lighthouse, across the street from a grove, just above the riverbank. The ground sloped upward. In the front, the main part of the building, with six bedrooms and the front porch, was on stilts, so it was protected from high water. In the back, the dining room and kitchen were at ground level. Under the bedrooms was a large storage area with lattice sides and a dirt floor. Above the bedrooms, accessible with a pull-down ladder, was an attic which could sleep four people in beds and up to a dozen on the floor. In the backyard there was a grape arbor, a garage, and a tool shed. To the side, were a stone-and-masonry goldfish pond and a yard large enough for volleyball, badminton, and croquet.

When Sarah's brother Harry returned from World War I, he stayed at the cottage for several months before heading west once again. He had volunteered to stay overseas for two years after the end of the war, and he had just heard his wife was divorcing him. Day after day, he puttered aimlessly along the beach, heaving stones and shells at unseen targets. Then in the fall, he headed west to start a new life. He left behind several trunks full of military paraphernalia and souvenirs from Europe, North Africa, and the Middle East. Those trunks gave the summer house an aura of the exotic.

***

After taking Charlie to *The Wizard of Oz* for three Saturdays in a row, Rachel wanted to take him to the summer cottage which she had heard about from Russ. Sarah insisted on going, too, so Carl took them all.

As soon as the car stopped, Charlie ran out with his bucket and filled it with sand, then dumped it, and did that over and over again, making many simple sandcastles along the waterline. Carl, Rachel, and Sarah all followed, making more such bucket castles. Then they all cheered as Charlie ran down the line, stamping on each and every castle.

Russ watched from a distance, surprised to see his fifty-year-old mother up to her ankles in wet sand, splashing like a four-year-old. She had never played with him like that when he was Charlie's age.

Not to be outdone, Russ scavenged in the storage area for Uncle Harry's World War I army gear. Then he crept across the street and hid behind tall grass near the main path. There he lay in wait.

When Charlie and Rachel came strolling up the path, Russ pulled a string, which lowered the grass, revealing what looked like soldiers dug in with guns at the ready. Then he set off firecrackers.

Rachel burst out laughing. But Charlie froze in terror until Sarah picked him up and carried him to the house, calming him with hugs and soothing words.

The next day, Russ sat on the porch and watched in amazement as, once again, his wife and parents played on the beach. He wanted to join in the fun but felt out of place. So instead, he rigged the cottage with water balloons.

Charlie, who was the first one back from the beach, was the perfect victim. Running through the kitchen door, Charlie was hit by the first water balloon, then tripped in confusion and triggered a second and a third. Rachel thought it was hilarious, and this time Charlie laughed, too.

After that, Charlie wanted Russ to teach him tricks that he could play like short-sheeting beds and putting grapes in slippers. And on cloudy, cool days, the two of them would get out the old army gear and dig foxholes on the beach and play war games with the neighbor kids.

Sarah remembered that summer as the time when she learned to enjoy her son Charlie. She was always grateful to Rachel and Russ for that. But at the same time, she felt guilty for feeling so happy and feared she would never be able to establish the same distance and same level of discipline with Charlie as she had with her other sons. She was afraid of what might become of him with such an unorthodox upbringing. But she couldn't help but roll in the sand and the waves with him, now that Rachel had shown her how much fun that could be.

***

That fall, Fred got discharged from the Army and returned to Gettysburg College. He became a Lutheran minister and moved to Illinois where he married Francine and had two sons, Jimmy and Georgie.

Russ finished college at the University of Maryland, became an actuary for an insurance company, and moved to nearby Rockville, Maryland, where he and Rachel also had two sons, Frankie and Eddie.

The beach house was where the cousins of the new generation met and played with one another and with their Uncle Charlie.

Charlie didn't belong in the generation of his brothers. He was 20 years younger than Russ, and eight years older than Frankie, to whom he was more like a big brother than an uncle.

The beach was where the extended family would gather—some of them for the whole summer, some for weekends, and some just for the Fourth of July. There were plenty of rooms. And when friends and more distant relatives showed up, as they often did, there was always space for more sleeping bags.

This was where Carl got used to being called "Grandpa" and Sarah "Grandma," even by their own sons and daughters-in-law and even by Charlie. It was also where they could act like kids themselves, joining Charlie and their grandchildren to build sandcastles.

And this was where Charlie could get away with devilishness. Now he was expected to be the practical joker and imaginative terror of the younger kids. Russ, who no longer indulged in such childishness himself, laughed at and encouraged Charlie's booby-traps and pranks, and prodded his own son Frankie to join in.

Charlie also developed an endearing manner with the older generation. When he went too far in his horseplay and was at risk for serious punishment, he could put on an apologetic look and admit his fault and nothing came of it.

Once, when Frankie was seven and Eddie two, Rachel asked Charlie to babysit.

Russ objected, "Charlie at the beach is one thing. But in this house with these kids, that's something else. No way. Absolutely no way."

But their regular babysitter had taken sick, and Rachel was determined to go to this party. There was no choice but Charlie.

"Now look, kid," Russ told Charlie. "To be on the level with you, I think you're too immature for this. Yes, you're thirteen years old. Yes, you're tall for your age. But from what I've seen of you at the beach, you're more of a kid than Frankie is. Today I want you to act older than your years, not younger. Surprise me. Show me you can act like an adult."

Charlie smiled broadly—too broadly, Russ would recall—and reassured him. "I can act like an adult. Just trust me."

From what Russ and Rachel could gather afterwards, Charlie did indeed fulfill his promise, after a fashion. When they got home, their neighbor Mr. Callahan was waiting on their doorstep, and their house was filled with cigarette butts and empty beer cans.

Frankie had woken up, heard talking in the living room, and peeked around the corner. He saw Charlie with a bunch of older boys, "grown men," he insisted, but they were probably about eighteen. They were drinking beer and swapping jokes. Frankie didn't understand what they were saying and fell asleep in the hall. When he woke up, the house was dark and quiet.

"Charlie!" he called.

No answer.

"Mommy! Daddy!"

No answer.

Eddie woke up screaming. Frankie panicked and screamed, too.

Mr. Callahan found Frankie on the sidewalk bawling, "Mommy! Daddy! Where are you?" Mr. Callahan fetched Eddie, too, and brought them to his house, and left a note on the door.

Charlie came over when he got back. "I thought Frankie was sound asleep," he explained. "I just went out with my friends to get more beer." That explanation from a thirteen-year-old did *not* go over well.

Russ was furious when he found out. But after a few years and many retellings of the tale, even Russ couldn't help but laugh at how Charlie did indeed "act like an adult."

***

Rachel maintained a special friendship with Charlie. When the family got together, she'd bring him presents, and she always had something she wanted to talk to him about—a new movie or book that she had seen or read. Charlie would ask her about her dreams and record them in a notebook.

Thanks, in part, to this practice with Rachel, Charlie developed a remarkable ability for getting along with adults. At fifteen, when he was taller than his father and taller than his brother Russ, Charlie played master of ceremonies at family gatherings— first as a joke, and then as his expected and natural role.

He enjoyed being the center of attention and being in control.

At parties he found just the right words to help strangers mix. At school dances, he made a habit of dancing with all the wallflowers. He was at ease with all girls—bright and dull, beautiful, and homely.

By the time he was eighteen, Charlie was confident enough to practice his powers of flirtation on any woman, regardless of her age. He'd give that woman his full attention, keeping her off-balance, while maintaining a respectful distance. This tension of desire and restraint was exciting and liberating, particularly to married women twice his age.

***

At Colonial Beach, Rachel luxuriated in Charlie's attention. Russ was inclined to get wrapped up in his insurance work and to take his work home. He seemed to forget that Rachel had interests of her own, aside from taking care of the kids, and that she liked to be noticed and appreciated. At the beach, the attention of Charlie, this virile and handsome teenage brother-in-law made Rachel feel young again. She wore a revealing two-piece bathing suit that would have scandalized Russ, had he noticed.

Rachel was proud of the figure she had maintained despite having given birth to two children. Her breasts were now more ample and, as Russ often reminded her, sexier than they had been when she was a teenage bride. Yes, there were varicose veins on her legs, but a summer tan soon masked those. Strangers found it hard to believe she was old enough to have a son Frankie's age.

On Saturday of Memorial Day weekend in 1960, when Charlie was a high-school senior, Rachel found herself alone with him at the cottage. Everyone else was downtown at a carnival and wouldn't be back for hours.

Rachel could feel the silence in the cottage as she stood half-naked in her room. The heavy silence was punctuated by footsteps that could only be Charlie, walking toward her door, hesitating, then continuing down the hall, out the front door and down the steps. She didn't know what she would have said or done if he had knocked or even opened the door to her room.

She felt ashamed of herself for having such thoughts. But it gave her pleasure to think that she was attractive, that he might want her physically.

She pushed her two-piece bathing suit lower at the bust and at the hips before she grabbed a towel and ran after him toward the beach.

Charlie was leaning against a pine tree in the middle of the grove. Out of the corners of her eyes, Rachel could feel his eyes following her. She walked with more than her usual sway.

She pretended not to see him and called, "Charlie! Where are you, Charlie? Did you go off to that carnival and not say a word?"

When he didn't answer, Rachel felt and acted like a mischievous teenager. She stretched out her blanket in a sheltered area below the bank where she couldn't be seen from the road, or from any of the houses up and down the river, and just a few feet out of the range of Charlie's view. There she boldly undid the top of her bathing suit and stretched out on her belly to sunbathe.

She heard Charlie take a few steps closer on the bank. She pretended to shut her eyes, but through her eyelashes she could see him ten feet away, stretched out on his belly on the bank above, gawking at her. She felt deliciously evil. She hadn't felt so desirable and desired since Russ first undressed her fourteen years before.

She sensed he was about to back away, but she wanted this sensuous tension to continue. So, gracefully, she rolled over, exposing her ample breasts.

She even dared to look him straight in the eye, quickly, so he knew she knew. Then she looked away, not to embarrass him or force him to speak or to leave. She leaned back on her elbows, thrusting her breasts up and forward to grant him the fullest possible view.

Rachel and Charlie lay like that, silently for nearly an hour. From time to time, Rachel would change position for comfort, but always giving him a picture-perfect view.

Then, still looking away, she stood up, put on the top of the bathing suit and walked back to the cottage as if nothing had happened.

That night, when Russ and Rachel were going to bed, Rachel asked, "What's the probability of a woman becoming pregnant from making love just once without a condom?" As he looked up, she slowly, like a stripper removed her bathing suit, revealed her now suntanned breasts. Her feelings of guilt from her outlandish behavior that morning added zest to the passion which drew her and Russ together, like a pair of teenagers alone at last, after months of groping and lusting. Nine months later, nearly eight years after the birth of Eddie, she gave birth to their third son, Johnny.

***

That same night, after everyone was in bed, Charlie went out to the beach alone. There, by the light of the full moon, he built a large and elaborate castle out of sand and wood using bits of lumber from the storage area under the cottage.

Just after dawn, Carl, on his usual morning walk, found him there. "That's a fine castle, son," he remarked. "I've never seen you do anything like it before. Have you been sneaking down here in the dark to practice?" he chuckled.

"No, this is the first. And it will be the last for a while, too."

"But we have a long summer ahead of us. We could work together on something like that. Indeed, I'd like to if you'd let me."

"Maybe some other time, some other place," Charlie stared down at his feet. He had come to the beach to be alone with his thoughts. This encounter was unexpected, but welcome. Charlie wanted to talk to his father in private. "Dad," he continued.

Carl smiled. "Yes, son."

"I'm joining the Army."

"Well, that's certainly a choice to consider, along with college, but I thought your heart was set on college in the fall," Carl responded in a friendly, but patronizing tone. "Let's talk about the Army after you've graduated from high school. Then we can weigh the pros and cons together."

"No, Dad. I've made up my mind. I'm not going back to school. I'm not going to take finals. I'm not going to graduate from high school. I'm simply going to join up. Please don't try to talk me out of it," he quickly added. "It's a difficult decision. Please don't make it any more difficult."

"But why are you doing this, Charlie? What's your dream?"

"I've got lots of dreams, Dad. Maybe that's the trouble. There are so many dreams floating around in my head that I don't know which one is really mine. Maybe I ought to be a builder like you, or a soldier like Uncle Harry, or a minister like Fred. Or maybe I could write books or make movies. I can see myself doing any of those things. But mostly, I see myself with women, all kinds of women. And that's confusing. I need to get away and sort it out before I make a total mess of things."

"Well, Charlie, I hope you do sort things out. Most folks never do." Carl shut his lips tight. He looked long and hard at the sandcastle, then sat on it, making himself comfortable, as he knocked over towers and walls. Charlie laughed and sat beside him. It was a very big castle.

"You know, I don't talk much," said Carl. "Your mother's the one for words. But this sandcastle of yours has got me to thinking. What matters is what you do, more than what you say. I like to think that what I do with my hands is what makes me who I am. I like to be in control. But time and again, I see dreams and stories and ideas making more of a difference than plain facts. I can't make sense of it, but it happens. Why am I a builder?" he asked Charlie.

"I suppose because you wanted to be one."

"Yes. And why did I want to be one? Where did the motivation come from? It was a dream, planted in my mind by my grandfather, the cabinetmaker. And Russ and Fred joined the Army in wartime, when they didn't have to, because of a dream their Uncle Harry had planted in their heads. And there are other dreams floating around in this family, just waiting to be picked up by somebody else and change another life."

"What do you mean, Dad?"

"I think of your mother and those house dreams she tells you about, and her superstitions about death not really being the end of things. I think about your dad, Russ, and the way he liked to stage practical jokes—like what matters isn't what you do, but how well you surprise everyone with it. It's okay to marry a girl you hardly know, if you can make a good story out of it. That's the kind of thing I'm talking about.

"Dreams like that can have a life of their own. They seem to move from person to person, from generation to generation, living and growing and changing.

"There's something risky and uncontrollable about them. I don't trust the way they can change your motivation and make you go in a direction that nobody would ever have expected, from the plain facts of the matter."

Charlie took a board from the castle and heaved it side armed so it skipped on the water like a large flat stone, then it floated on the waves. The two of them watched it quietly for a few minutes before Charlie answered, "It isn't a dream that's making me do this, Dad. I don't have an ambition to go in one direction that I see clearly. No, I'm doing this because I don't have a direction and need to find one."

"But your dropping out of high school when you're nearly done, and not going to college, that feels like me at your age, when I left my father's farm and went to D. C. to become a builder. That made no sense to my father, just as this makes no sense to me.

"Don't get me wrong, son. I know you need a sense of direction. I know you need to figure out who you are and who you want to be, and you need to follow through with what you promise yourself. But I'm scared, son. I'm scared of what dreams can do to a person. Please don't build your life on dreams."

Carl continued, "How can I tell you straight when it isn't straight to me. I loved building sandcastles with my grandfather. And I loved showing you how to do it. I'm a dreamer, too. I suppose that's part of being a builder. You don't make houses with just boards and bricks; you need plans, patterns, ideas, dreams to give them shape so they can fill a purpose. But my advice is stay in control. Keep your sandcastles at the beach. That's where they belong. That's the only place where building and then breaking doesn't bring harm to anyone."

10 ~ Recruited

The recruiter's office was barely large enough to fit one small table and two chairs. It was a temporary space in the Post Office building, used at various times by a dozen other organizations. The Army recruiter had it afternoons Tuesdays and Thursdays from three to five.

Charlie stopped in the doorway and looked around. The gray paint on the walls was peeling in large strips near the one window on the street side. There were no posters. There was no rack with brochures. A strong odor of disinfectant masked a faint odor of vomit. The recruiter, in well-pressed dress greens, with highly polished buttons, was hunched over a table, absorbed in a paperback book. His name tag read "Sergeant Camaratta." There were two stacks of books on either side of him on the table. Each book had one or more bookmarks.

Charlie had never been to a job interview. For summer jobs, he worked on construction projects for his father or his father's friends.

Standing here, quietly waiting, he was apprehensive, but saw himself as brave and important. He was proud to be taking charge of his life with this bold dramatic gesture.

Charlie was prepared for one brief, painful moment of transition, like diving into the river on a cold morning. Once he was in, he was sure he would do fine. Millions of others before him had gone through basic training and a three-year hitch in the peace-time Army. He was in good physical shape. He'd do fine. He just wanted to sign up and get it over with.

Charlie's feet itched. He could smell his own sweat.

The sergeant kept reading with a frown of intense concentration. He was heavy-set, with a square pock-marked face. His hair was cut short and flat. Only when he got to the end of a chapter, marked his place with a torn piece of paper, and reached for another book from the stack to his right, did he acknowledge that Charlie was standing in front of him.

"Hello, son, what can I do for you?" asked the sergeant.

"I want to sign up."

"Fine. And what do you want to do?"

"Like I said, I want to sign up."

"Yes, son, but are you interested in the Army as a career or are you looking for a chance to learn skills that will help you get a job in civilian life?"

"Mister, to be honest, I don't know what the hell I want to do. That's why I'm here."

"Okay. First things first. How old are you?"

"Eighteen."

"Have you graduated from high school?"

"No."

"How far did you get?"

"Mister, you're not making this easy for me. I was supposed to graduate in two weeks, but I just dropped out."

"Kicked out?"

"No, dropped out. My grades are okay. I was planning to go to college. But I just can't keep going like I've been going. I don't like myself anymore. I need to get away. I need time to figure out who I ought to be and how to become such a person."

"Hey, kid, don't we all? But what's the rush? This is the start of a new decade, kid. Believe me, you're going to need education to get anywhere. Go ahead, put up with another two weeks of high school. Then put in a few years in the Army, see something of the world, grow up a bit. Then you can come back and really get something out of college."

"Mister, please. I don't give a damn about college. Sign me up and get it over with."

"Just a second, kid. What's your hurry? Do you see a long line of people waiting behind you? Let's do this right. Whatever you do, do it right. Now, what subject turns you on?"

"I was thinking of maybe becoming a builder like my father or a minister like my Uncle Fred."

"Listen to the question kid. At school, what subject really grabs you?"

"I don't know. I might end up writing books or making movies or just stay in the Army. How can I know until I try it?"

"You have trouble listening, don't you? Look, kid, don't you hope that someday you'll be able to read *Finnegan's Wake* or understand quantum physics?"

"What the hell is *Finnegan's Wake*?"

"I haven't read it myself; never could finish it, that is. But if you like to read, and the way you keep looking at those books you probably do, then that's probably the biggest challenge there is. Do you like challenges, kid?"

Charlie stared in disbelief. He had never imagined that joining the army could be so difficult. Instead of being allowed to dive, he was forced to stand on the dock, getting splashed repeatedly, with a chill wind blowing. He felt vulnerable, and the recruiter was lording it over him, lecturing to him.

"Who or what are you running away from?" asked the Sergeant. "Did your girlfriend dump you? Did you get some girl pregnant? Are you in trouble with the law? Look kid, this isn't the French Foreign Legion. This is the peace-time Army."

Charlie raised and lowered his hands twice, as if he were trying to talk with them and had forgotten how. Then he grabbed hold of the back of the empty chair in front of him and said, "I'm not trying to sign up for the Marines. I just want to join the Army. Will you give me the papers to sign and get it over with?"

"Wake up, you smart ass," answered the recruiter. "Get your shit together."

Charlie let go of the chair and turned around toward the door. He wasn't used to hearing adults use language like that. Without looking at the Sergeant, he shot back, "I didn't come here to get interrogated. I just want to join the fucking Army." He was trying hard to sound tough, but the word "fucking" came out mumbled.

The Sergeant continued, "Didn't your father sit you down and tell you you're acting like an asshole? Go finish high school. Then come see me."

Charlie turned back, and grabbed the chair again, "I've made my decision."

"But there's more than one decision to make."

"What?"

"When you're drafted, you have little or no choice. But when you enlist, you get to choose your MOS, your Military Operational Specialty—provided you can pass whatever tests might be required."

"I don't want to choose."

"You have to choose."

"Just pick one for me at random."

"Look kid, this is my job. I take pride in my job, and I do it well, even when idiots like you don't give a damn."

"All right. I'll pick one at random. Then just sign me up and get me out of here."

"It's not that simple, kid. First you take the physical. We could schedule that for tomorrow. Then you pick your MOS. Then we give you tests. Then we schedule your training. The basic training is easy to schedule, but some of the specialty schools have few openings and only start once or twice a year. We want to schedule basic for you so when you get out, you can go straight to AIT, Advanced Individual Training."

"But why?"

"Because I've got a heart and a head, kid. Because that's the way it should be done. Because no one in their right mind wants dead time between training. Believe me. You don't want six months of nothing but polishing your boots and waiting to be put on KP or any other shit duty that comes along."

"I don't want to sit around waiting for training to be scheduled. What's the point of waiting? I would have graduated in two weeks."

"That's fine. Go back to school. We'll build that into the schedule. You can sign up now and graduate with your class."

"Don't you understand? I don't want to graduate. I've decided and I'm going to stick to it. I've made a decision and I want to get on with it as soon as possible."

"Life just ain't that simple, kid."

***

It took Charlie a couple hours to walk the ten blocks home.

"I kept supper warm for you," his mother offered hesitantly as Charlie shuffled by.

"Thanks, Mom. But I'm not hungry."

"Did you ... Did you actually do it?" she dared to ask.

"Yes and no," he mumbled. "It's complicated. I'll take the physical tomorrow." He dragged his feet as he climbed the stairs.

Sarah and Carl had decided not to challenge him on this. They knew from experience that overt resistance would make him more determined. They hoped that if they didn't make an issue of it, he might come to his senses and return to school and graduate.

Charlie shut the door to his room, pulled down the shades, and collapsed on his bed. He felt weak and tired. For a long while, he just lay there, his eyes shut, trying to fall asleep.

When he opened his eyes again, the room was dark, and he was neither awake nor asleep, but trapped in some in between state.

Moonlight shone through the shades, and he could make out the familiar shadowy shapes of his bureau, desk, and bookcases. He thought he was awake, but he couldn't move his head or his body, only his eyes. He scanned the room, anxiously. He was an avid collector of dreams, but this wasn't like any dream he had had or had heard of.

On the far wall, between the windows where no light could shine, purplish blue light appeared, as if a movie projector had been turned on, sending a beam of light against the wall as a screen. As he looked more closely, he realized that there was a range of colors, going from light blue at the top and fading into dark purple toward the bottom.

His every muscle was tense. His calves spasmed in cramps, but he couldn't move and couldn't scream.

Against that blue-to-purple background, a picture began to move upward into view, like a scroll unwinding. A white sleeve, as from a toga, appeared. Then came the shoulder, and he knew, while he was watching this vision, that that was the arm and shoulder of Jesus Christ.

He saw himself step forward and kneel, with head bowed low, before Christ. He felt the coolness of Christ's shadow where his bare knees met the gravel of the street.

There were many people around, but he didn't dare raise his head to look. They were speaking a language that he didn't understand, but he knew for a certainty that he could make three wishes.

He tried to say, "Fame, fortune, and love." But his tongue and lips were numb and unresponsive like from Novocain at the dentist. The once-in-a-lifetime chance would pass. With heroic effort, he forced out the words as loudly as he could. With horror, he woke to his own voice shouting, "Aunt Rachel."

The light vanished.

A fly was buzzing, caught between the shade and the windowpane. It was a loud buzzing—loud enough to wake people in the next room or down the hall, and they'd come running, wondering what was going on, why he was shouting his Aunt's name in the middle of the night.

He opened the window and let the fly out.

Then he lay as still as he could, trying to conjure once again that image of Christ.

The wall remained dark and blank.

When he got up the next morning, Charlie recorded this vision in his journal of dreams. He didn't tell his mother or anyone else about it. He was convinced that he must start his life anew and didn't want to give anyone an opportunity to talk him out of it.

He had to let go, to abandon control, to open up and be more aware and considerate of other people. Strangely, joining the Army was the first step in that direction.

As a test of his resolve to become a new person, he'd go ahead with his decision. He would quit school, without graduating, and join the Army even though he realized it was irrational, even foolish.

He would humble himself. This was an act of self-denial, a religious penance that he took on with youthful fervor and pride.

***

When Charlie entered the recruiter's office for the second time, he noticed not just the books, but also the titles and authors. There were several novels that had come out recently: *Dr. Zhivago* by Pasternak, *Exodus* by Uris, *On the Beach* by Shute. In addition, there were works by Plato and Aristotle, a *Bible*, *The Book of Mormon*, a dog-eared copy of *Finnegan's Wake*, and a German-English dictionary. The book Sergeant Camaratta was reading was in a foreign language.

"Excuse, me, sir," Charlie dared to interrupt. "What's that book?"

"*Der Schloss* in German," he answered with a smile. "In English that's *The Castle*, by Kafka."

"How did you learn to read German?"

"I taught myself," he answered proudly, "while I was stationed over there."

"And can you actually read this many books in a day?" Charlie asked in a tone of sincere admiration.

"No, not in a day. I read a chapter of this, then a chapter of that. That's my style. Some folks would be bored out of their minds with an assignment like this. But I love it. It gives me time to improve my mind." Seeing the kid was interested, he continued. "I'm not a college type myself. I taught myself everything from science to languages to history to literature.

"There's nothing sacrosanct about going to college," he added. "If you like challenge and drive yourself and work hard, you can learn a hell of a lot on your own. What matters is what you know and what you do with what you know, not how many degrees you have. But from what I've seen, college is good for a lot of guys. It makes learning a lot easier if you can afford to set aside four years to do nothing but study. I never had that luxury myself. I wish I had. Don't pass up your chance, kid."

"I know you're right," admitted Charlie. "But I also know I have to do this."

"Okay, kid. Then let's fill out some forms and take some tests."

***

Two hours later, as the Post Office was closing, the Sergeant was rechecking the test answers for the third time, scratching his head, and glancing out the window. Finally, he said, "Look, kid, I don't know if anybody's ever told you this but you've got smarts. I've never seen results like you got on those tests. Look, I think I can do something for you. What do you think of languages? I just saw an opening for a Russian language specialist, 98G."

"But I don't know Russian."

"That's the point. These tests say you have talent for languages, so much talent that the Army will send you to school—to the Defense Language Institute in Monterrey, California, for a full year of training. Then you'll go to Goodfellow Air Force Base in Texas to learn how to listen to Russian radio transmissions."

"What's the catch?"

"Yes, there is a catch. Together with basic, that's nearly two years of training. If the Army is going to invest that much in you, they want to get some payback. So you have to sign on for four years, instead of the usual three."

"And where would I be stationed?"

"Any of about a dozen places overseas. Most likely in Germany."

11 ~ The Pictures from Charlie's Wedding

"He probably got some girl in trouble," Russ concluded when he heard Charlie had joined the Army without finishing his senior year of high school.

Russ disapproved of almost everything Charlie did. He resented the fact that his parents treated Charlie so differently than they had him and Fred. With some justice, he claimed Charlie was spoiled. Russ wouldn't raise his own son that way, even though Rachel was inclined to. He'd rely on old-fashioned discipline, and it was just as well Charlie was gone because he wouldn't want his son Frankie to come under Charlie's influence.

Frankie, who was twelve, didn't pay much attention to this issue. He was caught up in Little League baseball. He had finally made the majors. Then, in July, his family moved from Rockville, Maryland, to Philadelphia. Frankie hardly noticed that Charlie was gone.

After basic at Fort Bragg in North Carolina, Charlie came home for a few days at the end of summer. Frankie saw him at the Colonial Beach cottage on Labor Day.

Charlie brought a super-8 movie camera, and all day he shot roll after roll of film of the family and the beach and the cottage. Everybody went out of their way to dress up, especially Rachel, who changed three times in one afternoon. Frankie got in front of the camera as often as he could and anxiously waited for nightfall when Charlie was going to show some of his movies.

"You won't be in them," Charlie explained. "I'm not a miracle man. It takes a week to get film developed."

"But these are real movies, aren't they?" asked Frankie.

"Yeah, sure."

"I've never seen home movies before," admitted Frankie, "just the junk on TV and in movie theaters."

"That's not junk kid. That's the kind of stuff I'd like to be able to make."

"Come on, Charlie. You're the greatest. You always have been. You always will be," Frankie insisted.

But when Frankie saw Charlie's movies that night with the rest of the family, he had his doubts.

Carl hung a sheet from the clothesline by the goldfish pond. Rachel dressed up like she was going to a Hollywood premiere. And Sarah popped popcorn.

"These are shots from the last few days of basic training," Charlie explained. "I'd just gotten the camera and was experimenting with light."

The movies went on and on. There was no sound, just light flashing and guys in uniforms running around. Frankie fell asleep long before it ended.

***

The following August, Charlie returned on leave again after a year at the Defense Language Institute in Monterrey, California. Now he nearly always had a book in his hand, either Russian, which he was studying for the Army, or German, which he was studying on his own, or chess, which he had learned from his bunkmate.

Charlie still had his 8-mm camera, but he was much more deliberate in his use of it.

Frank's baby brother Johnny was taking his first steps. Charlie had Rachel pose with Johnny, standing him up, moving away, and holding out her arms for him to run to her. Johnny stood still, confused by the camera and all the people, then fell on his bottom and cried.

Rachel kept holding out her arms, coaxing and encouraging Johnny. Russ lost patience, swooped down, picked up the crying baby, and deposited him in Rachel's lap.

"Terrific," shouted Charlie. "I couldn't have scripted it better."

Charlie asked Frankie to gather all the kids he could find. Then he filmed them as they ran this way and that. Frankie couldn't see any point to it.

The Navy was testing weapons and ammunition at Dahlgren across the river in Maryland. Charlie was delighted at this opportunity for "realism." He filmed the kids running up the beach, jumping to avoid dead fish that washed ashore after test explosions in the river.

Sometimes Charlie let Frankie hold the camera, and Charlie got into the action himself, telling Frankie exactly what to shoot and how.

Then Charlie took individual shots of everyone in the family waving their arms in odd ways.

The next day, Charlie drove to the University of Maryland where a friend let him use the lab to develop and edit the film.

That night the family gathered once again by the goldfish pond to see Charlie's latest creation.

Before starting the projector, Charlie began playing a record with electric guitars and words that no one could decipher.

Entitled *Arms*, this silent movie began with Rachel reaching out her arms to Johnny. Johnny fell. Rachel reached again and again. Johnny fell again and again, until he screamed, and Russ snatched him up.

Then a woman's arm appeared. Naked to the shoulder, it reached out and gestured, gently, warmly, "Please come." Then another arm patted a puppy. Another waved good-bye, slowly, reluctantly.

Another arm appeared suddenly, sticking out a thumb to hitchhike, only to be pushed aside by another arm with an abrupt "stop" signal.

Then a fist was raised high in protest, and another and another, one of which turned to an obscene gesture, followed immediately by an older woman's hand from the other side of the screen, with index finger waving "naughty, naughty," then "no, no," and finally pointing forcefully in accusation.

Charlie himself appeared alone in a field, pretending his hand was a pistol and aiming and firing it. He set up a can and stepped back with his hand in holster position. He drew and fired. Nothing happened to the can.

He drew and fired again. And this time the can jumped as if hit by a bullet. The punctured can lay on the ground.

The focus shifted back to his hand as he held the can and stared in surprise. He jokingly pointed the finger toward his own head, then warily pointed it away.

He set up another can, drew and fired again.

Once again, the can was hit.

Proud of his accomplishment, he blew on his finger as if blowing away smoke, then polished his finger on the sleeve of his shirt.

He swung in a circle, aiming at possible targets. A group of kids, including Frankie, was standing in the far distance, out of focus. Charlie slowly lowered his "pistol" hand and aimed and fired at the group — bang-bang.

Frankie dropped to the ground. Charlie grinned proudly.

The kids in the group gathered by Frankie's body. Some looked around, bewildered. One, then two, then three of them started gesturing angrily in the direction of Charlie. Charlie tried to look innocent, put his hands in his pockets, whistled, and turned to walk toward the camera.

He looked back and saw the group was running after him. He started running away from them, desperately.

The group was getting closer. Charlie could see them when he looked over his shoulder. While running, he pointed his finger back and "shot." Several kids fell as if hit by bullets.

They were gaining on him. Charlie stopped and fired again and again. Several more of the group fell, but there were even more kids chasing him now than there had been before.

The pursuers raced up the beach, dodging the dead fish.

When they were about to catch up with him, Charlie dropped to his knees and covered his eyes with his hands.

A subtitle appeared: "Lord, please let this be a dream."

The kids swarmed around him angrily, blocking him from view.

Then the group backed away, and Charlie appeared again with no arms, just the empty sleeves of his coat.

Charlie squirmed on his back on the ground.

A subtitle appeared: "Disarmament."

Then another subtitle: "Violence is as much a part of us as our arms."

Charlie's curled-up body filled the frame.

The kids pointed menacingly at him. They started to close in on him.

His eyes were shut. He was cringing in fear. Then he opened his eyes. He had an idea. He raised his right leg and started to swing it in a circle while lying on his back. He shook his leg as if it were a machine gun firing. Each member of the group fell as if hit with a bullet from the leg.

The movie ended with Charlie on his back in the middle of a circle of bodies, laughing hysterically.

The title was "Arms."

Frankie applauded wildly and insisted on watching the film three more times. He didn't know what it meant. But it looked like a "real" movie. And he was in it, and he had helped to shoot it.

***

The next time Frankie saw a Charlie movie was the summer of 1963 when Charlie was in Germany. In the meantime, the Berlin Wall had been built, Yuri Gagarin had orbited the Earth in a satellite, and Kennedy and Khrushchev had brought the world to the brink of nuclear war over Cuban missiles.

This film arrived by mail with instructions from Charlie not to look at it until the family was gathered. Sarah and Carl invited everyone to the beach for a special showing on a sheet by the goldfish pond.

There was an audio tape in the package that was supposed to be played in sync with the movie. According to the instructions, everyone was supposed to stay quiet until it was over.

The film opened with footage from family movies Charlie had shown them before. But the audio tape gave the pictures a new dimension. The live audience heard the voices of a recorded audience watching those same movies and reacting to them. The voices on the tape were like voices of other people in the same room with the people who were watching the film live now.

The recorded reactions were familiar and natural—how cute the babies were, how much Eddie and Frankie and their cousins had grown, how cousin Matilda had put on weight, how young Aunt Martha looked back then. Then there were shots of the whole family at the airport gathered to say goodbye to Charlie when he left for Germany.

Charlie never appeared in the film. He was the eye of the camera. People talked to him and waved to him.

There were shots of Europe—Munich, Heidelberg, Paris, Geneva. Two of the recorded voices said that they had been to those places before. Those voices sounded very much like Fred and Francine, who had visited those places and were now in the live audience. Charlie had not only guessed the kinds of things they would say but had accurately mimicked their voices.

The character in the film was named Charlie. This was a film with a story, and not just, as they had been led to believe, another showing of home movies. The Charlie in the film had always wanted to be a movie director, but his father had insisted on him becoming a lawyer. That was fiction. Charlie's real father, Carl, had never expressed an opinion on what Charlie should become.

The father on the tape, was proud of his son, proud that he had gone to college—which the real Charlie hadn't—proud that he had been through ROTC and gotten a commission, proud that when he got out of the Army he planned go to law school following in his father's footsteps.

The Charlie in the movie had a girlfriend, a doctor's daughter named Holly, who lived a few blocks away from the family house. Holly was a charming girl who always smiled the same sweet smile.

Holly, chaperoned by an aunt, had gone to Europe to visit Charlie. Charlie and Holly were due to get married back in the States next year. This summer Charlie was using his Army leave to show her around Europe.

Then one of the recorded voices, a young kid, asked, "Who's that other girl?"

"What?" asked the recorded grownups.

"The one with the short blond hair. There she is again."

"Yeah," replied the voice of a teenage boy. "She's been in nearly every one of the shots from Europe, standing off in the background."

Then this girl appeared alone on a hillside, tossing her hair in the wind, picking wildflowers, and throwing them at the cameraman. After a few seconds, the film cut back to Holly and her aunt at an outdoor restaurant in Paris, then to the stranger on the hillside again.

After that, it was impossible not to notice this stranger in every scene. Frequently, the camera would stray from Holly and linger on the stranger. Sometimes the stranger would pay no attention to the camera. Other times, she'd wink slyly.

Then the screen went dark for a couple minutes, and the audience heard the voice of Charlie himself for the first time. He said how important his family was to him, how he loved them all, how he had always struggled to live up to their high expectations of him. At first, it was hard to tell if he was talking to his real family directly and truthfully or if this was part of the movie.

"I want to apologize," he went on. "You all had such wonderful hopes and plans for Holly and me. I wanted to give you the pleasure of sharing my happiness. But love doesn't follow timetables. When you've met the woman of your dreams, a year is simply too long to wait."

Once again images appeared on the screen. A church, crowded with people. The camera, Charlie's eye, was near the altar, up front. The camera moved around, quickly, nervously—handheld camera effects. Finally, the camera turned and looked up the aisle toward the bride. She was out of focus, then in focus for a second, then way out of focus as she got nearer and nearer. Then she was next to Charlie in front of the altar; and, in sharp focus, it was clear what everyone had begun to suspect. He was marrying the stranger, the girl with short blond hair.

The credits came on, superimposed on her playful, smiling face, as they took their vows at the altar.

Produced by Charlie.
Directed by Charlie.
Starring Charlie and Irene Uhland.
Awarded third prize at a film festival in Germany.

That was the first time anyone in the family had heard of Irene.

Eddie and Frankie thought that film was a class act. They wanted to see it again and again. As they watched it, they paid special attention to this mysterious and lovely woman who Charlie had married.

12 ~ Irene in Munich

On his first weekend pass in Germany, Charlie and two Army buddies, Max and Griff, took the train to Munich from Augsburg, where they were based. They checked into the Drei Löwen Hotel near the train station. Max and Griff headed straight for the red-light district. But Charlie, map in one hand and small satchel in the other, strolled through the cobblestone streets of the medieval center of the city toward the district of Schwabing, the English Garden, and Schelling Strasse. His goal was the Schelling Salon, a gathering place for chess players.

He paused before opening the door, expecting to find here the *true Germany*, not just another Americanized beer-joint full of homesick GIs. The round tables of the huge room were crowded with young and old, mostly men. The lights were dim. Cigarette smoke hung like a thick fog.

"Was wollen Sie?" asked a hard-faced waitress in a black skirt with a white blouse.

"Essen, bitte," he replied with an American accent.

She looked not at his face, but at his insignia of rank—a lowly Spec 4. Then she reluctantly led him to table-for-two in the center of the room. She seemed annoyed at serving an American GI, an enlisted man. She handed him a menu, then disappeared into the smoke and the crowd.

None of the other patrons were eating. Most were drinking beer or coffee and talking loudly. There were a few chess players at tables in the corner, with kibitzers leaning over their shoulders.

He studied the menu and with the help of a pocket dictionary, decided to order a beef stew dinner. But the waitress was nowhere to be seen.

He felt awkward. He was the only soldier, the only American, and probably the only person in the place ordering dinner.

He was tempted to go over to the chess players and watch, in hopes of playing. But he didn't want to leave the table for fear of missing the waitress, who sooner or later would return for his order.

He used a dictionary to look up every word that he didn't know on the menu, dozens of words. Still the waitress didn't appear.

Finally, he opened his satchel, took out his chess board and set and a well-worn copy of *My System* by Aron Nimzovitch. No sooner had he set up the pieces, than the waitress reappeared.

She reached out her hand and said emphatically, " Fünf Marken." Confused, he picked up the menu again and, reluctant to botch the German pronunciation, pointed to the item he wanted.

"Ja, ich verstehe. Aber Sie spielen Schach hier and das kostet fünf Marken."

Charlie looked again at the menu. The item he had selected had a price of twenty marks and she was saying something about five marks. He was afraid she had misunderstood his order. He pointed again.

Again, she said, " Fünf Marken für Schach spielen." Her tone implied he was acting like an idiot.

"Excuse me, but I don't understand. Do you speak English, please?"

She glared at him as if grossly insulted, then knocked over the pieces.

He leaned over and caught the king before it hit the floor. As he sat up again, he saw a blond boy in a black jacket hand the waitress some coins and send her away.

"Please excuse her," the stranger said. "She doesn't speak English."

"Thank you. How much do I owe you, and what was that about?"

"Five marks. They charge five marks to play chess here. You rent the table."

"But I ordered supper," Charlie explained while repaying the boy. "That costs far more than five marks. And I only set up the pieces for myself, to go over games from a book."

"Yes, and she will bring supper. But it costs five marks to play chess. One rule for all. Would you like to play?"

"Why, yes," Charlie admitted.

"Sehr gut."

The boy took off his jacket, hung it on the back of a chair and sat down. Then, even with the bad lighting and the smoke, Charlie realized that the boy was a young woman, with short blond hair and dark blue eyes.

"You know how to play?" Charlie asked in surprise.

"A little," she smiled. "Women in America do not play chess?"

"A little. I mean, not very well. I mean, not very many of them play."

"Yes, it is a man's sport. The pieces are so heavy, " she took the king from his hand and hefted it with an ironic smile. "You come from America. You know Bobby Fischer, yes?"

"Yes, everyone knows— "

"You play with him often?"

"Never, I mean, yes, of course," he boasted and smiled back.

"Then you must play very well, yes?"

"Well, I have been known to win a few games."

"Sie sind Grossmeister, ja? I can from your eyes see you have great depth of mind. Your eyes, they are dark blue, like mine, yes?"

"Yes," he said automatically. He would probably have said "yes" to anything she asked. He had no control over the situation and didn't like being out of control, but despite himself, he was reveling in the attention of this intriguing young woman.

She set up the pieces and asked "Time? Have you the time?"

"Of course," he answered. "I have plenty of time"

"Die Uhr, die Schach Uhr, bitte? The clock, yes?"

"Yes, of course. It's three o'clock." He showed her his watch.

"One moment, please." She got up and disappeared into the crowd.

He wondered what mistake of language or local courtesy he had made this time.

A few minutes later the blond returned with a clock that had two faces. She set it down beside the chess board and pushed one of the two buttons on top.

He stared at the clock and at her, wondering what was expected of him.

"The move is yours," she said, gesturing toward his pieces.

"Of course." He quickly moved his king pawn forward one square.

She stared at the board, then at the clock, then at him. "The time," she gestured.

"Yes, of course." He hadn't the faintest idea what she was talking about.

"When you make your move, you must push your button on the clock," She pushed the button on his side of the clock then made her move and pushed her button.

He tried to concentrate on the board. His eyes were watering from the smoke in the air.

"Solch ein grosser Grossmeister. You have read this book of Nimzovitch many times?"

"Yes, I mean, not really. I bought it second-hand. I haven't gotten that far. It's complicated."

"Ja wohl. Do you play for money in America?"

"Yes, of course. Sometimes. It can make the game more interesting."

"Would you like to play for money now?"

"Yes. Why not?"

"Ja. Why not?" She put five marks on the table, so he did the same.

Once again, he tried to concentrate on the board and decide on the next move. But his eyes kept wandering to hers. She winked at him. He winked back.

"Too bad." She reached over to put her hand on both buttons of the clock. Then took his five marks.

"What?"

"The time, it is over, yes? Five minutes each." She pointed to the clock face nearest to him. "Would you like to play again?"

"Again?"

She pointed to her five marks on the table and he took five more from his wallet.

She reset the clock and turned the board around so she had the white pieces.

This time he shaded his eyes to stop himself from looking at her and concentrated on the board. He was weak at the openings but had good instincts in middle game. With practice, he had become the best player in his barracks in Monterrey and at the language-listening school in Texas. He was not going to let himself be beaten by a woman, no matter how attractive she might be.

He moved quickly and slammed the clock. This time he would make sure she didn't beat him on time.

He took a piece, then another piece, then a rook, then her queen. He was proud of himself for totally decimating her position. Then she announced, "Mate."

He stared in disbelief. His king was well-protected, surrounded by pawns and pieces with no empty square around it. She had checked him with a knight and the king couldn't move out of check, because of all those defenders. It was "smother mate."

"You play so well." She set up the pieces again. "I was so lucky, yes?"

"Yes," he answered, in a tone of annoyance. He couldn't believe he had been so stupid as to miss that.

She pointed to her five marks on the table. He put ten marks on the table. She nodded in agreement and added five marks.

This time Charlie attacked quickly with his queen, gobbling up stray pawns that she left unprotected. He could see no plan behind her moves. It looked as if she were trying to lose. Then his queen was trapped. All he could do was trade it for a knight or lose it outright. A few moves later, in a hopeless position, he resigned.

"Again?" he asked.

"Again," she affirmed.

He put twenty marks on the table, and she matched it.

Spectators gathered around the table, and the waitress finally delivered the beef stew, but nothing could distract him from his game now. Charlie hunched over, clenched his teeth and moved his pieces with authority. This time he got off to a great start. He was ahead by a rook, then two rooks, then a bishop as well. He focused on her king. He had her this time. He was sure of it. But she deftly eluded mate again and again. Then she stopped the clock, announced, "Time," and once again took his money.

"Again?" she asked.

He didn't answer. He put fifty marks on the table, and she matched it.

Now there were dozens of spectators gathered around, including the waitress, who once again held out her hand. "Zwanzig Marken, bitte. Für das Essen."

Charlie paid her quickly, made his move, and hit the clock.

Three moves later, he was mated. Scholar's mate. He had made one of the worst beginner's mistakes.

Someone laughed and muttered, "Was ein Grossmeister!"

Charlie took out his wallet, counted his money, set aside enough to pay his hotel bill, and put the rest on the table—200 marks. She matched it.

This time he could make no progress at all. It was as if she knew his every move before he did. If she had been moving his pieces for him, she couldn't have destroyed him any more efficiently than she did.

"Gute Nacht," she nodded, and disappeared into the crowd with his money.

***

In July, Charlie returned to Munich. Once again, he set out in the direction of Schwabing, but this time his intent was different. In his satchel he had his 8-mm movie camera and a few books: Kafka's *Castle* in German, short stories by Gogol in Russian, and dictionaries. Max and Griff had told him that on warm sunny days, nudists gathered by the stream that ran through the middle of the English Garden.

If the weather stayed cool, he'd read. If it got hot, he would enjoy the scenery and try to talk some young woman into modeling for him.

As he crossed the Marienplatz, the sun broke through the clouds and the temperature rose quickly. It was morning, and the park was almost empty. He settled beneath a weeping willow beside the stream and started struggling through a Gogol story in Russian, word by difficult word.

He fell asleep and woke abruptly when a drop of water hit his face. A group of young men and women, all naked, were playing in the water near him. He pretended to read again, so as not to seem to stare. He was both embarrassed and fascinated. Fully clothed city-dwellers, businesspeople on lunch break walked past on the path nearby, and naked sunbathers lay on both banks of the stream just a few feet away.

One young woman in a dark suit stopped on the other side of the tree that Charlie was leaning against. With her back toward him, oblivious to everyone around, she removed all her clothing and stretched out on her belly on the grass.

Charlie put his book away. Not even in movies had he seen such a beautiful womanly shape. She lay just three feet away. He tried to think of something to say to her, but before he did, she was on her feet again, putting her clothes on as calmly and quickly as she had taken them off. Soon she was strolling away, probably back to the office.

Charlie scrambled to his feet, grabbed his satchel, and followed her.

Her blond hair was shoulder length. Her brown leather pocketbook hung on a long strap from her left shoulder. She kept a tight grip on the top of it. The cut of her jacket and the skirt that descended to near ankle length obliterated any hint of the shape that had mesmerized him.

Seeing the gate toward which her decisive stride was taking her, Charlie raced down a side path, out another gate, and down the sidewalk toward her exit. There he pulled out his movie camera, braced himself against the stone wall and aimed in her direction.

She was still a hundred feet away. He zoomed in on her face. It was the chess player. He nearly dropped the camera.

As she strolled by, she looked him straight in the face, "Ach, mein Herr. Do you make movies as well as you play chess?"

"No, I mean yes. I mean— " He tripped.

She laughed and walked on.

He caught up.

"Are you free tonight?" he asked.

"You mean you cannot pay?"

"I mean ... shit! You know very well what I mean."

***

That night they met for supper at a restaurant near the train station. Charlie made no pretense of understanding the menu. He let her do the ordering. Her name was Irene. She worked as an administrator at the University.

"And what do you do with this camera of yours? Is that a tourist thing? Or is it a trick to pick up girls? Can you tell real stories in film with such primitive equipment?"

"I have a lot to learn. but I do what I can with what I have. I'd like to break into the movie business after my hitch in the Army. I have lots of stories I'd like to tell in film."

"And I, too, have stories."

"Tell me a story," he coaxed her.

"So you can steal it?"

"I'll trade story for story."

She hesitated, took a sip of beer, then continued. "In the *Bible*, the crucifixion story, the soldiers made a man carry the cross for Christ. The man's name was Simon of Cyrene, and hundreds of years later he was named a saint for this holy act. Imagine such a scene. Only this time the man about to be crucified is not Christ. He is a false messiah— not the Son of God. Do you see this with the camera inside your head?"

Charlie nodded.

"The false messiah drags the cross, then stops and falls to his knees, exhausted. Many who believe in him are watching. The crowd comes closer. The soldiers draw their swords. The captain picks a man at random from the crowd and makes him carry the cross for the prisoner. This man who was picked to carry the cross does not believe in the false messiah. But he is willing to help a suffering man. Like you this?"

"But what's the point of it?" asked Charlie.

"In the story, the messiah is false. Doesn't that raise questions? Is this man less holy than Simon?"

"No, of course not," Charlie answered without thinking. He couldn't see what the issue was. "Any unselfish act can bring you close to God."

"I like your God." She took his hand and squeezed it.

"But what other answer could there be?"

"Many think that God is a puzzle maker. If you follow the wrong messiah, you miss the Holy Grail. If you don't ask to be let in, you wait at the door of the castle forever. If you open the wrong door, you live the wrong life. Others believe there is no God, and the puzzles we face in life mean nothing. The puzzles happen by chance. So one story can lead to very different ideas about God and the meaning of life. That is a lot of story, nicht wahr?"

"But you could never make a movie out of that."

"Jawohl. Not me. But the next Bergman could make it."

"Who?"

"Ingmar Bergman. *The Seventh Seal, Through a Glass Darkly* ... "

"I never heard of him."

"Mein Gott! And you make movies? What kind of movies do you make, Herr Uhland?"

"I'm thinking of a scene," Charlie answered. "I'm not sure of the shape of the whole movie yet. But I like this scene. Imagine a boy, maybe sixteen, running along a deserted beach. In the distance he sees a sunbather. He slows. It's a woman. As he gets closer, he sees that she is completely naked, lying on her belly. She's twenty years older than him. She's beautiful. He has never seen a mature woman naked in person. He almost runs away. But her eyes are closed. She's sleeping. He steps forward to get a better look, slowly, quietly, but very frightened.

"Suddenly, she rolls over on her back. But her eyes are still closed, and she puts a towel over them to block out the glare of the sun.

"He stares long and hard. It's as if he were reaching out with his eyes and caressing her body.

"He's standing next to her. She smiles, and he realizes that she has been watching him from under the towel. She knows he's watching her and wants him to watch her.

"He's scared. She is more than just an object for him to fantasize over. She has her own wishes and goals. To her, he's an object. She grabs hold of his ankle, and with her other hand reaches up and caresses the inner side of his thigh.

"He cringes for fear that this woman may be crazy. But he doesn't run away. He stands stock-still while she pulls down his bathing trunks and pulls him on top of her and in her.

"When she is done with him, she gets up, puts on her clothes, and walks away, leaving him exhausted and bewildered in the sand."

Irene reached across the table and caressed his cheek. "I like your God and I like your dirty mind, too. Yes, you will do just fine, my Charlie. Yes, you will make good movies. Yes, we will make good movies together."

***

Charlie returned to Munich every weekend after that and stayed with Irene at her apartment in Schwabing. She was twenty-four. She had an advanced degree in literature and was a chess master.

That winter they planned the movie *The Pictures of Charlie's Wedding*, and the following spring they filmed it. They hired a minister to perform a real wedding ceremony as part of the movie.

They planned another far more ambitious movie as well, *Saint Smith*, based on a story of Irene's.

13 ~ Irene at the Beach

Rachel thought of Charlie as a generation younger than she was. She considered him sociable and attractive and presumed that many women would be out to snare him. She thought he was naive and vulnerable and that he needed to be protected from *women of the world*.

She appreciated Charlie's social skills at family gatherings. By showing off and taking center stage, he could turn a dull gathering into a fun party. When Russ was grouchy and didn't feel like going out, Rachel would prod him, "Why can't you be more like your brother Charlie? Why can't you relax and enjoy yourself?"

While Charlie was away in the Army, he was often a subject of conversation. And after the showing of the movie about his wedding, there was much speculation about his foreign bride.

Rachel and Russ met Irene for the first time in August 1964, two months after Charlie got back from Germany.

Sarah's first impression of Irene, conveyed in a letter to Rachel, was positive, "She reminds me of you at that age. No wonder Charlie is so smitten with her."

Rachel and Russ arrived at the cottage on the Potomac late at night, exhausted from the seven-hour drive and the interminable poking and squabbling of their three boys who had been sardined in the back of the car with the luggage and beach toys.

The next morning, Rachel was up before anyone else. She spread her blanket on the beach at the same place she had four years before, when Charlie gawked at her. Like before, she wore a two-piece bathing suit, but with a top that was a cup size smaller, which pushed her ample bosom upward, and made it seem all the larger. Her discomfort was balanced by her pride at being so well-endowed. If she were to pull back her shoulders, the strap between the cups might break, exposing her. That possibility gave her a tingle of excitement. It felt good to lie there in the hot sun, like in a spotlight, and know that any man who saw her would take pleasure in the sight. It felt especially good to imagine Charlie chancing upon her—Charlie, who was always an early riser. Not that anything would come of it. She didn't want anything to come of it. But she was sure that she, with her full-busted figure, must compare favorably with that mousy little German girl in the wedding movie. She remembered how good it felt to be wanted, unapproachable, but lusted for.

She heard footsteps coming from the cottage, covered her eyes with a towel, relaxed and waited. The steps were lighter than she expected. Whoever it was went past her quickly, not even pausing for a hello, and went straight to the water. She looked up in surprise, and saw Irene, in a white bikini. The top was just a narrow strip of cloth; her breasts, like those of a pre-teen, needed no support. The bottom, little more than a string, hid nothing. She dove into the river without a splash, with hardly a ripple.

Before Irene surfaced, Rachel was back across the street at the cottage. Rachel changed into everyday clothes and drove into town where she bought a one-piece bathing suit, one that smoothed out rough spots, which she had never noticed before, and flattened her tummy—which she used to take pride in.

"She's some kind of religious nut," Rachel told Russ that night in bed. "Did you hear her talking to Grandpa Uhland? She says, 'God is within you and me, within all of us. Everybody is holy. All men are brothers.' She's forever spouting sweet-sounding holier-than-thou phrases as if they were the latest discovery of modern man. She has the religious enthusiasm of the newly converted. I wouldn't trust her. She's hiding something, I tell you, not her body, that's for certain. Those skimpy clothes she wears and that scandal she calls a bathing suit. But I'm sure she's hiding something in her past. *Irene*, that's not a German name. It doesn't ring true.

"What do we know about her? Has anyone here ever seen or heard from a relative of hers? 'She's so spontaneous and natural. She doesn't dwell on the past, that's not her style,' Charlie says. Sure. A woman four years older than him. A model, or worse, from the looks of her. And that confident way of hers. She was all too *natural* in that silly film Charlie made. She's been in front of a camera before, you can be sure of that, and I doubt she had clothes on.

"You may think I'm being petty, but this is our Charlie that she's fooled. And because she's part of the family now, our children are exposed to her shenanigans. I feel it's my responsibility to get to the bottom of this. The last time she started that routine about we are all brothers, children of God, I asked her, 'Do you have brothers?' and she said no. And I said, 'And you have no children of your own, either. You've never driven seven hours with three boys in the backseat. It's easy for you to have idealistic notions.' But I couldn't provoke a reaction. She just smiled and asked, 'Could I have a cup of tea, please?'"

***

The next day, at high tide, and prompted by Irene, the Uhland kids went to the end of the pier and held a belly-flop contest. The aim was to make the biggest splash. Charlie joined the kids. Irene served as judge. She rated them based on how much water they splashed on her. Rachel sat back on the porch with Russ, Fred, Francine, Sarah, and Carl, and chatted and read the newspaper and watched the river roll by.

Charlie dove last. When he hit the water, the splash was enormous, and the front of him turned lobster-red. Irene, soaked from his splash, applauded, and awarded him a seaweed wreath as a prize. Then she slid smoothly into the water, blending as naturally with that element as she did with air.

Charlie belly-flopped again and swam after her, with huge churning strokes. The splashes rose high and far. But Irene, with a motion that seemed effortless and quiet, far out-distanced him.

Rachel left the old folks on the porch and hurried as fast as bare feet could carry her across the pine-cone-strewn ground to the beach where Charlie was wading ashore, while Irene kept swimming.

"What a sight!" Rachel laughed at his flop-bruised body. "Does it hurt?"

"Not that much," he answered distantly.

She handed him a towel and he put it over his shoulder and walked to the lighthouse. Once there, he planted his feet firmly in the sand and pushed with his hands on the foundation of the cement structure.

"Are you practicing for a role as Samson?" asked Rae.

"No, just working on muscle tone."

"Well, you and your Delilah are certainly a study in contrasts."

"Meaning?"

"Well, look at the different ways you dive and swim."

"Yes, definitely grounds for divorce, Aunt Rachel," he laughed.

"Oh, drop the *aunt*, please, Charlie. Hearing that from the likes of you makes me feel old."

"Okay, Rachel, so what's your point?"

"Just that she's the opposite of you. You go out of your way to do things the hard way, to push up against obstacles. And Irene, what little I've seen of her, she just slides along."

"And what's wrong with that?"

"I didn't say there was anything wrong with Irene. Don't go putting words in my mouth like I was trying to put her down. I'm sure she's a lovely person, after you get to know her. It's just ... well, look at yourself. Why do you always have to do things the hard way?"

"Get this straight, Rachel. Irene doesn't ask me to be like her. Au contraire, vive la différence."

"Well, why do you keep pushing on that damned wall?"

Charlie finally stopped pushing. He wiped his sweaty forehead with the towel and squatted on the sand. "Look, Rachel, it's all simple. I like to know what I'm up against. I like the feel of straining my muscles. Even if I don't move the wall, I learn something about the wall and about myself and maybe get stronger."

"And Irene, what does Irene say about that?"

"About what, Aunt Rachel? You're talking in riddles."

"And you're living in riddles, too. What are you going to do with your life?"

"Irene has landed a job teaching German at the University of Maryland. That means I'll have all the time I need to learn how to make movies, working on my own."

"Doing it the hard way, of course. And how do you expect to win when you play the game like that?"

"I'm not sure what winning means."

"What an attitude! Is that what you learned in Germany? Where's the old Charlie? Where's your drive? Your ambition? You have the talent to do great things. I'm sure of it. But the way you're going now, you're just an amateur, and you'll always be an amateur."

***

The following day, at Irene's prompting, the kids competed in cannonballs instead of belly-flops, and Frankie won. Carl, persuaded by Irene, served as the splash judge. It was the first time in years he had worn a bathing suit.

Sarah, sitting next to Rachel on the porch, leaned toward her and confided, "Ten years ago, you would've been the one coming up with the games. Not that you can't now, but you don't seem to want to anymore. Where's that contagious spark and zest for living that you used to have, that Sue had, that Irene has now?"

"Well, I have no desire to do belly flops or get splashed, and I think Irene's a bad influence on Charlie. I think he needs discipline and structure in his life, and clear tangible goals."

"Russ certainly has that aplenty."

"Thank God he does. It's not easy supporting a family with three boys, saving for college for all of them. I'm proud of Russ's success at work, proud of the orderliness of our lives. And Charlie has a shot at success, too—a more brilliant kind of success. I believe he has real movie-making talent. But Irene indulges him. She encourages him to play at movie-making rather than take his vocation seriously. She treats him like a child. She'll be the breadwinner. She'll take care of everything. And he'll squander his chances."

***

Every summer, Carl and Sarah, Russ and Rachel, Charlie and Irene returned to the beach. Each time, Rachel spent longer picking the right bathing suit. Each time, she spent more time on the porch than on the beach. Each time, she was a little more embarrassed to admit in public that Frankie was her son. She had married young and had had Frankie young and didn't like being pigeon-holed with other mothers of college-age kids. She didn't think of herself as that old, and she didn't want others to think of her that way. In public, she snapped at Frankie in the same tone she did to his younger brothers—as if he were as young as they. It was the summer of 1966, the summer before Frankie started college, that Rachel began to realize that he was looking at Irene as more than just an aunt-by-marriage. Like it or not, he was coming of age.

One day on the beach, Eddie started to say, "I got—" when Frankie clamped a hand over his mouth and pulled him to the ground. They had been skipping stones in the river, and there was no apparent reason for Frankie to attack him like that.

"What the—" Eddie tried to protest, but Frankie covered his mouth again and, with the other hand, grabbed him by his curly blond hair and turned his face toward the next grove of pines.

The tide was out. Below the eroded bank there was a patch of flat mud and rocks, shielded from view by the pines and bushes, a hundred feet or more from the dirt road. There, stretched out on her belly on a white beach towel, with feet dangling in the water, lay a naked woman.

Slowly, quietly, they crawled through the bushes.

With short blond hair, she was a full-grown shapely woman. She lay with her head on her arms, her eyes closed. Her well-tanned bottom was exposed, but the rest of what they were interested in was pressed flat to the ground.

"God!" Frankie started to whisper, "I think I know—"

But already Eddie had heaved a stone. It hit a rock off to her right and bounced into the water, where it skipped once before sinking.

Startled, she sat up. But before they had a chance to gawk at her, they recognized her face and ran as hard as they could back to the cottage.

"Charlie would kill us," Eddie whispered as soon as he caught his breath.

"Charlie what?" Rachel appeared out of nowhere. She had a way of appearing at awkward moments.

"Nothing, Mom. Honest. Nothing," Eddie insisted.

"Nothing? You think he would kill you for nothing? Well, I wouldn't put that or anything else past that uncle of yours. But from the look on your faces, I suspect there's more than nothing going on here. So, march back to the house and stay there, the two of you, until you're ready to tell me the whole story."

"But Mom—" Frankie objected.

"Don't *mom* me. I don't care how old you are or what fancy school you got into, you're my child," she repeated the familiar litany. "As long as you live under our roof and we pay your bills, you'll do what you're told."

"It wasn't our fault, Mom. Honest," pleaded Eddie. "Besides, it was Frankie who showed me. I wouldn't have noticed if he hadn't pointed her out to me."

"Thanks, buddy. Thanks. I'll remember that," Frankie noted with disdain.

"Who? What woman are you talking about?" Rachel pursued the scent.

"Irene," Frankie mumbled.

"Irene? Charlie's Irene? Your Aunt Irene? What's she doing? What's Charlie doing? Is Charlie here? They're not supposed to be here at all. We were finally going to have a Fourth of July at the beach with just our own immediate family. Charlie never said they'd be coming. But Irene? What about Irene? What's she up to? What did you see that Charlie would kill you for seeing?"

"You see she was—"

"Speak up, boy."

" ... sunbathing."

"Well, what's wrong with that? Though I can't understand why they wouldn't come to the cottage first and settle in before going off to the beach. That would be the neighborly thing to do. And they should have given us warning they planned to be here. But what was it about her sunbathing?"

"Nothing. Really, Mom. Nothing. Like you said, we were surprised to see her here."

"Nothing, yes nothing, indeed, I'm sure. Sunbathing, probably nude. Yes, from the look of you. I wouldn't put it past her, that little .... And here, at a family beach, with innocent children roaming about. I always said she was an exhibitionist, but I never realized how true, how literally true that is. Charlie, foolish Charlie, marrying a foreigner, and an older woman, at that. He'll live to regret it, mark my words. That marriage won't last long."

"They've already been married for three years, Mom," Frankie dared offer.

"Three years? That's nothing, nothing at all, little more than a honeymoon and no children, you see. She won't be spoiling her fine figure for something so unimportant as children. They won't last much longer as a couple, mark my words. I certainly hope they won't."

"But why, Mom?" Frankie asked. "What's she done to you that you're so bitter?"

"What hasn't she done?" Mom asked back, rhetorically. "She's a corrupting influence. Nude sunbathing at a place like this."

"You don't approve, Mrs. Uhland?" asked Irene. She caught them all by surprise, emerging from the bushes in a scanty blue bikini, with a red-and-blue plaid towel over her left shoulder.

Rachel regained her equanimity and went on the attack, "Well, Mrs. Uhland, what you do in the privacy of your own home is your own affair. But out here with impressionable young boys nosing about .... "

Irene smiled back.

"Don't give me that sweet puzzled look of yours," Rachel continued. "You've been around here long enough to understand English. And long enough to understand how to behave, too."

"You don't approve of the way I dress, Mrs. Uhland?" Irene asked pleasantly, not at all ruffled by the attack.

"That's right. I don't like the way you dress, Mrs. Uhland. And I don't like the way you undress either—in a place with young boys around. You'll be giving them ideas."

"But I thought they were quite bright."

"Bright?"

"Yes, that's the word, nicht wahr? I thought they had lots of ideas, all on their own."

That was the last time Frankie or Eddie saw Irene until their grandparents' Sixtieth Anniversary celebration back in Silver Spring a month and a half later. But they never stopped hearing about that incident, and it became part of their mother's repertoire of embarrassing stories.

"There she stood," Rachel told and retold the tale. "Her bosom, and she doesn't have much of a bosom really, it's just the way she flaunts what she's got. It reminds me of that movie *Tom Jones*, a horrid movie really. I'd have never watched it, except it was on television. Imagine putting a show like that on television, not even edited, so young children ... I wouldn't let mine watch it. I sent them out of the house to play when it came on. That's what they should do at their age, anyway, play with children their own age, rather than sit around the living room gawking at bosoms. They'll be old enough soon enough. No need to hurry it along. Soon enough they'll know more than enough, more than they ever need to know. 'The world is too much with us,' like they say in school. Television keeps flooding us with nasty facts like rape and fire and sin and war. The news is the most pornographic show on television with nothing but violence and sex. I don't let the children watch it. It's not good for them. Soon enough they'll be adults in a world full of adultery. Why rob them of their few brief years of innocence?"

14 ~ The Outhouse

After Carl Uhland retired, he and Sarah fell into comfortable habits. They each had favorite parts of the house into which to retreat to be alone. He'd go to the vegetable garden; to the workshop in the basement; to his study, with its floor-to-ceiling bookshelves; or to his rocking chair in the living room. She'd settle with a book in the alcove by the fireplace, or on a window seat in their bedroom.

One Christmas, Russ and Fred bought them a television set with a 25-inch screen. But Carl and Sarah never found time to watch it. They were too busy. They would have liked to donate the set to charity but kept it so as not to hurt their sons' feelings.

Carl always found things that needed fixing, and work that needed to be done in the yard and garden. Sarah always found some corner of the house that needed to be cleaned or dusted. They both complained regularly about how big the house was and how difficult to keep up; but when Russ or Fred suggested that they move to an apartment, they both objected angrily. The house was part of their lives. They didn't want to be separated from it.

It was more than nostalgia that tied them to that structure. Carl had designed and built it when he was young and prone to experiment. The exterior was of stucco and stone, accented with wood at the corners and around the windows. The roof sloped this way, then that, in multiple angles. Overall, it had the look of a Black Forest cottage.

Carl and Sarah stayed in touch with their local community. They bowled with the Senior Citizens Club. They were active in the Lutheran church and attended Reverend Schumacher's services every Sunday and then listened to Billy Graham and the Lutheran Hour on the radio.

Some of their children and grandchildren visited each Easter, Thanksgiving, and Christmas. But the first time in years that the whole family came together was in August 1966 at their Sixtieth Anniversary.

Russ and Rachel in Philadelphia had four children: Frankie would be a freshman at Yale, Eddie a freshman in high school; Johnny was six and Mark was just a few months old. Fred and Francine in Missouri had two sons, Jimmy and George. Charlie and Irene had been married for three years, but still had no children.

Irene and Charlie arrived first, then Russ, Rachel and their boys. When Fred and Francine arrived, they'd all go to church together, where the Reverend Schumacher would lead Carl and Sarah through a reenactment of their vows. Then they would have dinner at the Gateway Restaurant. Fred had arranged it all.

Frankie evaded the idle chatter in the living room and kitchen and settled down to read in his grandparents' bedroom. He was slouched deep in the stuffed chair, with his feet stretched on the window seat, when he heard steps in the hall. Through Grandma's free-standing full-length mirror, he saw Irene lead Charlie into the room and over toward the bed. Frankie didn't say a word, and they didn't know he was there. They could have seen him in the mirror, but they were too absorbed in each other to notice.

Irene was wearing a shimmering orange and gold sleeveless evening dress which was striking but out of place for a family gathering.

"Smile," she insisted. "You can't still be depressed about Bergman's *Persona*."

"Shit. There's that beach scene in that movie that's all too close to my idea, close enough to make my idea worthless. Whatever Bergman does, people will remember. And I bet someone will make a movie that's close to our *Saint Smith* idea, making that worthless, too. Like Rachel said, I'm just an amateur. I'll always be an amateur."

"Rachel? Your Aunt Rachel? When have you had time to talk to her?"

"It was a conversation we had years ago. Coming back to this house reminded me of it … of Rachel, of my life before I met you."

"You regret that you met me?"

"Of course not. I can't imagine life without you. But I've gotten nowhere and done nothing. Sure, your teaching supports us. I've got all the free time I need to study on my own and write and learn the craft of movie making. But let's face it, I don't know what the hell I'm doing. I'd be better off going to school and learning how to make movies the professional way."

"You mean learning how to do it the way everyone else does? That's not art."

"Well, here I am, still working on silent crap."

"But you've moved up to 16-mm."

"Yes, 16-mm crap, and still getting nowhere."

She kissed him to shut him up. Charlie tried to kiss her back, but she playfully avoided his lips. She undid a strap of her dress and pulled down her bra. "Bite-sized you call them. Well, have a bite," she offered and pulled his head to her breast.

He tried to force her onto the bed, but she slipped away.

He whispered, in frustration, "What do you want?"

"Just this," she replied, kneeling in front of him, unzippering him, then caressing and licking.

"God," he exclaimed. "Let me take you now, quickly."

"Do you always have to be in control?" she asked, between tender licks.

"No, not always," he whispered.

That was when Frankie noticed Eddie, who had stopped just inside the doorway. Frankie tried to signal to Eddie to go away, but Eddie had seen what was going on and was mesmerized.

Charlie started to moan. His eyes were shut. "Why do you do this to me?" he asked, as if he objected, but his hands urged her head closer.

As quietly as he could, Frankie slid to the floor, crawled over to Eddie, and the two of them got out of there.

"Don't you dare say a word," Frankie warned him, once they were out of earshot.

"No way, Jose. You think I'm crazy? Charlie would kill us."

***

After the family got back from the restaurant, Charlie brought out his 16-mm movie camera. He had a new plot he wanted to try, using family members for the parts. This time he was doing a movie called *The Out House*, using the toolshed in the backyard as the main prop.

He had everybody sit in chairs in the backyard and one by one go into the toolshed where he had painted a half-moon on the door to make it look like an outhouse. Since he was working without sound equipment, he could shout directions as he filmed.

"Okay, Jimmy, you go in now. Nobody pay attention to him. Now, Jimmy, come out and do whatever you please. Just stay out of range of the camera.

"Okay, everybody, you're all reading newspapers or talking to one another or looking off into space. That's right. Now, Irene, start looking itchy, like you've really got to go. Keep looking at the toolshed. Now go on over there. Knock on the door. Knock harder. Okay, you can't wait any longer. Open the door and go in.

"Dad, look up from your paper, like you're wondering what's going on. Eddie, you too, look like you're curious. Now, George you get up and go in."

One by one they all got up and went into the toolshed. They came out again as soon as the camera was pointed away but to the camera eye, they were all still in there.

Carl was the last one left. Looking very curious, hamming his part to the hilt, he got up and walked around the toolshed, scratching his head. Then he opened the door and stared in disbelief.

"That's where I'll splice in footage of Time Square at rush hour," explained Charlie.

"Way out!" said Eddie.

"Way out?" muttered Rachel. She had been skeptical, but now she finally got the point. "Yes, it really is an *Out House*."

"Yes, the ending is good," Irene affirmed. "Much better than Bergman's spiders."

"Can we eat now?" asked Eddie.

"Go ahead, run on in," Rachel told him distractedly, looking over the scene again, as if she still didn't know if Charlie's effort was clever and artistic or simply a waste of time. "Will you add sound later?" she asked.

"The whole point is to tell a story without sound," he insisted loudly. "I'm working within the limits of the medium."

"But that medium became obsolete as soon as talkies came along, back in the 20s," Rachel insisted.

"You don't get it. None of you get it. And I can't explain it," he complained. "Hell, if I could say what I wanted to say in words, there wouldn't be any reason for making a movie, would there?"

Then, without warning, Charlie grabbed Frankie and pulled him down to the ground. Maybe he just had to exert power over somebody, to get over a moment of self-doubt. But Frankie was scared. Charlie had struck so suddenly. The back of Frankie's head banged against the parched August ground. He had no way of knowing if Charlie had seen him spying on him and Irene upstairs and if he was angry about that.

Eddie looked out the door and saw them. "God," Eddie exclaimed. "Charlie's really going to kill him this time." He ran to the rescue, jumping on Charlie's back and pounding on him.

Charlie peeled Eddie off, and helped Frankie to his feet. "Hey, kid, are you all right? I'm sorry. I don't know what came over me." He smiled like it was an accident, that no one was responsible, and the family gathering could go on now as if that little tussle had never taken place. But Rachel sensed something was wrong.

"What do you mean, *this time*?" she badgered Eddie. "What reason would Charlie have for wanting to hurt Frankie *this time*?"

"Nothing, Mom, honest. Nothing." But Eddie's voice betrayed his guilt.

"You said something like that at the beach. Has someone been putting on a public display again?" she pursued relentlessly.

"No, Mom, honest. No. It wasn't her fault. It was just an accident," pleaded Eddie.

"What kind of an accident?"

"We just accidentally happened to be there."

"Where?"

"Grandma and Grandpa's bedroom."

"And what did you see?"

Eddie blushed.

Irene smiled and winked at Charlie, who shrugged and walked off.

"I don't blame you," Rachel told Eddie, with heavy emphasis on *you*. "Get in the house and eat your supper," she told him. "As for you, Frankie, you're old enough to know better than to play Peeping Tom. Get in the house. Get out of my sight."

***

Supper was served buffet style. Francine had made a massive casserole and a friend from church had made a wedding cake.

Eventually, the men settled on the back porch while the women straightened up.

Carl didn't want to go out on the porch. He preferred to rock in peace in front of the fireplace. The women went about their business, leaving him be—all except Irene, who, rather than help with the cleaning, sat down beside him and talked. She talked on and on and then he started talking, too, enjoying it.

Rachel and Francine were put off by Irene's behavior. "Some of that's fine, but enough's enough," noted Rachel. She poked her head into the living room to get another look at Irene, then stepped back into the kitchen. "After all, what's a thirty-year-old woman got to say to an old man?" Rachel asked, rhetorically.

"She's been married three years now, and still they don't have children, and none on the way," added Francine. "Irene won't be spoiling her figure."

"It's like she's trying to show up the rest of us by encouraging the old man's ramblings," Rachel said when Grandma was out of earshot. "Let him rest, that's what I say. Rest is what he needs.

"When I think of the troubles other people have, I realize what blessings I've got," she went on, as Francine passed her another dish to dry. "Poor Charlie. How he gets along with Irene is a mystery to me. She's simply so ... foreign. Terrible things the Army does by putting our fine young men in the hands of foreign women.

"I've always had my suspicions ... about Irene, I mean. She's sweet and all smiles to your face, but these foreigners, all they want is to get their hooks into an American, and abracadabra they're citizens. She speaks English well enough, brilliant girl, but foreigners think differently, you know what I mean?"

"Yes," agreed Francine, "it's hard enough for any two people to get along and make a marriage work; no need to make it tougher."

"That's what I say to my boys. Don't go making trouble for yourselves. Not that I'm prejudiced or anything, but why look for trouble? I don't like the look in her eye, like she's saying one thing and thinking another. I never could trust anyone with a look like that."

***

Later, the men got out their instruments. Fred played the violin, Charlie the trombone, and Russ the clarinet. Sarah sat at the piano, and everyone sang. That is everyone but Carl and Irene, who continued to talk, until Rachel insisted that Carl get out his violin and join in the music. "Let us hear you," Rachel coaxed. "It's such a pleasure to hear the whole family playing together, and I do enjoy singing along. You know, I always wanted to learn a musical instrument myself."

Rachel smiled, pleased that she was the one who persuaded him to join in, that she hadn't entirely lost her old touch, that it was she, not Irene, who drew Carl into the party.

15 ~ Saint Smith

While the rest of the family played their instruments and sang in the living room, Frankie, still humiliated by his mother's outburst that afternoon, stayed upstairs, sulking and reading in Sue's old room. Then he heard a noise down the hall and found Irene alone, stretched out on her back on the bed in Charlie's old room. With her dress awry, the upper part of one thigh was exposed. Frankie stopped and stared. Then she sat up, looked at him, and smiled.

"Was denkst du?" Irene asked. At the beach, she had let him practice German with her, for the beginner's course he would be taking in college. When he didn't answer, she asked again in English, "What are you thinking?"

Frankie asked, rather than answered, "How did you get your name? Irene isn't a German name, is it?"

"I chose that name," she said. "My parents called me Helga. Ich heisse Helga, Helga Heinz."

"Then Helga's your real name," he concluded.

"No, my real name is Irene."

"And what does Irene mean?"

"Peace. And before Irene, Iris was my name."

"Iris?"

"The rainbow—messenger of the gods. A bold name, nicht wahr?"

"Why change your name twice? Were you trying to hide something?" he asked.

"When you change, your name should change. Your name should be in harmony with who you are."

"What?"

"Have you ever felt the presence of God?" she asked, gesturing for him to sit beside her on the bed.

From downstairs, the volume of the music increased as the family reached the refrain of "A Mighty Fortress Is Our God."

There were two single beds in the room. Frankie's father and Uncle Fred had slept there as boys. Later, the room had been Uncle Charlie's.

Pennants from the University of Maryland, where Charlie had been accepted and planned to go, still adorned the walls.

Charlie's high school wrestling trophies filled a bookcase in the corner. Grandma had interspersed glass elephants and giraffes among the trophies and on the bureaus and windowsills. She had hung a brass crucifix between the windows. Over one bed, the one that had been Charlie's, the one that Irene and Frankie were on now, hung a framed reproduction of a painting with a determined-looking young man, very much like Charlie, holding the steering wheel of a ship and looking up and ahead, while Christ stood behind him with a hand on his shoulder.

"You think I'm a crazy woman, a religious nut, nicht wahr? But you should have seen me back in Heidelberg when my name was Iris."

She put her hand on his shoulder.

Frankie looked up at the painting of Christ and the ship's pilot and felt a twinge of guilt. Irene was the most sensuous woman he had ever known. He was hoping for the miracle of a caress. Instead, she spoke of God.

"Have you ever felt that God was beside you? God Himself, living and breathing?"

He stared at her, lost in her dark blue eyes.

"Imagine that Christ returned, and you made his return possible," she said. "Or imagine that each of us is Christ. A spark within us comes from God. And, sometimes, that spark can flare and burn brightly.

"You think I'm silly," she continued. "Sehr gut. Perhaps my words hold no truth. What could this crazy lady know?

"I will tell you a story. The story of Saint Smith. His parents called him Heinrich Schmidt. We came to call him Heilige Schmidt, Holy Schmidt. You would call him Hank Smith or Saint Smith.

"I was ambitious and proud of my cleverness, like Charlie now. I would make my mark on the world.

"I studied drama and literature at Heidelberg. One day I would write great literature. Already, the world was a stage to me. What I did and said would make a masterpiece."

"Performance art?" Frankie suggested.

"What you say—yes. Only not so big a deal. At the beer Keller, my friends and I made tales and jokes, not just with words, but with what we did and how we did it."

"Practical jokes?".

"Yes. Heinrich sometimes joked with us, but he was shy and quiet. We mocked him. We at laughed at him. We tricked him."

"He was the butt of your jokes?"

"Yes, he was the perfect victim. He believed everything."

"He was gullible."

"Yes. We made *ghost bags*."

"What are those?" Frankie asked.

"Home-made hot-air balloons. You have probably made such things at school"

"No," he admitted.

"Ach! You must learn how to do this. First, take two pieces of stiff but light wire, about two or three feet long. Cross the wires and join them by melting the bottoms of a bunch of birthday candles at the intersection of the wires. Then take a dry cleaner's plastic bag and tape the ends of the wires to the inside of the bag, so the wires hold the bag open."

"Okay. So what can you do with that?" asked Frankie.

"At night, go up on the flat roof of a tall building. Hold the bag open and light the candles. When the bag fills with hot air and smoke, let it go. The bag will fly for miles. And because it is filled with smoke and lit by candles, it will shine brightly and look like a ghost. And it will go for miles.

"We did this from the roof of Heinrich's building—ten bags, one after the other. One of us who was with Heinrich in his room made sure that he looked out his window as the bags went flying by. He ran through the halls shouting, 'Fliegende geiste!'"

"You mean 'flying saucers'?"

"Yes. He was so embarrassed by the spectacle he made of himself that he missed a week of classes. Then we pulled the telephone trick."

"What trick?"

"You need lessons on pranks? It's simple. All you need is a telephone and a couple of ball point pens. The old style telephone that has a receiver and a cradle. When you put the receiver in its cradle, the buttons go down and the call ends. Take the metal clips from two ballpoint pens, the clip that holds a pen in your pocket. Break off the rings from the clips and put them around the buttons that the receiver rests on. Then the buttons won't go down when you put the receiver down and the call won't end.

"I rigged Heinrich's phone that way. The receiver was down, but the phone was on. I played with the dial while talking to Heinrich in his room. I dialed the phone in my room. When I returned to my room, the phone was still ringing. When I picked up the receiver, I could hear everything from Heinrich's room."

"Like a bug?"

"Yes, a homemade bug. It cost nothing. It was just for fun. My friends and I listened from my room. Heinrich was practicing lines from a play. We laughed at him. He heard our laughs, but he didn't know where the laughter was coming from. He shouted. We laughed louder. He ran here and there and looked everywhere. Where was this sound coming from? We laughed louder."

"He must have been freaking out."

"Freaking, yes. That word. He was scared. He ran fast and far. He thought the room was geistlich."

"Haunted?"

"Yes, haunted. We had a good laugh."

"Okay. So you pulled some pranks on him. What's the big deal?"

"The big deal came next. I wrote a play I called *All God's Children*. In it, Satan tells God, 'Why do you bother to go to Earth? Why do you want to send your Son to Earth? Why do you play such games? All people are your children, right? Just wake up any random man. Just let that one man know the truth—that he is God, that God is in him.'

"In my play, God says, 'Yes, I should make miracles from the inside, from the God within. I will wake up one man to this truth, and he will be a guide to the rest.'

"In my play, God chooses the son of a carpenter. And to wake him up to this knowledge, God doesn't use angels or a burning bush. Rather, He gives the idea for a prank to the brothers and friends of this carpenter's son.

"Imagine Jesus at age twelve. To his parents, he is obedient and trustworthy and a fine young man. He works with his father. He helps his mother. But to his brothers he is proud and pompous. They call him 'Little God'.

"One night, while he sleeps, his brother James waves a torch near his face, then runs. Outside the window, others shout, 'I am the Light!' Jesus doesn't wake up. Nothing happens. The next night, they try again, and again Jesus sleeps through it. And a third night, again he sleeps through it.

"Then on the morning after the third try, Jesus wakes up like he is a new person—selfless, humble, kind. He listens to everyone. He cares about everyone. His look and his words comfort and inspire everyone. He becomes *a light unto the world*.

"I was proud of this idea. But my friends mocked me. They said that real people don't act this way. To prove my point, I tried an experiment. I tried a modern version of that same joke, with Heinrich as victim,

"I placed a tape recorder and a camera flash, with a timer, near his bed. In the middle of the night, the bulb would flash, and the tape recorder would boom, 'I am the light!' What would he think? How would he act? I thought that, like before, he would run down the hall and scream. He would tell more wild tales. about ghosts or flying saucers, and we'd have more laughs at his expense.

"But nothing happened. He slept through it. I tried again, and yet again, as in the play, nothing happened. I gave up.

"Then a week later, Heinrich changed. He glowed with warmth, concern, and tenderness. His dark blue eyes became compelling. His voice resounded. People started following him everywhere. He roamed the streets, night and day, with these followers. He spread good will and joy. He gave help to the poor and homeless. He didn't preach. He just acted. He showed great confidence, great strength of will.

"Me and my friends, we who had believed nothing, we, too, became his followers. *Der Heilige Heinrich, Der Heilige Schmidt, Saint Smith* we called him. And my friends named me *Iris*, crediting me and my play, my prank, for this miracle. To this new cult, I was a messenger from God.

"Heinrich didn't know about my trick. No one had told him. He had no idea that a joke had brought about this change in him. I felt I had to confess this to him.

"I told him in public where his friends and followers could hear. I told him what I had done. I knelt before him like before a god and begged his forgiveness.

"His eyes went blank and cold. Who was he now? He no longer looked like Saint Smith. And he didn't look like the old Heinrich either. I screamed. I grabbed him. I hugged him. I shook him. He was gone. The magic, the godliness was gone.

"Then I knew that I had loved him. As God-in-man I had loved him. I had loved that holy man.

"The cult ended. The followers blamed me. They called me *Fräulein Judas.*

"I stayed with him. I loved him with my body. But he had no soul, no magic. When we made love, it was just flesh rubbing against flesh.

"I became pregnant. I had an abortion. I left Heinrich. I left the university. I now called myself *Irene* because I needed Peace."

As she paused, Frankie became aware of the music from downstairs, the chorus of "Gloria In Excelsis Deo." His muscles were stiff. He hadn't moved during her narration. His right leg had gone to sleep, but he didn't dare shake it. He didn't want to disturb her concentration. He wanted her to continue.

"You stare at my eyes," she noted, "not in them, but at them. Yes. They are blue, like Heinrich's, but not holy. When he was God, when the God in him shone brightly, his eyes drew you out of yourself.

"Sometimes Charlie gets that look that Heinrich once had. When I first met Charlie in Munich, he had that look. He, a GI with a camera, stopped me on the street and, in broken German, he told me he needed my *face* for photographs. He would pay me. I knew it wasn't my face he wanted. He followed me, taking pictures of me while we walked. At the corner, I stopped, turned, and smiled. 'Okay,' said I in English, 'let's talk about your pictures.'

"We went to a beer Keller. I told him the story of Saint Smith. But I told it not as a story I had lived, but rather as a story I had written. That night his eyes looked dark blue like Heinrich's. On and on we talked about the Saint Smith story, about making a movie based on that. But before making it he would have to master his craft.

"At our wedding, too, his eyes had that dark-blue look. And sometimes, even now, his eyes flash that way when he wants me and only me."

"Frankie," his mother bellowed from downstairs. With a start, Frankie reawakened to the world in which his parents treated him as if he were still a little kid. He hated being called *Frankie*. "Frankie," she bellowed again.

"Yes, Mom?" he called back automatically.

"Get down here this instant. It's time to go home."

With his right leg still painfully asleep, he hobbled to the door. Irene kept looking in the same direction and with the same expression. He didn't want to disturb her, and he had to hurry. But he wondered if she continued to talk, after he left, and what she said.

16 ~ Blind Date

Frank, not *Frankie*, now that he was in college, woke with a start as the car lurched to the right. Nick, an upperclassman, was at the wheel. In the back sat Frank's roommate Brian. This was the last weekend of September 1966, their freshman year. They were on their way from Yale in New Haven, Connecticut, to Mount Holyoke in South Hadley, Massachusetts. Mary Jane, a girl Brian had met the summer before in Cape Cod, had set the other two up with blind dates. This was Frank and Brian's first trip anywhere off-campus since school started. They saw it as the beginning of a new stage in their lives. Much as they joked about blind dates, and they had never been on blind dates before, they were nervously optimistic.

The Vietnam War and its protests were just getting started. College students were deferred from the draft. Many presumed that the war would be over by the time they graduated. For the moment, college campuses were a sanctuary where an upcoming test or paper or upcoming dates loomed larger than international news.

At Mount Holyoke, every dormitory had its house mother who ruled like a benevolent tyrant. Male visitors weren't allowed beyond the Victorian-furnished sitting room. And only juniors and seniors could have cars on campus.

Mary Jane, Brian's girl, was waiting for them, reading a history book while sitting on a tree stump near the front gate. She had met him over the summer while waitressing at a restaurant in Hyannis where Brian was working as a dish washer. Mary Jane led the boys to Brigham Hall, a large yellow-clapboard Victorian house, with a winding staircase leading to the second- and third-floor dorm rooms. It looked like the setting for a pre-World War II movie. Nick's date, Doreen, greeted them in the lobby.

Waiting alone for his date, Frank scanned the geometric patterns of the silk wallpaper and the gargoyle shapes hand-carved in the molding that ran round the top of the room. His optimism was fading. Then a pair of blue-green eyes flashed at him from the top of the stairs.

Marge was five foot three, with jet black hair and a Botticelli face. She was wearing a plaid knee-length skirt and a white bulky wool sweater.

After making eye contact, she stepped forward quickly, then caught herself and held back, then rushed forward again.

They started talking, not with the usual first-date chatter, but rather about things that were uppermost on their minds. She rambled on about her older sister who was in the Peace Corps in Ghana and who she had just gotten a letter from, after two months of ominous silence. And Frank talked about Charlie, his prodigal uncle who would one day be a great movie director.

"We should get going now, Laurel, and catch up with the others," Frank suggested, offering her his hand.

"Laurel?" she asked.

"You are Laurel, aren't you?'

"No, I'm Marge. And you ...?"

"I'm Frank."

They laughed, realizing that they weren't one another's dates. Then with a look of complicity, they dashed for the door, delighted to have found one another, and not wanting the evening to be ruined by the arrival of the people they were supposed to be with. A few hundred yards from the dorm, they slowed down, out of breath, and laughed again, relieved that they had escaped. That's when they realized that they were holding hands, and with a warm squeeze, they continued to hold hands.

They passed the library, academic buildings, and the student center. Then they strolled down paths lined with hundred-year-old elm trees.

An hour later, they stopped by the pond, and looked in one another's eyes in silent anticipation. Frank had had a girlfriend in high school. They were the focus of one another's romantic fantasies and physical curiosity until they got into colleges on opposite coasts and hence, to the relief of both, could break up without the risk of either of them being hurt. Standing here with a woman he had just met, Frank wasn't sure what he could or should do next. He didn't want to botch this opportunity if it was an opportunity. The bulky sweater revealed little, but he imagined well-developed breasts. He was afraid of going too fast, and afraid of not going fast enough. The tension mounted until he finally summoned the courage to lean forward to kiss her. She met him halfway. Their dry lips brushed against one another, repeatedly, as they hugged.

She held him tight and offered no resistance to his hands as they roamed to the sides of her breasts, and even when he slipped a hand inside her sweater, inside her bra, and firmly held her breast, shapely, firm, and far larger than he had imagined.

For a moment, Frank felt proud of himself, like he had made a conquest. Then he sensed she wasn't responding. He pulled back enough to look her in the eyes, while keeping his hand in place. She didn't push his hand away, but she clearly preferred that he not do that, not now. So, he withdrew his hand, and, as if in thanks, she kissed him again, this time opening her mouth. Tongue touched tongue.

He was relieved of the burden of trying to figure out what to do next. Now he could simply enjoy the moment. It was as if they had confessed their mutual attraction and pledged their mutual respect.

"Can you come down to Yale for a weekend?" he asked.

"Yes."

"Next weekend?"

She hesitated, then replied, "In three weeks."

"Terrific. Then it's settled," he concluded.

"Yes. It's settled," she smiled. She, too, was relieved.

They walked to the College Inn and continued talking over ice cream and cokes.

"When I was growing up in Rockville, Maryland—"

"I grew up in Rockville, too."

"That's funny. You remind me of someone I knew back in grade school. We lived next door and were in the same class at school, but we hardly saw one another outside of school. Only once did we spend time together. We were seven then, and his babysitter had taken off and left him alone, and he came crying over to our house, and he and I stayed up half the night playing Monopoly."

"Maggie Callahan?"

"Frankie?"

"Good grief! That's incredible. We were ten when you moved away, and I never imagined ... "

"What's Rockville like now?"

"We moved away not long after you did," he replied. "We live in Philadelphia now."

"And we live in Boston. God," she exclaimed, "I can still see your panic-stricken face when you came to our house that night. I thought it was grown-up of me to help you and play with you at a time like that. I thought we'd be friends forever. But after that you ignored me just as you had before."

"I was embarrassed. I was afraid you'd tell everyone at school what had happened and how scared I was. What a crazy kid I was not to have made friends with you then."

"And what a crazy babysitter you had."

"That was my Uncle Charlie, the one I mentioned before, the movie-maker."

"Yes, Charlie, I should have recognized the name. The legendary Charlie. My father still tells that story with lots of embellishment. And what does Charlie do now aside from make amateur movies?"

"They aren't amateur. He has professional talent. One of his first flicks won an award in Germany. That's where he met his wife, Irene. She teaches at the University of Maryland. She's an extraordinary woman, with a remarkable imagination."

"You say that with such passion," she noted.

"Well, if you could just see her and hear her, you'd know what I mean. Why one night last summer ... " And he told her about ghost bags, and began the tale of Saint Smith, but before he could finish, Brian and Nick showed up, and it was time to leave.

***

Frank paused in front of the bathroom mirror to brush and re-brush his hair, though it was so short now—after his first haircut in six months—there was no need to comb it. He donned the dress winter coat his mother had insisted on giving him and which he had never worn before. Then he dashed off to the bus station on Orange Street.

It was half an hour before Marge's bus was due, and the station was a ten-minute walk away. He jogged to get there in plenty of time and then sprinted, when it occurred to him that the bus might arrive early. When he got there, he realized he was sweating. He wiped his face with his handkerchief and hoped there was no odor from his armpits. He had applied a double dose of anti-perspirant.

The bus was half an hour late, and she wasn't on it. He went to the information counter and waited in line to find out when the next bus was due. She must have missed her connection in Springfield.

Then he noticed a young woman standing by the front window, looking out expectantly. Her hair was gathered in a bun in the back. She was wearing a blue winter coat. She repeatedly checked her watch and tapped the floor with her high-heeled shoes.

"Sir. Excuse me, sir," said the man at the counter.

Frank had momentarily forgotten what he was waiting for, absorbed as he was in imagining what the young woman looked like and hoping she would turn his way.

"What? Oh, yes. The bus. The next bus from Springfield. When is it due in?"

At the sound of his voice, the young woman turned around abruptly and stared in disbelief, "Frankie?"

"Maggie?"

"Marge. Call me Marge now, remember?" she smiled.

"And call me Frank," he smiled back.

He reached out to hug her, but he could only put one hand on her shoulder before she handed him her suitcase. It was small, but heavy.

"Books," she explained. "I have a psych test on Monday. That's going to be my major. And you?"

"What?"

"Your major?"

"Maybe math. Maybe English."

"Maybe?" she laughed. "That's decisive."

He hesitated, not having a ready answer. He wouldn't have to declare a major until the end of sophomore year. He would just as soon postpone that commitment, any commitment, as long as possible. And he didn't want to go into that now with this woman he barely knew and wanted to impress.

She took his right sweaty palm in her left white-gloved hand, and said, "Lead the way, Macduff."

"Oh yeah," he answered, as if he had just woken up. He started walking toward the Old Campus, the freshman residence area. Then he abruptly changed direction. "I guess we should go to the Taft first, check you in, and drop off your bag."

"The Taft?" she asked. "That's really the name of the hotel?"

"Sure."

"The Taft. Just like in the movie *The Graduate*?" she laughed.

He failed to see the humor. His left arm was aching from the weight of the suitcase, but he didn't want to shift hands because she was holding his other hand, and he didn't want to let go.

"You did see *The Graduate*, didn't you?"

"Yes, of course."

"Well, maybe we can talk about movies. It's funny how little we know about one another. We've just had a few hours together, and that was three weeks ago."

As they got closer to College St. and merged with the flow of Yalies and their dates going to and from the Taft Hotel, Marge slackened her previously confident pace and fell silent. Some of the girls were wearing jeans, some were in skirts, and none of them wore high heels, none had their hair pulled back in a bun, none wore gloves, and none had lipstick or noticeable makeup. Everyone seemed to stare at Marge as if she were an alien presence, a refugee from a secretarial pool.

When they were crossing Chapel St., her right heel caught in a crack in the pavement, and she nearly fell. Frank dropped the suitcase, helped her, then, with great relief, switched hands. She, despite the autumn chill, removed her shoes and walked the rest of the way in stocking feet.

When they got to the room on the fifth floor of the Taft, Marge paused in the doorway. The cracking plaster and the dilapidated condition of the furniture did *not* resemble the movie set in *The Graduate*. And in the mirror straight ahead of them, both stared at themselves and each other with a bewildered lack of recognition.

Marge took a deep breath, let go of Frank's hand, strode straight ahead, threw the shoes aside, took off her gloves, freed her hair from the net in the back, then grabbed her suitcase from Frank, who was still immobile, and headed for the bathroom.

Standing in the doorway, Frank remembered the movie poster with Dustin Hoffman in the background, standing in the doorway of a room in another Taft Hotel, watching expectantly while in the foreground Mrs. Robinson pulled a stocking down over her knee.

He shut the door behind him and sat down on the bed. It had been a mistake. He had nothing in common with this girl. He didn't know what to say to her or how to act around her. This was going nowhere. He wished he had never met her, never invited her. He could be in his room right now, writing the paper on *Paradise Lost* that was due on Tuesday, or studying German vocabulary. How did he get himself into this mess?

When Marge emerged from the bathroom, she was wearing jeans and a bulky wool sweater. On her feet, she had flat brown shoes and white socks. Her black hair was like she had worn it three weeks ago—curling out at the sides, "perky," a bit unruly. Her smile and the sparkle in her eyes reassured him. He was delighted.

"Now what do you have planned?" she asked, walking toward the door.

He hadn't planned anything but didn't dare admit that. He would have been happy to stay in the hotel room and make out. "Well, there's a football game against Columbia this afternoon. And there will be a dance at Calhoun tonight."

She turned toward him, took his hand, and said. "Okay. From the look of you, you're about as excited about that stuff as I am. I get it. You feel awkward. I feel awkward. We've only been in college for a few weeks. You're at an all-boys school, and I'm at an all-girls. I've never been in a hotel before except with my parents. I don't know what to expect, and you don't either. Let's go for a walk. Don't do the campus tour thing. I don't need to know the names of the buildings. Let's just wander, like we did at Holyoke. You can talk about whatever matters to you, and how math and English will get you there."

As they walked from one side of the campus to the other and back again, Frank spewed forth his life story, with nervous intensity. He explained that his younger brother Eddie, who was a toddler when Marge moved away from Rockville, was now fourteen. And he had two other brothers now who were so young they seemed like they were a separate family. Frank said, "I guess Mom isn't ready to give up the role of mother. She had the youngest when she was forty-four. I guess it's her way to fight off the onset of middle age. The new kids are giving her a new round of Little League and Boy Scouts and PTA. And she enjoys the company of the younger parents of her younger kids' friends."

He told about the sandcastles that his grandfather and his grandfather's grandfather used to make, so close to the waterline that they would be destroyed by the incoming tide. He told about his Great-Uncle Harry and his tales of World War I and secret missions in Europe after the war, and the ranch where he raised camels in Colorado.

But his narrative kept coming back to Charlie, from the disastrous babysitting night, through his volunteering for the peace-time army, to his precipitous marriage to Irene, with detailed descriptions of Charlie's homemade movies, along with the story about Saint Smith that Irene had told him. He fervently believed in Charlie as a movie-maker. He admired Charlie's drive and ambition and was convinced that sooner or later his talent would be recognized by the general public.

"Well, what about you?" Marge interjected.

Frank tripped and nearly fell. He had been talking non-stop. Her question caught him off-guard. He grabbed hold of a lamppost to regain his balance.

"What was that?" he asked.

"Don't just talk about your uncle. Tell me something about yourself. For starters, what physical trait makes you memorable?"

"What do you mean?"

"Well, if something happened to you and you lost your memory and you were disfigured, how could I know that you were you? Not your teeth. Teeth are a cop-out. Do you have a distinctive scar, a birthmark ...?"

"My tongue."

"Do you mean *tongue* as in linguistics? Are you great at languages?"

"No. I mean *tongue* as in being able to touch the tip of my nose with my tongue." And he stuck out his tongue and did that.

"Yuck. Gross."

"Well you asked for unique."

"And what's your driving ambition?

"I'm a writer, a novelist."

He had never thought of himself that way before. But he needed an answer and needed it fast. It was bad enough that he had answered the question about choice of major with maybes. Crossing Elm Street gave him a brief reprieve, then he launched into what, for him, was a creative improv, inventing an ambition and elaborating on a plan for the future, surprising himself with what he had to say.

"I'm a lot like Charlie. That's probably why I talk about him so much. We're both into story. Charlie tells stories through film. I'll tell stories with words, with books, with novels. My parents hoped I would become a doctor. That was their idea of a successful life for someone with the intelligence for it. But I told them, years ago, that a doctor just prolongs life, while a novelist can give people reasons for living."

"Have you written anything yet? Have you been published?"

"I have lots of notes and beginnings. I need life experience before the pieces will come together. But I do have a working title."

"What's that?"

"*Restless*. The main character feels both driven and directionless. He feels he has a destiny to fulfill but doesn't know what that destiny is. Think Thomas Wolfe. Think *The Razor's Edge* by Maugham. I'll model the main character on Charlie—talented, energetic, charismatic. Someone who makes abrupt changes in the direction of his life like when Charlie joined the Army and when he married Irene."

The idea took shape as he talked about it. For him, this was a quantum moment. From hundreds of possible futures, he might have considered, he chose this one. And to Marge he spoke with new self-assurance. He was proud to be such a person and pleased that Marge took him seriously.

"What about you?" he asked.

"What?"

"What physical trait makes you memorable?"

"I thought you knew already. Your eyes wander there often enough. It's hard to keep eye contact with you."

"What do you mean?"

"Oh come on. It's my bosom, my knockers, my rack, my breasts. You were quick enough to put your hands on them when we first met."

He laughed. He would have never imagined her saying such a thing. She was a delightful bundle of surprises. "And your ambition?"

"To prove that sex is good for memory."

He laughed again. She was hilarious.

17 ~ Exchanging Dreams

That night, after dinner in Freshman Commons, when Frank and Marge got to his entryway in the Old Campus, the hall light on the third floor was out. Frank took her hand, guided her through the semi-darkness, and unlocked the door to his suite.

She scanned the living room—tattered sofa, purple rug with wear marks and stains, and metal bookcases over-stuffed with paperbacks. In the bedroom to the left, the bunkbeds, desk, and floor were cluttered with books.

She shuffled through the stack of records beside the stereo.

"Mahler," she exclaimed, picking up the album on top, delighted that they had similar tastes in music.

"That's Brian's," Frank admitted. "All those records are his. But we're free to use them. Just put it on the turntable."

"But there's electrical tape over the switch."

"No problem." He sat down on the sofa and pushed buttons that were tacked onto the armrest. The stereo started, the overhead light dimmed, and soft-colored lights flipped on.

"Brian's work," he explained. "He's good at electrical wiring." Frank fiddled with the switches, adjusting the volume, and making the lights go bright, then dim again.

Marge laughed. "That's the kind of thing my Dad would do. He's an electrical engineer, always tinkering with gadgets."

They heard a tapping at the door.

"Who's there?" Frank hollered.

No one answered, but the tapping became louder and more insistent. Frank swung the door open.

A woman stood in the darkness of the hallway.

Before his eyes had time to adjust, Marge hit the buttons on the sofa, and every light in the room went bright, and the stereo blared full blast.

"Mein Gott! What a reception!"

"Irene?" Frank answered, then called, "Marge, it's Irene, Charlie's wife."

Irene was wearing a waist-length white leather jacket, and a red miniskirt.

Marge dimmed the lights, turned off the music and smiled in recognition, "The ghost-bag lady."

"I didn't know if this was the right room," Irene apologized. "The light in the hall is out so I couldn't see the number. It's our first visit here, Marge. Did I get your name right? Yes, Charlie and I are on our way to Boston, and I said, 'Why not stop and see Frank.' Charlie's right behind me."

A 16-mm movie camera appeared over her right shoulder. "Smile, you're on candid camera," said Charlie.

Charlie was a couple inches taller than Frank, and more solid and muscular. At first glance, he reminded Marge of an actor, but she wasn't sure which one. His hair was short, dark and curly, like Warren Beatty. But the shape of his face and his general build reminded her more of Robert Redford.

Slung over his shoulders, he was carrying two bags of equipment, which he quickly unpacked, including an assortment of camera lenses, a projector, sound-gear, and bulky batteries. He set up his camera on a tripod, focused it on Marge, and started shooting.

"Are you doing a documentary?" asked Frank.

"Capturing raw footage for future films," Charlie winked.

"He bought this camera last month," explained Irene. "He takes it everywhere and shoots everything."

"But what kind of story are you trying to tell?" Frank persisted.

"The story will come from the reality I record," explained Charlie. "Beautiful moments happen all the time, and we don't notice them. The more I record, the better the chance that I'll capture such moments. Then later, through editing, I'll tell the stories those moments suggest to me."

"That's his latest theory," Irene explained proudly. "He gets this all on his own from reading, observing, and experimenting. Ja, isn't it wonderful how his art grows in new directions?"

"But will it sell?" asked Frank. "How will you make money with films like that?"

Charlie pointed the camera and microphone at Frank, "Great, Frank, tell me more. Tell me what art's all about."

Frank hesitated, self-conscious in front of the camera. He stepped aside to get out of range, but Charlie kept the focus on him. Frank sat down on the arm of the sofa, and tried to answer, "The quality of art is measured by results. It's what lasts, what gets reproduced over and over, by one generation after another."

Charlie laughed, "By that definition, no film will ever be art because the technology keeps changing." He swung the camera and microphone in Marge's direction. "And you, young lady?"

"Marge," she replied with a broad smile. She seemed to glow when the camera was pointed her way.

"Tell me, Miss Marge, what is art?"

"Art assists memory, like rhyme and rhythm do in poetry," she suggested. "The better a thought is expressed, the better it will be remembered and passed from person to person and from generation to generation." She was surprised and pleased by what she had said.

Now Charlie aimed at Irene, who added, "Art is experience, a special kind of experience. Ja, art helps us recognize and pay attention to the fleeting moment. Also, art captures that moment and preserves it so we can savor it over and over again"

Charlie handed the camera and microphone to Irene who now pointed it at him, as he lectured, "I agree with my sexy mini-skirted wife that art is experience. The artist picks particular moments as deserving attention and shows them from a perspective of his choosing. He gives focus and clarity to moments that otherwise would pass unnoticed."

They were interrupted by another knock on the door. Marge opened it.

"Mary Jane?" Marge asked in surprise.

"Hi, kid. Is Brian here?"

"You didn't mention that you'd be coming here this weekend."

"Oh, I'm here every weekend."

"Thanks for the great advice on how to do my hair and how to dress." Marge added. "I had no idea that you were putting me on."

"I should have taken pictures," Mary Jane laughed. "You were so cute with your hair tied back in a bun. So, where's Brian? And who's the guy with the camera? It's time to head over to Calhoun. The party's about to start."

"Party? What party?" asked Marge.

"Didn't Frank tell you? There's always a party on Saturday night."

"It's no big deal," Frank quickly explained. "People just drop in at Nick's suite. It gets crowded and noisy. I usually don't go."

As he spoke, the others, including Marge, followed Mary Jane.

Dozens of couples were crowded into the living room at Nick's suite. Irene made a bee-line to the stereo and shut it off, as Charlie, Frank, Mary Jane, and Marge marched in with the camera equipment.

"Just what we need—an audience," Irene exclaimed. "Show them *Traffic Jam*, Charlie."

"What's that?" asked Marge

"It's a film about fate and free will," answered Irene. "The meaning of life. Unanswerable questions answered in a ten-minute black-and-white film. Charlie did it with a rented camera. It was his first film with real sound not just sound synchronized with a tape recorder. It's one of my favorites."

"Ten minutes?" asked Frank. "How can you expect to make a buck with ten-minute movies?"

"Who wants to make a buck?" asked Irene.

"But people can make millions in the movie business," Frank persisted.

"And lose millions, too," Irene corrected him. "We're not in that league yet. We can only afford to lose thousands."

"On ten-minute flicks?"

"Yes, this one cost nearly eight thousand dollars. The editing is expensive when you have to rent the equipment by the hour."

"Eight thousand dollars for something that has no chance of being shown in theaters?"

"But it's a success," Irene insisted. "I've seen it dozens of times and still enjoy it. And Charlie enjoys watching the reactions of the audience when we show it."

***

Traffic Jam

[A couple drive down a highway.]

CHARLIE: Driving, driving, driving – it's all so unreal.

IRENE: What, dear?

CHARLIE: It's unreal, I tell you. We're sitting here like we're in our living room and things just go by.

IRENE: Just drive, dear. We'll have plenty of time to talk about things like that when we get where we're going. Just keep your eyes on the road.

CHARLIE: But the world looks two-dimensional and fuzzy through the windshield.

IRENE: Well, when was the last time you washed the windshield, Charlie?

[A second couple is in another car on the same highway.]

MARY: Dear, where are we going?

ED: Don't you know? I thought it was your idea.

MARY: No, it was your idea. I remember distinctly. We were at breakfast. You were reading the newspaper. I was listening to the news on the radio, and Tommy had dropped the Wheaties all over the floor.

ED: Yes, dear, but what did I say? Where did I say we were going?

MARY: Oh, I don't remember that.

[Two other cars, both convertibles with the tops down, are going side-by-side down the same highway at the same speed. One man is in each car. They start to talk to one another, shouting above the noise of the traffic.]

RALPH: Man, what a view.

AL: What view? There's nothing but cars and cars and more cars.

RALPH: Yeah, man, ain't it beautiful. Just look at all them cars. I've never seen so many cars.

[Back at the first car.]

IRENE: You look tired, dear. Do you want me to take over?

CHARLIE: That would be fine with me, but there's no way we can stop in all this traffic. It's unreal how much traffic there is. Where can they all be going?

[Back at the second car.]

MARY: Where are we going, dear?

ED: I just told you I don't know.

MARY: Then why are we going there?

ED: Because we have no choice. There's no way we can stop or turn around in all this traffic.

[Back at the two convertibles, Al waves and tries using signs to catch Ralph's attention and tell him to move. Finally, Al gives up and shouts.]

AL: Look, buddy, can you let me in your lane? My exit's coming up.

RALPH: Cool it, man, cool it. It's a beautiful day. Just look at all them cars. That's a Rolls over there, isn't it? That red one?

AL: Look, buddy, my exit's coming. We're jammed up. The only way I'm going to get out of this ...

RALPH: Like, crazy, man. I'd like to help, but this car won't slow down for anybody. She's just driving herself.

AL: God, that was my exit. Thanks, buddy. Thanks loads. Now there's no telling how long I'll be stuck on this damned highway.

[Car one.]

CHARLIE: Is it my imagination, or is the road getting wider?

IRENE: What was that, dear?

CHARLIE: Is it just me, or is the road getting wider? I can't see the side of the road. Just cars and cars and cars.

IRENE: And trucks. Just look at all those trucks. I'm sure it's just the trucks, dear. They block the view, and they take up so much space. I hate driving when there are trucks on the road.

[Car two.]

MARY: Where are we, dear?

ED: I wish I knew. I haven't seen a sign for hours. Can't say I've seen anything but cars and trucks and highway for hours.

[Car one. Charlie is puzzled. He taps on the gas gauge.]

CHARLIE: Something's strange, dear. When we started, the gas was on empty. I meant to fill up before we got on the highway, but I forgot.

IRENE: Oh, no, you mean we're running out of gas?

CHARLIE: No, dear, I don't think so. But I wish we were.

IRENE: And why would you wish that?

CHARLIE: Look, we've been driving for hours on an empty tank. That doesn't make sense. That isn't natural.

[Car two. Ed looks at his feet, moves his feet up and down on the gas pedal, then on the brake, and then on the clutch. The car doesn't respond.

Mary looks out at traffic on all sides. She's upset too, but for a different reason.]

MARY: Do something, Ed! Do something! Don't just sit there like a lump and let this traffic hem us in. Here we are wherever we are, and we don't know where we're going, and we've been going for hours on end. Do something. This is insane.

ED: Yes, dear, yes. I've been trying to change lanes. But there's no gap at all. And no matter how much I signal that I need to move over, nobody slows down to let me in.

MARY: Then stop. Just stop.

ED: I tried, dear. But I didn't want to alarm you. When I hit the brakes, the car doesn't slow down. I've been hitting the brakes, the clutch, the accelerator; but nothing happens. Somehow, we just keep going, staying even with the traffic around us.

[The convertibles. Al shouts, pointing to his wrist.]

AL: Hey, buddy, have you got the time?

RALPH: Sorry, man, but my watch stopped.

[Car one. It's now dark outside, except for the headlights of cars and trucks.

Charlie is spooked by the moving lights and keeps ducking to avoid their beams.]

CHARLIE: It's so dark. And those lights over there are racing at us. And these lights all around us. It's eerie.

IRENE: Calm down, Charlie. Calm down. Just pull yourself together. It's night. There's a perfectly rational explanation for everything. The gas tank was probably full, and the gauge is broken. Just take it easy. Slow down and try to pull over.

CHARLIE: But the car's driving itself. I'm not doing anything. I'm not even steering it.

[Charlie drops his arms to his sides. Irene shrieks, reaches for the wheel, falls across his lap. But nothing happens – no crash, no change of direction. Charlie helps her up, and she settles back in her seat – numb and helpless and frightened.]

[Car two. Ed's arms hang helplessly at his side. He's making no effort to control his car.]

MARY: Where are we going, Ed? Where are we going?

ED: I don't know. I just don't know.

[Car one.]

CHARLIE: It's like we're on a rocket ship, and there are thousands of other rocket ships just like ours, soaring through space on automatic pilot. Some computer somewhere has set us on this course, and it has set thousands of others on the same course. And here we are racing through space with our headlights bright like so many stars or meteorites. We worry about where we're going and how we'll get there; but it's all just a light show. The object isn't to get anywhere. Somebody just wanted to see the lights.

[The convertibles. Ralph, smiling, raises his arms.]

RALPH: Man, this is the life. Just look at them lights, man, just look at them lights.

[Car one. Charlie gestures, suddenly animated.]

CHARLIE: Look at the lights, Irene. Aren't they beautiful? Look at all the lights.

***

While the audience broke out in cheers, catcalls, and applause, Frank leaned toward Charlie and mentioned, "I think I've seen that somewhere before, but I'm not sure where or when."

"Shit," said Charlie. "People say that kind of thing time and again. And nobody remembers what or where. Do you have any idea how frustrating that is?"

Brian shouted from the other side of the noisy room, "Hey, you're good, man. What the hell are you doing fooling around with 16-mm stuff? Why aren't you out in Hollywood getting your foot in the door? Or in some film school? If you're serious about this stuff, what's your excuse for not getting on with it and turning pro?"

When Charlie didn't answer, Frank followed up, "Yeah, Charlie, you could be making real movies in Hollywood."

"Doing what I'm doing is exactly what I want to do," Charlie defended himself.

"Oh, get off it, Charlie," Nick piped in. "Go for the big time. You've got talent. Use it."

"But he is using it," explained Irene. "Thanks to my job, teaching at the university, Charlie has the free-time he needs to study and experiment on his own."

"And who is there to guide him and show the way?" asked Frank. "You can't make real movies alone. It takes lots of people with special skills to make a professional movie that can make it into theaters."

"He learns by watching the masters," Irene insisted. "We want to create art."

"He or you?" asked Frank. "Is this his ambition or yours?"

"Okay, okay," Charlie answered for himself. "You think I haven't had those thoughts myself? Maybe I am spinning my wheels. Maybe I should be in Hollywood. Maybe I should get any kind of nothing job out there just to get started."

Irene took his head in her hands and looked him straight in the eye. "If that's how you feel, then we should go. Right now, we should go."

"And you give up your job? When and where could you get a job as good as that? The college teaching market stinks right now. You love what you do. It pays good—good enough to give me the freedom to screw up my life by kidding myself that I can teach myself while I'm getting nowhere. Look, lady, I'm scared. Do you understand? I'm fucking scared I won't make it. As long as I don't take a shot at the big time, I can kid myself that I have talent. But what if I try and miss?"

Someone turned on the stereo and everyone started dancing again.

At two in the morning, the party crowd climbed the long winding stairs to the castle-like parapets on the roof of Calhoun College, singing "Scarborough Fair" and "Sound of Silence." At Irene's prompting, they were going to launch "ghost bags." They had gathered all the materials, to her specifications, and she had pre-assembled half a dozen bags in the living room.

Charlie took the camera with him. Nick and Brian carried the battery packs and sound gear.

Charlie shot film every step of the way, following Marge and aiming the camera up her dress as she scampered up the stairs ahead of him.

It was an Indian-summer night, with a gentle breeze heading toward the sea.

Marge stood near the corner, just above the traffic light at the intersection of Elm Street and College Street, facing the Old Campus and the Battelle Chapel. She sat on a parapet and scanned up and down the streets, which were still busy with students unwinding after a long hard week. When she half-closed her eyes, she could imagine that the gargoyles and other stone sculptures were alive, hiding under that stone camouflage, waiting years, decades, even centuries for the right combination of circumstances, when they would leap down on unexpecting passersby.

Charlie came over for a closeup of Marge with the tops of hundred-year-old oak trees and the New Haven Green in the background. Brian and Nick scurried obediently after him with the sound gear. Frank stood nearby and watched and listened. Meanwhile Mary Jane helped Irene hold the ghost bags in readiness, waiting for the wind to die down.

Charlie addressed Marge, "Okay, young lady, it's time for you to tell our viewing audience what you would like to be when you grow up."

She posed and smiled but didn't answer.

Then he asked her, "If you had one shot at greatness, one shot at making the world a different and better place, what would it be?"

Under the hypnotic gaze of Charlie's drunken but serious eyes, Marge found herself saying things that she had never said before. She talked about her father, who had been an electrical engineer. Physically, he was healthy for a seventy-year-old, but he had just been diagnosed with Alzheimer's. "I would like to do something that would stop that kind of suffering and waste," she said. "Even if the body deteriorates, if we could keep the mind alive and active, to keep building on all those years of experience and knowledge. Imagine the benefit, not just to the old folks themselves and to those who love them, but to all mankind. Just imagine if the elderly, with all their experience, could apply their full faculties to the problems of the present-day world."

"And how would you propose doing this?"

"Senility seems to be a breakdown of short-term memory, and I have this theory ... " she hesitated, embarrassed.

"Go on."

"I have this theory that dreams are important for memory. They're part of the mechanism for translating short-term memory into long-term memory. I understand that short-term memory is electrical, and that long-term is chemical. I need to study to figure out the details. At this point, all I have is a hunch. My father can still remember events from his childhood, but he can't remember where he just put a cup. I think that the short-term memory gets filled up, unable to take any more. Maybe it's like a blackboard, covered with chalk to the point where there's no way to distinguish anything new that's written on it from what was there before. It needs to be erased to be useful again. He has lost the ability to clean the slate and transfer recent information to long-term memory."

"But how could that lead you to a cure?" asked Charlie, switching lenses for an extreme close-up.

"That's where my theory comes in, and where I stray from what they teach us now in school. I believe that the mechanism for doing that translation is triggered by sexual stimulation."

Charlie smiled broadly.

"Freud made a big deal about the connection between dreams and sexual fantasy," she continued. "He presumed that sex is the be-all and end-all, at the center of all our creative activity. I would put the emphasis on memory instead. I would say that we dream not to fulfill unconscious sexual desires, but rather to renew our memory so we can continue to function as productive human beings. I would say that there's a connection between erotic dreams and the mechanism of memory translation. I would say that we dream about sex not because sex is important, but because memory is important. Sexual arousal triggers a set of events that puts our short-term memories into long-term form and then erases the short-term slate so it's ready to record new experience. Sex is a mechanism to renew memory."

"So you'll open up a chain of sex clinics to help memory," Charlie chuckled. "Well, you've got a dream. I'll give you credit. That's a whopper of a dream about dreams. That's your impossible dream. Go for it."

He wrapped his arms around her and gave her a quick avuncular kiss on the forehead.

"I intend to," she replied with determination. "And you should go for yours as well."

"Of course," he answered dismissively.

"Seriously. Don't let Irene talk you out of it. She's holding you back. Frank told me how she woke you up to your calling as a movie-maker. But now she's holding you back, treating you like a talented kid, a perpetual amateur, like she's afraid that you might fail in the adult world."

"So you think I should become an adult film maker?" he joked.

"She mothers you. She smothers you. She Peter Pans you. Maybe she's afraid she'll lose you if you grow up and don't need her anymore."

"And you say all this from knowing me for how many hours?"

"Yes. Because it's obvious to everyone but you. If you're serious about making serious movies, not just doing an adult version of show-and-tell, screening your creations in living rooms to audiences of family and friends, you need to go where the professionals live and work. You need to learn how teams of experts work together and how to manage them, instead of doing everything yourself. You need to make contacts and pay your dues in that community. You need to learn your way around and get known by people in a position to help you; and you need to put yourself in a position where you can help them in return."

"Mein Gott!" Irene called to them. "Come, bitte. The conditions are perfect. It's time to let the ghost bags fly!"

Following instructions from Irene, Nick and Brian held the top of one of the plastic bags high. Frank and Charlie held the sides apart. Irene held the clump of candles where the two wires met, and Marge lit the candles with a cigarette lighter.

The bag began to fill out with smoke and hot air. When it was completely filled, Irene shouted, "Now," and they let go and stepped back.

Slowly it rose as a gentle breeze moved it sideways toward the parapets. The bundle of candles, attached to the wire, hanging half a foot lower than the edge of the bag, barely cleared the wall. But after a flight of just ten feet, the bag caught on a branch of a tree, and the candles became dislodged.

"This doesn't look safe," noted Marge. "We could start a fire this way."

"They're just birthday candles," Charlie reassured her. "That was about the worst we could expect—getting stuck in a tree. The candles will blow out harmlessly on the way to the ground."

They tried again, adjusting their starting position so if the wind stayed steady, they would miss the tree this time. And it did miss, climbing slowly and gliding outward, over the streets of New Haven. The light of the candles refracted by the smoke in the bag made it clearly visible against the dark sky.

Charlie, Nick, and Brian kept an eye on the pedestrians below and laughed heartily when several of them spotted a ghost bag flying overhead and pointed at the eerie shape as if it were a UFO.

Frank put his arm around Marge, and she leaned back on his shoulder as they watched the bag rise against the background of the stars, going for miles, over Long Island Sound, until it disappeared from view.

18 ~ Thanksgiving

When Marge arrived at the bus station the following Saturday, she had her hair in pigtails, and she wore brown corduroy slacks and a parka. Her suitcase was even heavier than before.

"More books," she explained to Frank as he struggled to lift it. She insisted that they take turns carrying it to the hotel.

"I didn't realize that you were that serious about your studies," he noted.

"I wasn't," she admitted. "But now I am. Charlie's right. That theory of mine is my shot at greatness. I should give it my best effort. I'd never forgive myself if I didn't. By the way, is Charlie likely to drop by again?" she asked.

"No."

"Are you sure?"

"Well, normally, I'd say, 'Who can tell what Charlie will do?' But from what I hear, as soon as they got home, they sold their furniture, threw the rest of their belongings in a U-Haul, and drove to California. I don't think we'll be seeing them for a long time."

"Well, that's good," she concluded. "It's high time he took his movie-making seriously and tried to become a professional."

"I'm not so sure," answered Frank. "I wonder about Irene leaving her teaching job in the middle of the semester with no notice. That will be a black mark on her record. Leaving that way, she's throwing away her career."

"I wouldn't worry about her," noted Marge. "She'll find a way to enjoy the Hollywood experience."

"I'm surprised—you don't seem to think much of her."

"On the contrary, I think she's extraordinary. Teaching is just a job to her. It's what she does; it isn't who she is. I wouldn't worry about Irene. She'll always be the star of the story of her own life."

"Well, from what you say, I guess I'm the only one of us four who doesn't have a shot at greatness."

"What do you mean? You're the novelist, remember?"

They didn't say anything more until they got to the hotel room, but the suitcase seemed lighter to Frank now. He carried it the rest of the way and even forgot to switch it from hand to hand.

"Well, even without Charlie, there'll be another party at Nick's tonight," Frank promised, while Marge was unpacking her bag.

"That's not where my head's at now. Can we avoid the crowds this weekend? Can we just stay here in the hotel?"

Frank smiled and moved closer to her, looking for an opportunity to put his arms around her.

"I mean alone together with our books," she explained. "I really do have to study this weekend," she added. When their lips brushed against one another, she lightly touched his upper lip with her tongue.

Frank had a sudden inspiration. "You're really serious about that theory of yours, aren't you?"

"I certainly am."

"Well, then why don't we put it to the test?"

"How?"

"If it's true that there's a connection between sex and memory, then sex could help when cramming for a test."

"Well, I do have a big test on Monday," she whispered suggestively, her lips brushing against his earlobe. "You will help, won't you?" she added, with an electric flick of her tongue.

Marge took out her books, and Frank ran back to his room to get his. Then they stretched out on the hotel bed to study, punctuated with occasional kisses and caresses, until she asked, "Would you like to play with the twins?"

"What twins?"

"Don't be dense."

She pulled off her sweater and unhooked her bra, and Frank put his long tongue to good use.

They fell into the habit of spending their weekends together, studying and making out. Then the question of Thanksgiving arose. "I can't get out of going home by saying I have to study," Frank told her. "Mom has invited Grandma and Grandpa and is making a big deal out of the occasion. There's no way I can back out. God, I wish you could come with me."

"Why not?"

"You mean you could?"

"My folks don't make much of a fuss about Thanksgiving now that my sister is off on her own. They're delighted that I've set my sights on grad school. They think you're a good influence on me. Yes, of course I've told them about you. And I'm sure they'd be happy if I was happy. Yes, I could go to Philadelphia with you."

***

Frank borrowed Nick's car. Nick was flying home to St. Louis for the holidays. He picked Marge up in front of Brigham Hall after her last class the day before Thanksgiving. A few flakes of wet snow fell as they headed south on I-91. At first, she listened to classical music on the radio and worked on homework. But when night fell as they were on the Cross-Bronx Expressway, she slid over close and rested her head on his shoulder. "Getting tired?" she asked.

"No, I'm doing fine," he answered, expecting she might offer to share the driving.

"Well, I wouldn't want you to get drowsy in all this traffic," she whispered in his ear. "Maybe I should help keep you alert."

Her hand slid to the inner side of his thigh and caressed gently, moving upward, until she brought a broad smile to his face and a very alert look to his eyes. She kept up her caresses, with occasional variations, for the rest of the trip.

Then, a few blocks from Frank's house, she insisted that they park on a side street. He reached out to hug and kiss her, but she backed away. "Cool it now, Frank. Just cool it, and I'll make you very happy."

He sat on his hands and waited patiently while she made up her mind whether to go ahead with what she had been thinking about doing. Then she reached over, unzipped him, reached in, and held him.

Frank remembered the time he had seen Irene alone with Charlie in his grandparents' bedroom. He pleaded, "Could you ... could you please kiss it?"

She hesitated, then whispered, "Will you promise not to come on me?"

"Of course, of course, whatever you want, I—"

"One more word," she warned him, "and I won't do it."

Then her wet lips made quick contact with his exposed flesh.

***

At his parents' house, Frank slept on the living room sofa, and Marge in his old room, which, much to his annoyance, his mother had redecorated. He couldn't see anything of himself in the *collegiate look* she had tried to create. His grandparents shared his parents' room, and his parents used the sofa bed in the basement recreation room.

Rachel had gone all-out to make everything *perfect* for this holiday, and she made no secret of the effort she had expended like giving an expensive gift and deliberately leaving the price tag on.

Grandma Sarah stood at Rachel's bureau, looking at herself sideways in the mirror, "It feels so strange not being at our own house for Thanksgiving."

Grandpa Carl laughed, "No cooking to do, no dishes, yes, it must be like you've died and gone to heaven."

"No, just strange—detached, not belonging. It's like being inside somebody else's body."

"Sarah, just leave it to you. You come up with the spookiest, creepiest notions. You should write stories for one of those television shows, like *Twilight Zone: Caught inside somebody else's body.* What a notion."

"Well, how I feel is how I feel."

"But you know, Sarah, Rachel is going way out of her way to make us feel comfortable. Why, here she and Russ gave up their own room for us."

"Well, we should be the ones in the basement. We're the guests, aren't we? It's not fitting. I'll go along with it, since that's what she wants, but I'm glad I can tell you how uncomfortable I am, glad I can talk to you about this or anything else. You'll put up with any and every nonsense of mine. After all these years, you're still a love." She kissed Carl hard on the lips. "Okay, Grandpa, let's move it."

Carl nearly tripped over Marge at the foot of the stairs. "Ah, you must be Margaret. Rachel said that Frank was bringing a friend from school."

"Yes, Mr. Uhland. And Frank has told me a lot about you."

"And what's your major?" he asked gruffly.

"Psychology."

"Psychology? You mean dreams and such? You might want to go talk to Sarah. She's always been big on dreams."

"Yes, dreams are interesting," Marge noted, "dreams and memory."

"Now, memory, that's more my department." Carl went on, "I can remember everything as clear as looking out a picture window. If only I could hear as well. Why I can just shut my eyes and see scenes all over again that I first saw seventy and more years ago. And I can remember where I left my keys, too, unlike some of our friends. I've still got my wits about me."

All day, Eddie ogled Marge the way he and Frank used to ogle Irene. Just before dinner, he took Frank aside and asked, confidentially, "Does she go all the way?"

"Eddie!"

"Well, how far does she go?"

"Grow up, kid. Going out with a girl isn't the same as playing a game of grope."

"Sure, Frankie, sure. Like that isn't what you're thinking with a doll like that? How naive do you think I am?" He looked like he was proud of having used the word *naive*.

"Well, don't go playing peeping Tom, right? Find some girl of your own."

"Oh, but I have found one; I most definitely have, dear brother." He winked and smiled in what he must have imagined was a sophisticated and knowing manner.

Rachel went out of her way to make Marge feel at home. "I always wanted to have a daughter," she rambled on, repeating herself. "I guess Frankie didn't tell you. How could a mother expect a boy to say anything about his mother? It's as if mothers don't exist. It's good when we get a chance to see someone *special*. Not that Frankie brings home *special* people all the time, or that he ever has before. But I'm sure he's never said a word about his dear sweet, self-effacing mother who would do anything she could for him—and does over and over, you can be sure. Why he wouldn't be at Yale today if it weren't for me. His father took one look at the tuition price and wanted him to go to a state school instead.

But I stood up for Frankie. He's worked so hard and done so well; he deserves the best, the very best that money can buy. It's only money, after all. And what good is money in the grave, I ask you? But we won't have that problem, believe you me. All we'll leave behind are debts — the debts we took on to give our children the very best. But, as I was telling you, I never had a mother, or never knew her, I mean. I was an orphan raised by an aunt and uncle. My uncle was in the military, so we were always on the move and never staying long enough to put down roots. So never having had a mother, I always wanted a daughter who I could be a mother to and do all the things I had wished my mother had done with me.

"I'm glad Frankie brought you home for Thanksgiving. And I'm sure it must have been your idea because Frankie never has considerate ideas like that. So that makes me think all the more of you. Yes, he's a lucky boy to have found someone like you, I'm sure of that. Not that luck has ever mattered that much for him. He's a hard worker, you know, and incredibly brilliant. Why all his teachers from the first grade on, I'm sure, knew that he would go to the best schools and that he would make something of himself. Yes, you're lucky to have found him.

"But it's sad, too, for a mother you know, when her son brings home a full-grown marriageable woman. It makes me realize that in a year or two, perhaps even sooner, I could be a grandmother. Me, a grandmother? Why the thought of it is simply mind-boggling.

"Of course, I'll love my grandchildren. And I'll want dozens and dozens of them to love and cuddle and do grandmotherly things with and give grandmotherly gifts to. I never had a grandmother, you know.

"But I'm not ready to think of myself that way — to think that I'm old enough to be a grandmother. Why little Mark, my youngest was born just last year, and Johnny is only seven. I made close friends with a couple of mothers who were in the maternity ward with me this last time. They're half my age, if truth be told, but I feel I have so much in common with them. My mind is young, you know. I read all the time to keep my mind young. And we have lots of friends who are young parents with children Johnny's age and younger. Our whole life revolves around the younger set now that Frankie is off in college and Eddie is in high school and dating the Tomkins girl, Dr. Tomkins' daughter. We hardly ever see him either, and when we do, he doesn't talk to us.

"So, when I think that you or someone like you could make me a grandmother soon, I can't help but think how wonderful that would be and yet how scary it is, too. Life goes so fast; one minute you're just beginning and then it's over."

***

"That Margaret is a joy, isn't she?" Grandma Sarah noted that night when she and Carl were alone in bed.

"Yes, she's like Irene, I'd say. She had no trouble understanding me. She listens and cares what I say."

"A fine young woman, isn't she?"

"Yes, she has her feet on the ground. Frank would do well to win that one."

"Win indeed. You men are all the same, as if she were some prize in a game. No, she's a fine intelligent woman. All her talk about memory made sense to me."

"Wasn't she cute the way she was embarrassed, how she talked about sex without saying the word?"

"I'm sure she was sincere in asking us about things we remember. It's been years since anyone aside from Irene seemed to care what we had to say. Yes, I like the girl, and Frankie or no Frankie, I'd like to see her again and be friends with her. That's what I told her, Carl. Frankie or no Frankie, she's welcome at our house. I told her to come on down to Silver Spring. There's plenty of good colleges in and near Washington with graduate schools like she's talking about. She should check them out and stay with us and visit. We'll always be glad to see her.

"And that's a fine theory she has," Sarah went on. "I can't think of a better way to try to keep your memory alive and active. That's a theory I can see the point of. Right or wrong it gets you to do what you want to do and ought to do."

"You've got me there, Sarah. I'm right proud of my memory, and I give you full credit. The very sight of you stimulates my memory," he smiled.

"I don't know whether to thank the Lord that your eyes are failing or to thank Him that you have such a good memory that when the lights are out you can remember the way I looked decades ago."

"Sarah, the way you are right now, you're all a man could wish for. And praise the Lord for that. It hasn't been a bad visit after all, you must admit." He stretched out naked in bed, then added, "You have such a way with me, woman. You can breathe fresh life into these old bones."

"You dirty old man. So, you want me to take care of your Jack Robinson? Well, you're off to a good start without me having to do a thing. This looks like it will be a fine night for memory renewal. Yes, we have a lot to thank Marge for."

19 ~ Betrayal

After the intimacy of the ride to Philadelphia, Frank had hoped for more of the same on the ride back. But Marge repeatedly warded off his groping hand.

"I'm not ready to get married," she told Frank as they approached Mount Holyoke.

"Of course not now."

"I mean not now and not next year. Not until I've finished college. Not until I've finished grad school."

"Oh."

"That might be six or even ten years, depending on how well the dissertation goes. And even then, I don't know about children."

"I never said anything about children."

"Well, I want to make sure we understand each other up front. Children will have to wait. My career comes first."

The next weekend in New Haven was a downer for both of them. Marge felt put upon and Frank felt frustrated. Neither of them got much work done despite spending hours staring at their books.

With exams coming up, Marge decided to stay at Mount Holyoke, alone, the following weekend. That was when Frank met Gillian, a 20-year-old New Haven secretary with a British accent.

Nick had brought Gillian to mixers at Calhoun a couple times. In that context, she looked out of place. She wore her long hair piled high on her head, in the cone shape of a beauty-parlor hair dryer. Her eyes were done up as if she were in a play with thick mascara, false eyelashes, and bluish powder under her eyes. She wore a black, leather miniskirt, and a pink silk blouse with padded shoulders.

When Nick was mellow from a few beers, Frank had asked him what he saw in Gillian. "Are you kidding?" Nick answered. "She puts out. And she doesn't charge much, either."

"You mean you pay her for it?"

"Well, she's a working girl. 'Nothing's free in this world,' she says. 'You never pay more for sex than when you don't pay for it,' she says.

And she's right, you know, even in terms of hard cash. What does a weekend with Marge cost you?"

"More than I can afford."

"Sure. And I bet she doesn't put out either."

"Well ... "

"Give Gillian a call. I don't own her. That's why I pay her—so I won't have to own her, and she won't own me. Here's her number. She expects a hundred dollars and a fun night like dinner, maybe a movie. Don't rush her. Don't treat her cheap. Just give her the money as a present, up front and you'll get your money's worth at her place before the night's out."

Frank called. He paid. They had pizza. He took her to see *I am Curious (Yellow)*.

At the end of the evening, back at her place, she did exactly what he wanted her to do. On request, she knelt in front of him and caressed his privates with her lips and tongue, as he had seen Irene do to Charlie. Then she opened a bureau drawer, took out a handful of condoms, picked one she said was her favorite brand, and put it on him quickly and efficiently. But he came and went limp before she had a chance to undress. It was humiliating, and he had cheated on Marge for nothing. But he pocketed a couple of condoms on the way out. If and when he got lucky with Marge, or with someone else, he wanted to be prepared, and he would be too embarrassed to buy them in a drug store, to ask the clerk to get them from behind the counter.

Over Christmas vacation, Frank felt uncomfortable during his phone calls with Marge. He kept remembering scenes from movies and television shows where a secret came between two lovers and poisoned their relationship.

He was confused to discover that he thought that sex with someone who did it often with many partners was meaningless, but sex with a virgin was a declaration of love and commitment. It was the same act, so why was the meaning different? And if he confessed to Marge about his time with Gillian, how could he convince her that that wasn't betrayal?

He thought that if he didn't tell her about this stupid mistake of his, he wouldn't be able to feel close to her. If she cared for him as he did for her, she would understand and forgive him, and his confession would bring them closer together. He also told himself that he shouldn't be ashamed to admit how it had turned out. With this other woman, who was completely accessible to him, he hadn't been able to perform. That was tangible proof of his love for Marge. But he couldn't bring himself to say the words.

Over vacation, Frank bought a used 1960 Ford Falcon for three hundred dollars, borrowed from his parents, "so he could come home more often." It had over a hundred thousand miles on the odometer and a rust hole in the hood. Its headlights flickered when he hit the brakes. But it gave him a new level of independence.

On the first weekend back from vacation, he drove up to Mount Holyoke and took Marge for a spin through the country. Proud of himself and his new wheels, keeping his eyes, responsibly, on the road ahead, he blurted out the story of Gillian, in detail, as he had rehearsed it to himself. Marge sat quietly, staring at her fingernails. When he came to a halt at a stoplight in Northampton, she shouted, "I hate your guts," and stormed out of the car, slamming the door behind her. By the time he found a parking space, she had disappeared.

He spent two hours walking the streets, going in and out of shops. Then he drove back to Mount Holyoke. There he found Mary Jane, but she had no idea where Marge might have gone and wasn't cooperative because, from his own account, it didn't sound like Marge wanted him to find her. He had no choice but to head back to New Haven.

On subsequent days, he phoned repeatedly, but she didn't answer, then her phone was off the hook, then it was disconnected. She probably got a new unlisted number.

Two months after his confession, Frank saw Marge at a mixer at Mount Holyoke. She was standing by the punch bowl, turning down every guy who came along. When she spotted Frank, there was anger in her eyes. But the old electricity was there when their fingers touched. Hand in hand, they walked out of the auditorium, across the campus, down to the pond and around it three times, without saying a word. Then they got in his car, drove to a dark spot at the far end of a parking lot, and climbed into the backseat.

He reached under her sweater and unhooked her bra. She made no effort to help or to hinder him, sitting passive and disinterested, staring at her fingernails. She asked, "How could you go with a whore? I don't do enough to satisfy you? You want more? Okay, well let's do it and get it over with."

"What?" he asked in disbelief.

"You're curious, and I'm curious. And we're both yellow. That's the only reason we haven't done it, right? Scared. Well, let's do it and find out what the hell it feels like. Except that wouldn't satisfy you, would it?" she asked. Then she matter-of-factly lifted her skirt and pulled down her pantie-hose and panties. "Hurry up and take me, you idiot, before I change my mind."

Frank fell on the floor, scrambling to get out of his trousers. He laughed self-consciously.

Marge lay back, put her hands behind her head, and spread her legs as far as she could in those cramped quarters. She stared out the window as if something important were going on in the sky above the empty parking lot. But before he had touched her, she closed her legs tight. "Don't go in. Get as close as you want, but don't go in."

He hesitated. In his pocket, he had the condoms he had taken from Gillian's room months ago. But if he brought one out now, Marge would think he had sex all the time with other women., or that he had been planning to find her tonight and thought she was easy and intended to take advantage of her.

He lay down on top of her, and pressed himself against her, and hugged her, and kissed her. She wept. He begged her forgiveness and told her he loved her. They laughed and kissed tenderly, and he felt closer to her than he ever had.

Then she said, "My God!" and jumped up. "You didn't come, did you?"

"No," he mumbled, taken aback. "Not really."

"What do you mean, 'not really'? Either you did, or you didn't."

"I don't know," he said, and he didn't know if he was limp because he had come or because of their talking.

"I mean, for God's sake, I could get pregnant."

"Since when do you swear?"

"Since whenever I feel like it. And I definitely don't feel like getting pregnant. I have grad school and a career ahead of me. And I don't want anything like this getting in my way."

"A baby, you mean?"

"Of course. You know I don't want children."

"Not right away, of course. That's what you said."

"'Never is what I said and what I meant."

"Well, we haven't really talked about that. There's a lot we haven't talked about."

"And there's a lot you should understand without our having to talk about it. How could you do this to me?"

"Do what?"

"Oh, shut up with the what-the. How could you take such a risk with me?"

"But you wanted it. You asked for it."

"And I expected you to have sense enough to restrain yourself."

"But I didn't go in."

"But we were close, weren't we? Very close?"

"Yes, of course."

"And could you guarantee that nothing dribbled?"

"Dribbled?"

"You don't like the word? Well, fumbled, bumbled, fouled up my life. How could you do this to me?"

"You're not pregnant. There's no way," he insisted.

"Leave me alone," she cried.

After that, Marge and Frank didn't see one another or try to call one another for over a month. Then Marge called to say, "I missed my period."

It took Frank a while to absorb that statement and come up with a response. "How late are you?"

"A week."

"That doesn't mean anything."

"I'm regular. It's never been this late before."

"But you have mid-terms. You're tense."

"It's not just late. I've missed it. I'm sure."

"Don't panic. That's physically impossible. Believe me."

"You know it's possible."

"You're still technically a virgin."

"Technically—thank you."

"The odds are astronomical. It's too remote for words. Just hang in there. Another week. It'll come," he insisted, but his voice didn't have the confidence he wanted it to have.

"How could you do this to me?"

"But you're not pregnant."

"I could be. Odds or no odds, it's possible. And you damn well know it. How could you give me this worry, and now, of all times? My grades matter. All my grades matter. I don't just need to get into grad school. I'll need a fellowship. I need to ace all my exams. This period nonsense is driving me batty. What will I do if I'm pregnant? You might have messed up my life for an experience that amounted to absolutely nothing. Whether I'm pregnant or not, I hate you for this. I hate you for gambling with my life. You ..., you bastard. You should have stayed with your whore. I hate your guts."

20 ~ California Dream

When Charlie and Irene first arrived in California, they stayed in the apartment of Charlie's old army buddy Griff. They slept on the sofa-bed in the living room among boxes of film and books and movie equipment, and heaps of plumbing tools and odd bits of pipe.

Griff was a short, fat plumber, whose belt was always overloaded with tools and whose pants were always falling down in the back. "I wish I had connections or could tell you something helpful or even encouraging," he said. "But the closest I've ever come to a movie magnate is my buddy Matt, who's got a master's degree in film, with a concentration in screenwriting. He works as a janitor at the USC Film School."

Irene laughed, "You see, Charlie, how much good it does to study film in college? Better you should do the thing itself—make movies."

First, they played tourist at Disneyland and Universal Studios, checked out the beach in Santa Monica, and took a bus tour of the homes of the stars. Then they went to Central Casting at Universal, and Irene wound up in crowd scenes in a dozen movies. Charlie was never picked, but he went along with Irene and watched her in action. Often the camera would scan the crowd, then stop and linger on Irene before passing along. He was reminded of her appearance in *The Pictures of Charlie's Wedding*.

Meanwhile, Charlie scoured directories at libraries for names and addresses and then typed query letters and sent them to agents and studios, hoping to get an opportunity to show his work. After a week, most had been returned, unopened, by the legal department of each company. The rest simply went unanswered.

Next, he went to the studio offices, hoping that in person, with his persuasive manner, he could get an appointment. From that he learned that there were long waiting lists of people who had been to film school and were begging for jobs as secretaries and go-fors. It was Kafkaesque seeing all these people waiting for a magical opportunity. He wanted to shoot a film about people trying to get into the film business, but the studios wouldn't let him bring his movie gear through the gates.

Even staying with Griff, Irene's sporadic work as an extra didn't bring in enough to cover expenses. So, Irene got a job waitressing at the Golden Nipple, a topless bar in Hollywood.

"You're a bit old for it, and your breasts are small," said the owner, Mr. Garvey, with cold objectivity. "But I like your style. You could add class to the operation. You aren't just another high school brat hoping for a break into the movie business."

She did far better in tips than the other girls. Charlie sometimes sat in a corner watching the customers watch her, watching her fend them off with panache. He took notes for movies he hoped to make one day.

The gimmick at the Golden Nipple was the gold-colored thimbles the waitresses wore over their nipples. After a few beers, Charlie would be mesmerized by the reflections from those thimbles. He would deliberately unfocus his eyes to see a continuous pattern of light and motion, like time-lapse photography of traffic at night, with the beams of multiple passing headlights making continuous lines of light. He wanted to capture that effect on film.

When he shared that thought with the manager, Garvey suggested, "Well, you find the right shtick and there's plenty of money in movies."

"All I'm interested in are the images," insisted Charlie. "It'll be an art flick, not something to be shown in theaters."

"I tell you what, kid. I'm kind of a patron of the arts. You make your flick here. If it shits, it's all yours. If I like it, I have the option to buy the negative, a print, and all rights to distribute and screen it for a thousand dollars. You put that in writing up front, and you can shoot all the footage you want of my girls and my bar."

Charlie shot every night for two weeks getting over fifty hours of film. Even using his own 16-mm camera and volunteer actresses, the expenses ran to more than he was going to get paid. But the project had captured his imagination, and he was determined to do it right.

Griff's friend Matt let him use the editing room at USC after hours. Charlie worked from midnight to four a.m. for four weeks, trying to capture the right rhythm in a snappy collage of motion.

When he was done, he felt like the princess who promised to give her first born to Rumpelstiltskin. Garvey loved the film and for a thousand dollars, as agreed, he walked off with it.

Irene looked at the bright side of the venture. The film he had made was excellent. He had done it all on his own and for an incredibly small sum by Hollywood standards. He had learned a lot by doing it, and a print, which they kept, could be useful to showcase his talents. Besides, with the tips, her job was bringing in good money now. It was time to celebrate and rent an apartment of their own in nearby Glendale.

Having made a quick profit reselling the film, Garvey wanted more. The next time Charlie stopped by the restaurant, Garvey propositioned him. "There's a market for flicks with lots of flesh," he noted. "The more flesh the better. I'm not talking about big movie-house big bucks. I mean the mail-order market for private home screenings. Between me and my connections, and you and your know-how, we could do well."

"I'm not in the porn business," Charlie insisted. "And if I wanted to do that kind of thing, I wouldn't know where to start."

"There's no better place than home," Garvey insinuated. "Your wife has qualities that would show well on film."

"Get off it, buster."

"Seriously, she doesn't seem to have a problem with nudity. Do some beaver shots of her alone, and I could find a market."

"Forget it."

"Well, if you've got something against her showing her stuff, then find other chicks to pose for you. The money could be good, and it's a way for you to get experience and work your way into the business."

A week later, Charlie applied for work at a temporary secretarial outfit. He did so out of pride. He felt he had to contribute something to the household, while waiting for a chance to show what he was capable of in the film business. While sitting on a bench waiting to take the typing test, he noticed that he had worn a hole in the sole of his right shoe. He also noticed a young girl, no more than eighteen, avidly reading *Variety* while waiting her turn.

They left at the same time, and he struck up a conversation with her. It gave a boost to his wounded ego that she readily responded to his advances. Molly was the prettiest girl in Farragut, Nebraska, and wasn't shy about announcing that. She had had the lead in the high school play for three years running, and everyone in town agreed that she "should be in pictures." She had arrived a month ago and was staying in a run-down rooming house. She spent her days going from studio to studio, hoping someone would notice her.

Charlie flattered and cajoled her back to his apartment. Irene was at work. His equipment was set up. He had used similar lines to recruit models before he met Irene, when he was in the Army, using photography as a ploy to pick up girls. He soon had Molly out of her clothes. He shot an hour of film, paid her a hundred dollars, and got her to sign a release.

He knew that Garvey would be willing to pay for raw footage of "beaver" shots like this, but from professional pride he felt the need to edit it. Matt was more than happy to let him use the equipment at USC in exchange for a print.

Garvey wanted more of the same, and Charlie obliged — hanging out at the bus station in downtown Los Angeles and picking up lost-looking young girls who arrived with large suitcases. He shot the footage at the apartment at night when Irene was working at the Nipple

To explain the money he was making, Charlie told Irene he had found a job as an assistant cameraman on a project at Paramount. But that lie obliged him to be out of the house during the day, so he and Irene saw little of one another.

There was an element of sexual attraction and tension in recruiting actresses for his films, and it seemed natural for him to snatch an occasional kiss and feel. He maintained a level of professional distance from his actresses and technically remained faithful to Irene, but the temptation to do more mounted, and he began to get headaches. He suspected that Garvey had told Irene about the porn operation, but she didn't let on that she knew, and he didn't have the courage to tell her. He had nightmares of her walking in on him in the middle of a shoot, and then disappearing never to be seen again. The headaches got stronger, despite heavy doses of Anacin, even after he ended the operation and told Irene that the project at Paramount was over and he was unemployed again.

Finally, Irene convinced him to go to a doctor, who suggested he see a dentist. At first, the dentist thought the generalized excruciating pain sounded like an impacted wisdom tooth. But once Charlie opened his mouth, the dentist smelled the rot. There was a crack in an old filling in a molar and decay had set in under it, infecting and killing the root. He drilled out the decay and patched it with a temporary dressing which stopped the immediate pain. The tooth was dead. The root canal and gold cap on top of that wound up costing eight hundred dollars, which to them, at that time, was a small fortune.

His tongue kept worrying over this shell of his own tooth that was now dead-matter in his mouth. While the specialist worked on him, in weekly session after weekly session, Charlie imagined a police pathologist using this dental work to identify his dead body.

Anesthetized time after time as he went back to the dentist for treatments, he resented the fact that he had no say over what was happening to him. He just had to sit and wait and hope it turned out okay. Gradually, he began to see the movie business in the same light.

"In this business, you have no control over your life," Charlie explained to Irene. "Somebody's always doing something to you or for you. You're always trying to sell yourself. And you don't know why you're picked or why you aren't. And you don't know whether or where you'll be working next week. That's not the kind of life I want. I want to build something, to make something that's mine and that I can be proud of. It makes no sense for me to try to break into the movie business in Hollywood, where no one, not even the money people, have control — where even if I succeed, I fail. I've got to get out of here."

In March of 1969, shortly after the dental work was done, the transmission on their second-hand Pinto broke. It would cost more to fix it than the car was worth.

Griff came to the rescue, "What the heck, I've had enough of California. I'll drive you back east. They must need plumbers out there."

They headed to Washington, D.C. where Griff stayed with their army buddy Max the housepainter, and Charlie and Irene stayed with his parents, Sarah, and Carl.

21 ~ Reverend Schumacher and Son

After Thanksgiving, Marge sent thank-you notes to both Rachel and Sarah, as a formality. Much to her surprise, Sarah sent a long chatty response. Marge replied, and they kept up a lively correspondence.

Sarah repeated her invitation, and Marge did want to check grad schools during spring break. But having broken up with Frank, she felt awkward imposing on his grandparents, especially since she suspected she might be pregnant from her one close encounter with Frank.

Then she heard that Irene and Charlie would be there and remembered the Saint Smith story and that Irene had said she had had an abortion. Perhaps Irene could give her advice if she still needed advice. Marge accepted. She stayed in Sue's old room.

Irene and Charlie were down the hall, beyond the stairs, in Charlie's old room. Irene and Charlie were trying to save enough money to start over. Charlie wouldn't accept a loan from his parents as a matter of pride. They would make it on their own, but he did concede that they needed to stay with his parents while they got their act together.

Irene worked nights as a nurse's aide. Charlie worked for his old Army buddy Max as a house painter. The weather was warm that spring, and the painting season was starting early. When he wasn't on the job and Irene was at work, Charlie went out with Max and Griff, dealing with his depression in the bars of Georgetown. For her first few days, Marge didn't see Charlie at all.

Marge visited American University, Catholic University, the University of Maryland, Georgetown, Johns Hopkins, and William and Mary. The responses they gave were similar:

"We have few openings in our graduate program in psychology. The competition is stiff. We have even fewer fellowships, and the competition for those is even stronger. Of course, if you were to do fantastically well on your Graduate Record Exams that might influence our decision. But realistically, with the sort of preparation you're likely to have, that possibility is remote. Have you considered teaching? There's a shortage of elementary school teachers, particularly in inner-city schools. Or nursing? Many women find that a rewarding career."

"Your hypothesis sounds interesting in an off-beat way, but that's not the kind of work we do here. We do experimental psychology based on principles of behaviorism. How are you at handling rats?"

"If you want to pursue that hypothesis of yours, you should approach it from another discipline. You would be more likely to find the answers you want from the perspective of biology or chemistry."

After a week of being hammered with that kind of advice, Marge didn't know whether to head home, or to join the Peace Corps and forget about finishing college. But she still hadn't had her period, and she hesitated to do anything until she knew if she was pregnant. There were no do-it-yourself pregnancy test kits. She was ashamed and frightened to go to a doctor with such a question. And she was afraid that if she went home, her mother would see her anxiety, and guess its cause. She had another week of vacation. Sarah and Carl seemed to enjoy her company and urged her to prolong her stay. She did and went out of her way to spend time with Irene, hoping that her problem would go away, but at the same time looking for an opportunity to confide in Irene and get her advice.

Irene played chess with Marge a dozen times, then took her to a weekend tournament at the Hilton in downtown D. C.

At first, Marge resisted, "Women don't play chess."

"And why not?"

"It's just not done. We could be the only women there."

"Oh, my dear, what a terrible problem! Yes, indeed, just the two of us girls and a couple hundred young men. How will we ever survive?"

Irene won prize money in the expert section. Marge won three out of her four games in the novice. Two of Marge's opponents, ones she had beaten, tried to ask her out, but she declined. She returned to the Uhlands' house in much better spirits.

Irene emphasized that Marge should be her own person and take charge of her life. "That's one of Charlie's best qualities, you know. Even when he makes mistakes, he takes charge and moves on and takes on new challenges. One day he decided we had to go to California. Then he decided we had to return East. Maybe the first decision was a mistake. Maybe both were. But he's in charge of his life. I respect him for that."

"But what about you?" asked Marge. "Why should Charlie's choices be your choices? Why should he control your life?"

"It's simple—I love him" she answered with an ironic smile. "But it's you we are talking about, nicht wahr? It's you who must stop assuming this is a man's world. It's anyone's world who is willing to take it. If you were a man, with the same ambition and drive and original ideas, would those schools be giving you the same advice? The world has changed from when Sarah was a young girl. We have the pill. We have our freedom. We can use our bodies for pleasure; and if and when we wish, we can have children. You are on the pill, nicht wahr?"

"No," Marge admitted, wishing that she could confide in her now.

"But you simply must."

"But I've never—"

"No matter. It's time you got over Frankie. Get the pill and use it, just in case. That way you can be spontaneous when the right guy comes along. I'll take you to the doctor tomorrow and make sure you get a prescription."

Marge brightened. Irene must have guessed. She would make it all simple.

Irene stayed with her the whole time, and Marge, much to her own surprise, lied to the doctor about the timing of her period so he wouldn't suspect her problem.

***

The next morning the Reverend Schumacher joined the Uhlands for a pancake breakfast. It was a monthly ritual for him to stop by.

Sarah and Carl had many rituals. For instance, every morning before breakfast, Sarah would ask Carl, "How's your memory today?"

"Couldn't be better, thanks to you," he'd reply with a wink.

Each time she overheard that, Marge blushed, but she couldn't help but be pleased that she may have helped these remarkable seventy-year-olds keep alive the sexual aspect of their love for one another, the culmination of a lifetime of love.

When Reverend Schumacher arrived, Sarah quizzed him, as she always did, seeking explanations for puzzling passages in the Bible.

"Have you ever wondered, Reverend, about the meaning of the word *with* in the New Testament?"

"But Sarah, you know that that's a translation. In different passages, the Greek for that word could be quite different."

"We've talked before about the beginning of John, where the Word is *with* God. But now I'm wondering about another passage you quoted last Sunday. I believe it's from *Matthew*. 'When his mother Mary had been betrothed to Joseph, before they came together, she was found to be *with* child."

Marge coughed into her napkin to hide her embarrassment.

"Bless you my child," Sarah patted her gently on the back and then continued her inquiry. "Just think about it, Reverend — Mary is *with child* and the Word is *with God*. If the passages are parallel, could that mean that God is inside the Word, like a child is inside its mother and the Word will give birth to God, like a mother gives birth to her child? The etymology probably won't support such an interpretation, but the thought is intriguing. And might not God be responsible for echoes of meaning like that, even if the author of the *Gospel of Matthew* did not consciously intend it?"

The Reverend hesitated, then confirmed, "That might make a good subject for a sermon. I'll take note of it. That calls to mind passages from hymns that call Jesus *the Word made flesh*."

"*Bathed in the blood of the lamb*," Marge blurted out involuntarily, then blushed and tried to cover up and explain. "That's another phrase that shows up in hymns and that I could never make sense of. Yes, lots of lines in hymns are confusing when you stop to think about them."

"Mystery is at the heart of Christianity," the Reverend reassured her and quoted in a loud voice, "*Behold, a virgin shall conceive and bear a son, and his name shall be called Emmanuel.*"

Marge pretended to choke on her pancake and quickly excused herself from the table.

That night Sarah insisted on taking Marge to see Disney's *Alice in Wonderland*, which was being rerun at the local movie theater, and which Marge admitted she had never seen. Sarah gleefully recounted the tale of Charlie's first trip to the movies to see *The Wizard of Oz*. Sarah said that *Alice* was the next best thing to the *Wizard*.

For Marge, it was a nightmarish experience. She cringed, involuntarily, at every mention of the white rabbit and at the blood-like look of the red paint on the roses. The image of growing up in an instant was terrifying. The Cheshire Cat was fiendishly diabolical. She wished she hadn't gone but nevertheless, to her own surprise, she readily agreed when Sarah offered to take her to church the next day — Good Friday.

"I guess by your Irish name you're Catholic."

"Yes," Marge admitted. "But my parents never made a big deal about religion."

"Well, big deal or not, Good Friday is Good Friday. If you like, we could go to a Catholic service. I'd be glad to go with you. I've been before with friends and I like the mysterious sound of the Latin. I'd go to an Orthodox church, if there was one nearby, just to hear the Greek or the Russian."

"That's all right. Your Lutheran Church will be fine."

"It's settled then. That way you'll get to see the Reverend Schumacher in action. He and I have been friends for thirty years. And his son Bob will be there, too, I'm sure. Bob's a pre-ministerial student, a senior at Gettysburg. A fine boy. You should meet him."

"Really, Mrs. Uhland."

"Sarah."

"Yes, Sarah, I'm not in a frame of mind to be meeting *boys my own age.*"

"Why that thought never crossed my mind. But, yes, you're right. That's all the more reason to meet him. By the way, what did Frankie think?"

"About what?"

"About religion, about the fact that you're Catholic and he's Lutheran? If there had been children, how would you have raised them?"

"Well, we weren't that serious. The question of religion, or children never came up."

"Indeed? I guess you young folks these days have so many things on your minds, and school of course. It isn't like you were face-to-face with a decision or anything."

"Face-to-face with a decision?"

"It calls to mind an expression of Samuel Johnson's, *When a man knows he is to be hanged in a fortnight, it concentrates his mind wonderfully*. Your minds weren't concentrated, so you never got down to the business of deciding important matters. If there had been a real deadline for decision-making, you would have looked at each other differently."

"I don't know what you mean."

"Things are so different nowadays. But in my day, if a girl wasn't married by twenty-five, she'd be an old maid for the rest of her life, and that was worse than getting caught by the boogey man. It was a fate to scare little girls with. And if a girl had compromised her honor, or even gone so far as to lose her virginity, then if she didn't get a man to the altar pronto, she was an outcast for life. That's what I mean by a deadline. But I'm sure those ideas are old-fashioned now. And I wonder how young folks today make decisions about getting married without a deadline like that *to concentrate the mind*. Maybe you could try it as a thought experiment."

"What?"

"That's what Einstein called experiments you make by imagining. I think the Reverend Schumacher used that in a sermon a few years back. Imagine what it would be like to be married to Frankie or some other young man, to wake up beside him every morning, to care for him when he's sick, and to rejoice with him when the Lord blesses you. Imagine what it would be like to bear his children and raise them together with him and to put up with him when he's being himself, not putting on a show to win a bride or when he's a frog and not a prince. Imagine what it would be like to do all that for sixty years and more."

"Not many people stay married for sixty years these days."

"That's what I mean when I say people have no deadlines these days. And they seem to have poor imaginations, too, so they can't do good thought experiments."

"Have many of your friends been married as long as you have?"

"None that are now living. But there are some who are so well matched that I'd say it's certain they'll stay together for the rest of their lives even should they live to be a hundred or more."

"You mean like Charlie and Irene?"

"No. It's hard to imagine them staying together long. Not that I don't love the two of them dearly. But I can't fathom them and their ways. No, I meant like the Reverend Schumacher and his wife Emily. They've been together now for over twenty years, and they'll stay together for life."

"Theirs must have been a traditional marriage, like you're talking about."

"No, my dear, not at all. They were facing a nine-month deadline, and it concentrated their attention quite well."

"A minister? I would have never thought."

"No, my dear, you misunderstand. He is not the father of his son."

"Oh."

"Yes. We've been good friends for many years. He was such a comfort to me when Sue died. That brought us close, and we've stayed close, as if he were a member of my family. I can remember him playing Monopoly with me and Rachel and Charlie, before Frankie was born, and when Charlie was so young he didn't understand how to play, but he was pleased and flattered that grownups were including him in the game.

"The Reverend Schumacher and I have confided in one another at difficult times. Emily was pregnant when he married her, and he knew it, though he didn't know who the father was. I don't think in all these years he's ever asked her. And it was a blessing. It turned out later, although he didn't know then, that he couldn't have children of his own."

Marge said, "I can understand how, in retrospect, that would seem like the right thing to do. But what did you think back then?"

"I advised him to marry the girl. I didn't say so directly, rather the way we sometimes talk to one another about Bible passages. I chose a passage about Joseph and Mary, she being pregnant and not by him before they married. He could see the parallel without being hit on the head. The Lord works in mysterious ways. Even our mistakes and sins may turn out to be part of his handiwork."

The sermon at the Good Friday service was on the miracle of birth and the miracle of God and how, mysteriously, the two were one.

22 ~ Modeling for Charlie

That night, Charlie, racing down the stairs, nearly collided with Marge and Sarah.

"Charlie, how are you doing?" asked Marge. "I've been here for nearly two weeks and I haven't seen you. Where are you off to now, in such a hurry?"

"I'm going to hit the bars in Georgetown with Max and Griff."

"On Good Friday?" Sarah objected.

"Hey, Ma, it's just a way to unwind with my friends. It's been a long day."

Marge asked, "Those are what they call 'dating bars,' aren't they?"

"Yeah, sure, but we just—"

"Can I come along?" she blurted out.

"Well ... "

"Good," Marge replied before he could say no. "Let me freshen up, and I'll go with you."

Max and Griff were a Mutt-and-Jeff pair. Max was tall and thin, Griff short and fat. Even without his tools, Griff's pants hung down in the back, revealing the top of his hairy rear end.

They were six years older than Marge and neither had gone beyond high school. Before this night, she would never have imagined *going out* with either of them. But she danced with one or the other or both until three a.m.

As a pleasantly intoxicated Max clung to her during a slow dance and let his knees bend and his legs spread so he'd be low enough to press his obvious hard against her crotch, she performed thought experiments. What would it be like to be married to such a man and to wash his dirty laundry, feel his naked body pressed against her in bed? She surprised herself. It was imaginable. It could even be desirable as an end to all the tension and striving and competition. Just have sex and babies and keep house, have a purely physical and practical relationship and a clear and simple life.

As she relaxed against him, she felt a warmth well up inside her. The emotion shocked her. She didn't realize that she was that vulnerable to the friction of a male member against her fully clothed genitals.

When she felt wet down there, her first thought was that maybe he had come, and the flood of moisture had gone right through his pants. But there had been no change in the rhythm of his dancing or the hardness of his member.

Then she thought that maybe it was she who had come.

Finally, she recognized that sticky, itchy, uncomfortable sensation — she was bleeding.

She ran to the bathroom. The flow was stronger than ever before. She wondered if this was a spontaneous abortion or a delayed period. In either case, she was relieved.

Returning to Max, who was still standing, but looked lost in the middle of the dance floor, she laughed to think that a short while before she had considered him as a possible mate. Perhaps the mental concentration that came with an impending crisis didn't always lead to good decisions. The Reverend Schumacher had been lucky.

She was lucky, too. It had been foolish for her to take that risk with Frank. Even now, in relative calm, it was easier for her to imagine herself married to carefree, mindless Max than to Frank who was a selfish curious adolescent.

On the Saturday night before Easter, Sarah and Carl went to a viewing for their retired mailman, Rem Jones. It was an awkward time for someone to die—out of sync with the symbolism of the church calendar. The funeral would be held on Monday.

"Rem was ninety-two. He was retirement age when Charlie was born," explained Sarah. "He knew everyone and remembered everything about everyone. There were people who died years ago, and he was the only person who knew and remembered them. Now that he's gone, they're gone too, finally, completely. We're not just mourning him," she added. "A piece of our world has passed away."

Irene was at work. That left Marge and Charlie, who, for the first night in weeks, was staying home. He dashed around the house with a still camera, taking shots of all the rooms from multiple angles, as if he wanted to preserve them just as they were. In passing, he took shots of

Marge as well, curled up in the armchair in front of the little-used television set.

The first time he came around, she smiled for him. The next time, she stood up and held a mock pose, like a model and he, without missing a beat, took on the role of a fashion photographer, going down on his knees, then his belly, to catch her from different angles. Then in keeping with that role, he started a fire in the fireplace and had her stand in front of it in the alcove. Following his instructions, she brushed out her hair with her fingers, then shook her head to make her hair flare out freely.

"You're good, you know, very good," he flattered her blatantly, sensing she enjoyed it. "You're the one who should have gone to Hollywood. With your combination of looks and intelligence, you could go places. And your knockers, lady, your rack is truly exceptional. There's just one problem."

"What's that?"

"You come across as prudish. Many photographers and directors want to capture a look of innocence, but an innocence that's free and uninhibited, not uptight and buttoned down."

"What exactly are you driving at, Charlie?"

"You've got it, honey, but you've got to be willing to show it."

"You mean, lift up my sweater?" she asked, raising it to fully expose her bra, and striking what she thought was a sexy pose.

He put down the camera and delivered a line he had delivered many times before, recruiting in California. It came naturally to him. "To be honest, if you really wanted to make it as a model or an actress, and you've got the looks for it, you'd have to have a portfolio of photos of yourself in all kinds of dress and undress. A first-class portfolio can cost big bucks, but even if you wanted to spend that kind of money, it would be a waste for you, because you've probably never taken your clothes off in front of a man, much less a camera."

"Are you asking me to strip for you?"

He picked up his camera and started to walk away. "I knew you'd take it wrong. What can I say? Look," he turned again to face her, "I know you have no ambition to be in show business though, with your looks, that's a crying shame. I know you're into this psychology stuff and grad school, and I'm sure you'll get into the best damned grad school in the country, and you'll be the best damned psychologizer who ever came along."

"Actually," she admitted, "much as that's what I want, it's very unlikely that I'll go to grad school."

"Is money the issue?" he asked sympathetically. "I hear it costs a fortune these days."

"I'm not likely to be accepted at a first-class school. I'm simply not good enough." Her body shook involuntarily. He walked over to her, put his arm around her, and led her to the sofa.

"Okay, honey, okay. It's not the end of the world. There are lots of things a woman can do aside from psychologizing."

"Yes, like teach and nurse—"

"And model," he suggested.

She smiled through the tears that were welling in her eyes. "The world's a lot more complicated than I thought," she admitted.

He reached in his pocket, but his hand came out empty. "I'm sorry. I thought I had piece of mushroom that could make you little and safe and comfortable again."

"Growing up is scary, isn't it?" she smiled again.

"Want to tell me about it?" he offered, holding her close, so her head rested on his shoulder.

Feeling his warm hand brush her hair protectively, and not having to look him in the eye, it felt natural for her to unburden herself to him. So she told him about Frank, his tale about his experience with a hooker, her breakup with him, her close encounter with him in his car, her fear of pregnancy, and the fact that her period had started last night in the bar when she was dancing with Max.

He gave her a quick kiss on the lips and hugged her. She hugged back. She had needed to tell someone. Now she felt relieved of a burden and light-headed.

"Did you ever consider that film might be the way to approach that memory theory of yours?" he suggested.

"How?"

"What is film but memory? And what is film best used for but sex — showing sex, suggesting sex, stimulating sexual feelings? Yes, memory and sex are closely linked in film. Maybe you'd be better off studying that relationship in Hollywood rather than in grad school."

She laughed at the absurdity of his idea but looking him in the eye, she couldn't help but find him charming and attractive. She did a quick thought experiment and concluded that if this were a Moslem country, she would be content as Charlie's second wife. She'd feel no jealousy toward Irene, but rather would welcome her companionship.

"Look, young lady, whether you want a portfolio or not, I want one and need one. To get a real job as a photographer, I need to demonstrate my ability. This house-painting is the pits, believe me. It's time for me to pick up the pieces and get on with my life. So, do me a favor. Put aside your notion of propriety. If you could add a dash of abandon to that innocence of yours, I could put together a portfolio that would get me photography jobs and, if you ever wanted to give it a try, the same shots could be your portfolio as model or actress."

"What would you want me to do?"

"I'll show you." He took her hand and led her upstairs to his parents' room.

"For starters, check out my mother's dresses in the back of the closet. She never throws anything out. That's where she keeps her oldest dresses, all folded and stacked, as if she thinks one day she'll be twenty years old again and able to wear them."

"But what will she think?"

"She'll never know. They won't be back for hours. And I don't think she'd care anyway. Imagine you're a kid playing dress-up. I won't look. I'll step out in the hall while you change."

She picked a pink dress with two rows of pearl-like buttons that went from the hem all the way up to the high collar. It fit her remarkably well, as she saw in the free-standing full-length mirror. Then, in the mirror, she noticed Charlie watching her from the hall.

She turned quickly, "You promised."

"I lied," he answered puckishly, taking photos, one after the other, as he walked into the room. "Now comes the tough part. The look I want is the combination of old and new, prudish innocent girl and modern liberated woman. I'd like you to unbutton all the buttons."

"But they go all the way to the floor."

"Exactly. The dress will be like a shell that is being opened."

"But I'm not a stripper."

"Of course you're not. But you're wearing a brassiere and panties, aren't you? And those cover far more than your bathing suit would, don't they? And you don't think underwear ads in women's magazines are pornographic, do you? Is what I'm asking all that unthinkable?"

She looked him in the eye. Yes, she could imagine being his second wife—sixty or seventy years ago as Mormons in Utah. She unbuttoned slowly and calmly. As she did so, he took shot after shot, from one angle after another, sometimes adjusting the light by twisting lampshades in different directions.

"Now take hold of the sides of the dress and open it wide. That's right. Wider now. Now spread your legs apart and reach your arms back, high and wide."

The intense attention he was giving to her body through the lens of his camera was embarrassing and demeaning but at the same time it was exhilarating, and the exhilaration grew as she warmed to the role of model.

"Now try on another dress. See if you can find something in blue with the same style and cut. Yes, that will do. And, no, I won't go through the charade of standing out in the hall. What could you show me that I haven't seen already?"

She laughed and let the pink dress drop to her feet. She felt naughty and playful. She had never stood in her underwear in front of a man before. She had let Frank touch her everywhere in the dark, but no one had seen her like this. Charlie's gaze excited her.

She slid into the blue dress.

"Don't bother to button it," he ordered firmly. "Come over here by the mirror. That's right. I want to get some shots from the side here, of you looking at yourself in the mirror. Let me play with the lights a bit." He brought in a floor lamp from Sue's room. "That's right, yes, look at yourself, and enjoy looking at yourself. I'm catching both you and the image of you in the mirror. That's the effect I want. Your look of surprise is perfect—like Eve in *Paradise Lost* seeing her own naked form reflected in the pond and falling in love with herself. Yes, reach your arms high and wide, like you did before and while you're doing that, look at your breasts. See how they rise and swell, pressing against the fabric of your brassiere. Spread your legs. Wider. Yes, that's right. Now, thrust your hips forward. In the mirror, look at yourself down between your legs. Focus on that mound there, and the little cleft. Yes, it's noticeable. Even in a bathing suit it's noticeable and, believe me, men do notice. Just like when a man gets a hard-on, clothes don't make much of a secret of it."

Through the mirror, as he had probably intended, she noticed the bulge in his trousers. She didn't know where this game would lead. She felt good, whole, desirable and she wasn't sure how she wanted this to end.

"You're good at this," he encouraged her. "I don't mean just your looks. You take orders well, and that's important in a model. You're in the flow of the moment, riding the wave. You're both relaxed and excited. You enjoy taking orders. For these few brief moments, you're taking a vacation from thinking and deciding, just letting yourself go and being excited by the demands you know you're going to fulfill. Let's take that look one step further. Come over here by the bedpost. That's right. Now raise your hands high, stretch, and take hold of the top of the bedpost. Perfect." He took several shots, then added, "Just hold that now."

He stood on the bed and took a piece of rope out of his back pocket.

"What are you doing," she protested, but she kept her hands in place.

"Just a prop. I'm not going to tie you tight or hurt you. The rope will add to the drama of the photos. It gives a message of submission and abandon—to add to your natural innocence in that shell of an old-fashioned dress. And I would be very surprised if that rope, the sign that you're helpless, doesn't give rise to fresh expressions and poses as you discover aspects of your personality that you never imagined."

He stood on chairs and shot from above. He got down on his back and lay with his head between her legs and focused the camera on her crotch, with her breasts and her face in the background.

"Are you finished?" she asked, growing frightened.

"Yes, that's what I'm looking for," he exclaimed enthusiastically, stepping forward to take extreme closeups of her face. "That expression of confusion and, yes, fear, that's perfect."

"Please, untie me. I've had enough," she pleaded.

"Not quite yet. We have a little further to go."

He knelt in front of her and took hold of her panties.

"No, please, don't do that to me," she begged him. Then she added, in hopes that it might dissuade him, "Remember, it's my period."

"No problem."

He pulled down her panties and brought his head close.

"Schweinhund!" resounded from the hallway. "Ach! You disgust me!"

Marge looked up and, in the mirror, saw Irene watching the two of them.

Charlie rushed toward her, "Irene! Darling!"

She met him with a fist to the nose and a knee to the crotch that doubled him over on the floor. He crawled away down the hall as Irene untied Marge, who was in a speechless state of shock.

"This isn't the first time," Irene comforted her. "I don't hold it against you, Marge. It's like there's two of him. There were times when I saw a divine spark in him. But now he's all ego, and control, and needing *success*, whatever that means. If you've got a thing for him, he may be available soon, very soon, and you'd be welcome to him. Playing pranks like this behind my back. He likes them busty and young, very young. You're older than most of the ones he had in California."

Marge picked up her clothes and started to put them on. "How long were you watching?" she finally dared to ask.

"Five minutes. Maybe more. Charlie saw me in the mirror. Our eyes made contact, and yet he continued. It turned him on to know I was watching. He had no notion of how deeply he was hurting me. I was paralyzed with anger. All he could think of was heightening his own pleasure. He's still an adolescent. Scheiss! I hate him almost as much as I love him."

Irene helped Marge fold Sarah's dresses and put them back in the closet. Then they put the lamps and lampshades back in place.

"Honestly, Marge, I'm not surprised, and I'm not mad at you. It's me that I'm mad at for wanting him too much—for wanting him all to myself. Scheiss!" she pounded on the bedpost. "This whole scene reminds me so much of how we met in Munich. Now, thanks to me, he has no career, and he has no children. I've done this to him. I've driven him to this—this need to keep proving himself in adolescent ways. I'm no good for him."

"You're too hard on yourself," insisted Marge. "You had such faith in him and his talent for living, not just for making movies. You were willing to reshape your life however you could be close to him and please him. Yes, you talk a good story about the independence of women, but that's not the way you act. You're not only a wife, you're a mother to him."

"Yes, an over-indulgent mother—that's me. I have no children, so he's my child. I love him too much for his own good, and he listens to me too much."

The next morning, Easter Sunday, Marge took a train home to Boston. She was no longer afraid to see her mother. Besides, as she explained to Sarah, it felt right that she should be home on Easter Day. Sarah understood that reasoning and gave her warm hugs when seeing her off at the train station.

23 ~ Rebirth

After his breakup with Marge, Frank tried going to a few mixers, but his confidence was at a low ebb, and women sensed it, avoiding him like a non-entity, thereby adding to his depression.

Just before spring break, he got up the courage to call Gillian again. "I must apologize for the last time we were together."

"Apologize? Whatever for? I had a great time. I remember it well, love."

"I meant afterward. I'm sure I didn't live up to your expectations. You see, I tried to act sophisticated and experienced, but I'd never done it before. Honestly, I'm still a virgin."

"Well, that's nothing to be ashamed of, love. All of us were that one time or another. And that's a problem that can be easily fixed. In fact, I would enjoy fixing that for you."

"You would?"

"Of course, love, after dinner and a movie. Let's make a night of it."

"Sure. That's great. And is there anything I should do beforehand?"

"You mean warming up exercises?" she laughed.

When they returned to her apartment, rather than manipulate him to make him hard, as he had expected, she taught him how to turn her on and to bring her to orgasm, which drew his attention from him to her, making him less self-conscious and building his confidence. Entering and finishing was simple and pleasurable.

Then, to his surprise, she asked him to "finish her off."

"But I thought you already came?"

"You are a love," she gave him a long kiss with an active probing tongue. "I was faking it, of course, to help you along."

"Faking?"

"Oh, don't get so down in the mouth, love. It felt real enough to you, didn't it? It got you just what you wanted, didn't it? So what could be wrong with a little untruth that brings on such results? Don't sulk now. Just get on with it. Do more of what you were doing before, and I'll come for real now, and we'll all be properly satisfied."

A few days later when he was home on vacation, Frank began to feel a tightness and pain in his penis. It hurt to urinate, and yet it seemed he needed to urinate more often than usual. After a few days, it was hard to keep a straight face in public, and risky to stray more than a hundred feet from a bathroom. He was afraid he had contracted a venereal disease. He checked a medical encyclopedia at the local library but couldn't learn enough from that to diagnose himself. His family's doctor, Dr. Tomkins, was a long-time family friend, and Frank couldn't imagine telling him that he had been with a hooker and might have caught something dreadful.

Desperate, he told his parents he wanted to visit a friend in Connecticut. He drove north, with a receptacle near his feet, in case on the turnpike he didn't have time to get to a service area and it was dangerous to pull off to the side. He went straight to Yale Health Services, which was open over vacation for students who didn't go home.

He swallowed his pride and told the whole story to a doctor he had never seen before, who matter-of-factly examined him and jotted notes. Frank gave test samples, then spent an agonizing two hours in the waiting room, imagining one scenario after another of what he would do if he had a serious disease. He might never be able to have children. He might never be able to have sex. He couldn't believe his own stupidity for taking such a risk.

The doctor's voice awakened him from his thoughts, "It's just a urinary tract infection."

"And that isn't serious?"

"It's quite common. Here's a prescription. It will change the color of your urine while you're taking it, so don't let that frighten you. That should take care of it. But if the problem persists, you should come back and see us in a week of two. By the way, you should tell the young lady. She might want to see her gynecologist. She's probably got a yeast infection that should be taken care of before she experiences discomfort herself or passes it on to you again or some other young gentleman."

Driving back to Philadelphia, he felt older and more sober. When school began again, he returned with renewed seriousness. It was as if he had been granted a new life, and he didn't want to botch this one.

On the Saturday of Memorial Day weekend, while he was bouncing back and forth between making notes in his creative writing journal and studying for his last final in German, he got a phone call from Marge.

"I think it's only fair to tell you that you won't be a father—not soon anyway, and not with me."

"False alarm?"

"That's a handy phrase to toss away the whole experience as if it never happened."

"I'm sorry. What more can I say?"

"Your belated apology is accepted. I don't hold grudges. Irene suggested that I call you and set the record straight."

"You saw Irene?"

"And Charlie." She hesitated. "I stayed with your grandparents over spring break. But, of course, you don't write to them or call them, so how would you know?"

"I've been busy."

"Yes, haven't we all. It was while I was with them in Silver Spring, while I still thought I might be pregnant by you, that I was able to sort things out, to put our relationship into perspective."

Frank was tempted to tell her about his latest experience with Gillian and the resulting infection, but this time he held back and listened.

"Irene thought that I should call you to make sure you know that I don't love you and that I never loved you. Of course, you and I never talked about love. I was afraid to say out loud what I thought we had, like that would jinx it. Now I realize I was in love with the idea of being in love, not with you in particular. You were a transitional object for me. I'm beyond that now, in a different place. I wanted to tell you, and Irene wanted me to tell you, but I've been procrastinating. Then today, I was reminded by a letter I got from Sarah."

"Sarah?"

"Your grandmother, stupid. By the way, in case no one has told you, Irene and Charlie have broken up. Charlie and his friends Max and Griff took off for the cottage at Colonial Beach. No one knows where Irene is. At least that's what Sarah, your grandmother, says."

"God! I thought Irene and Charlie were the perfect couple."

"You would, wouldn't you? Well, I've done my duty. I've been honest. Have a good life. Good-bye."

Frank checked his mail on the mantelpiece. Brian had been picking it up, and Frank hadn't been paying attention, what with exams. Halfway through the stack, he found an unopened, week-old letter from his grandmother.

Dear Grandson Frankie,

Warm weather is here at last. And it's welcome. The furnace was giving us trouble all winter; and tell him as often as I do, I can't keep Grandpa from trying to fix it. He gets all worn out and has to call the oil man anyway.

So many things have happened I hardly know where to start. Grandpa was out already today weeding the garden, raking the lawn. The exercise does him good.

Fred and family were here last weekend. Went to church together. It's so nice to have the boys come back.

Your friend Margaret was here over Easter, looking at graduate schools. Too bad you couldn't have been here, too.

We miss you. Haven't seen much of your Dad either, and he's no better correspondent than you are. Say hi to him from us when you get around to seeing him.

Charlie and Irene are getting divorced. Your mother never liked her from the first. But I don't know. If there's fault, it's probably his. Poor Charlie. Will he ever grow up? Now he's gone to the cottage at Colonial Beach. He's probably chopping wood and making movies of chipmunks, trying to get a handle on who he is and what he wants.

It's a terrible thing when a marriage falls apart, but there's a lesson to be learned. Marriage shouldn't be rushed into. You're choosing a helpmate for life.

Marriage is a sacrament. Remember to read your Bible.

Have you seen your friend Margaret lately? I was glad she stayed with us. It gave your Grandpa and me a chance to get to know her. She's a lovely girl. As your Grandpa says, "She has her feet on the ground." There's no nonsense about her. She knows what she's about; and the fact that she once thought highly of you, makes me think higher of you.

You must remember that it's not just the things you learn in books that matter. Your Margaret has common sense, which is an uncommon quality. When she listens, you know that she truly hears and cares about what you're saying. And she's close to her family, with respect for tradition.

You're lucky to have met her, and I hope you have sense enough to try to get back together with her. Only don't rush into marriage. Even if she's the right girl for you, you're both too young. Give yourselves time to grow up and get settled. Even the right people can't make a marriage work if it's the wrong time for them. There's a time and place for everything, as your Grandpa says about his cabbages. Be patient. Restrain yourself. Treat her with the respect she deserves, and you'll have many happy years together.

Grandpa has been feeling low these last few days. He thought the world of Irene and can't believe that she and Charlie have separated. He wants to try to patch things up between them before it comes to divorce. It's not likely that Charlie will listen to his father at a time like this, but he writes to Charlie every day.

I'm sure your studies keep you busy but let us hear from you sometimes. Read the enclosed church bulletin. On the back, there's advice for the young about how they should try to understand their parents. Remember, God is our heavenly Father; and if we can't understand our earthly parents, how can we hope to understand God?

Send our love to your Margaret.

Enclosed is a dollar for gas for your car.

With love,
Grandma and Grandpa

***

Frank also found an unopened letter from Marge. Perhaps that was why she was so abrupt in her phone call. Perhaps she had tried to patch things up, and he had blown it by not checking his mail.

Dear Frank,

Someday, when you're not too busy with yourself, you should make time to visit your grandmother and get to know her. She's a remarkable woman.

She's seventy-six years old now. "Be reborn in Christ," she says often. I wonder if we are always on the brink of being born. The mantelpiece, the buffet, the walls, and the top of piano are all covered with photos of previous generations and of the present generation at all ages.

You once told me, "It's a shame your father is so much older than you. It must be difficult talking to him, hard for him to understand you and you to understand him."

I didn't know how to answer you at the time. But meeting your grandparents and seeing Irene with them made clear to me some things I've taken for granted for years.

I have tremendous respect for the wisdom of older people. I believe that memory helps transform the material of our lives into tales worth telling and learning.

Every day, we're bombarded with unconnected experiences and sensations and emotions, and life often seems disjointed and meaningless. But afterwards, through memory, we're able to sort things out, see similarities, make connections, see story lines, and figure out what's important. The natural, unconscious editing work of memory is what enables people to find meaning in life.

When I see an elderly person relaxing in a rocking chair, I like to believe that he or she is looking over a collection of jewels that memory has formed from his or her experience.

I'm a bit of a romantic — Wordsworth rewritten for a modern audience by Proust and Jung.

I've always thought of my father as a source of quiet strength. The less he said, the more I presumed he knew. He'd nod his head and smile, and I would be sure that he understood my concerns. I've never drawn him out in conversation and tested that assumption. I doubt that I ever will. It would be like eating the forbidden apple — by the act of challenging his wisdom, by treating him like an ordinary human being, I would lose my childlike faith in him. And I need that faith.

Your grandparents are totally different from that, especially Sarah. She chooses her words carefully, and afterwards, when thinking back, you realize she understood and meant far more than first appeared.

Irene, too, is extraordinary. She listens well, without being judgmental. It's easy to open up to her. She'd make a good therapist. The night before I left, she got me to thinking and talking about my future. She showed such sincere interest in what I had to say that I began to take my own thoughts and words more seriously than I had before.

We even talked about God. Ordinarily, I avoid religion and other questions that can't be answered. But I was curious because of what you had told me about her and Saint Smith. Somehow the tone she set made me believe that something could be resolved, that we were on the brink of some important discovery.

I forget now what I was trying to prove. I did most of the talking, and yet I was coming to accept many of the things she had said to start with.

She has this notion of a personal God, with kind intentions and limited power — rather like a Greek sun god, beaming life-giving rays at man, but unable to do much more.

An omnipotent God would be responsible for all the misery and evil in the world. But Irene's God is more human than that. He wouldn't let anyone suffer if He could do anything about it.

I'm sure Irene and I weren't on the brink of Truth. It was just some wild set of thoughts she'd started whirling in my mind. It was just an effect of her peculiar personality like the way she talks to people gets them thinking and talking. She isn't afraid to get awkwardly intimate and make people feel ill-at-ease. She doesn't see barriers that other people see.

Sarah takes the notion of a personal God a step further. She literally believes that God is her father and your father and my father. She claims she talks to Him. She tries to console Him when things aren't the way they should be, and she does what she can to set them straight.

Unfortunately, the phrase God is your father cuts both ways. It doesn't necessarily mean that we're close to God. Our relationship to God may be just another dimension of the generation gap.

Or perhaps God holds all of us in His memory, together with all we have done and will do. And maybe He can understand the meaning of what we do before that meaning becomes clear to us. But He doesn't tell us, because He loves us, and He understands the importance of our coming to our own conclusions. That's why He blessed us with the transforming power of memory so we can revisit what we've done and try to make sense of it.

I hope that Irene and your Uncle Charlie resolve their differences. As your grandmother says, Charlie needs to grow up; and I hope he will before it's too late. Irene is such a caring person.

The Greeks believed that a rainbow was a bridge from heaven to earth. Iris, the goddess of the rainbow, ran back and forth across that bridge with messages from gods to men and from men to gods.

Irene believes in a personal God who talks and acts as if there were bridges everywhere, as if there were no gaps separating man from man, and man from God, as if there was no such thing as loneliness. And yet she and Charlie are miles apart. She is that far from her own husband. That's what her bridges amount to.

And what's a rainbow, after all? Just light bouncing off raindrops.

It's painful watching two people who love each other break apart. I wish there were something I could do to help.

So, have a good life, Frank. And try to find time to get to know your family. They're much more interesting and important than you have given them credit for.

Peace.
Marge

***

Frank stuffed the letters in his pocket and went outside. He felt numb and empty – like Charlie must feel without Irene.

24 ~ A Portrait of Irene

After Charlie broke up with Irene, he drove to Colonial Beach and started to build a cabin of his own on the back of the lot where the family cottage stood. Sometimes Max and Griff would drive down and join him. They'd fish in the morning and spend a couple hours in the afternoon helping Charlie, who hammered and sawed mindlessly, as long as there was daylight.

Charlie was building from scratch. He didn't want anything pre-fab or done by contractors. He was interested in the challenge and the struggle more than the finished product. The more he worked, the less he had to think, and he didn't want to think.

When Frank arrived on Memorial Day weekend, Charlie's car was in the driveway, but Charlie wasn't in the cottage or in the roofless shell of his cabin. Frank made himself a sandwich and sat in a screened-in porch that served as a dining room, waiting for Charlie to come back from wherever he was. Then he wandered across the street toward the grove and the beach.

"The sea, the sea!" a voice called from above. "She is our great sweet mother. Come and look."

At the window at the top of the lighthouse, Charlie was calling.

"How the hell did you get up there?" Frank called back.

"A six-pack to the watchman. I like to come up here to chug beer and to savor the literary ambiance. If I'm going to be useless, I might as well do it in style. Come to the lighthouse, lad. Yes, this isn't Kansas, it's Virginia. And Virginia, yes, there is a Santa Claus. There's nothing to fear. The door's unlocked, and there's only one door. You can't fail to choose the right one."

At the top of the spiraling staircase, Charlie was stretched out on a lounge chair. Beside him lay a knee-high stack of dog-eared Modern Library classics. "Sea, Sea, sénor," he babbled. "I'd be in the heavy house or the dark house if I could find one. But all I've got is a lighthouse and light beer to numb my dark heavy soul."

"Taking a break?"

"Six days shalt thou labor, till the long thin week becomes a broad and work is forgotten. For all our Saturdays have lighted fools their way to drunken beds, that our accidents may be fruitful and fill the earth. So we multiply allusions and illusions and therein clothe our works and days, for the joy of unbuttoning, unzipping, and pulling off to see what we always knew was there."

Max and Griff arrived that afternoon and when it got dark, Charlie started up the generator and projected his movies on a white sheet hanging from a clothesline in the backyard. It was a marathon beer-drinking event. First came his silent films: *Arms* and *The Outhouse*; then his audience films: *The Pictures of Charlie's Wedding* and *The Television Experience*. And while Max, Griff, and Frank watched, Charlie recorded their reactions as raw material he might use in future films.

Similar to *The Pictures of Charlie's Wedding*, *The Television Experience* consisted of two interacting parts—a show and an audience for the show. Charlie had written the script a couple years before he left for California and tried to sell it, unsolicited, as an episode for *Twilight Zone*. He mailed copies to the producers, the studio, and even actors who had appeared on previous episodes. All the copies bounced back without comment. He attributed the reaction to Hollywood's paranoia about lawsuits, when different people come up with similar ideas and claim they were stolen. Only when he was in California did he find out that he had typed the manuscript in the wrong format, and it was the wrong length. With glaring mistakes like those, no one in the business would have taken the idea seriously. Eventually, he made the movie himself, using volunteer actors.

In this movie, college students were watching television. The movie audience saw what the students saw and heard their reactions, but their faces never appeared. In the audience, you felt like you were in the room with the students, watching television with them. The students mentioned their friend, Charlie, who was missing.

They watched a PBS special on insanity in modern society, then switched to a news show, to a production of *King Lear*, to a cops-and-robbers series, then back to the PBS special.

In the first scene of the PBS show, the moderator talked in the background as the camera moved around a blank studio, centering on a figure in shadow, huddled in a chair. This figure was one of the examples for the moderator's talk. There were other examples that the camera moved to in sequence, as he gave a brief commentary on each.

You began to hear the prerecorded outcries and incoherent babbling of the examples, interspersed with the words of the moderator.

The central figure used to be a TV addict. He spent every waking moment watching or talking about TV. Now he claimed he was in a TV set, literally inside it, trapped in another world. He believed that the real world was outside this box he was in. The viewers were out there. They could hear him and see him, though he couldn't hear or see them.

The moderator quoted him, "That's right. Of course I can't hear them or see them. I'm inside the TV. People on TV never see the people in the living room."

Then the screen that the students were looking at went blank as if somebody shut off the TV. You heard them dispute whether the TV should be on or off and what they should watch.

After the TV was turned on again, students could be heard commenting, reacting, chattering. There were four of them—Bill, Eric, Kathy, and Irene.

Irene was waiting for Bill's roommate, her boyfriend, Charlie. Charlie was a TV addict. Irene used to think that TV was boring, but now she, too, was addicted. She remembered the names of people mentioned in credits from every show she watched, even the makeup and costume people.

Nobody knew where Charlie was. Irene was upset.

Kathy wanted to watch the news. Eric, her boyfriend, wanted to watch the local production of *King Lear*. Irene wanted to watch the show they had on before, the special on insanity in modern society. She liked the moderator. Bill wanted to study for a psychology test. He was the one who turned the TV off.

In the ensuing argument, the TV was switched on and off, and the channel was changed again and again.

Finally, the channel changing stopped at a news show with Walter Cronkite as anchorman. After a brief summary of events came images of destruction from a terrorist bombing. You heard the voice of a newsman on the scene. In the background, a victim was carried out, tightly bandaged from head to toe. The victim shouted, "Let me out of here. I've got to get out of here. I'm in the tube. I know I am. I have to be. These things that are happening aren't real. People don't do things like this. The real world isn't like this. This only happens on television."

Irene tried to remember the name of the newsman. She knew that she had seen and heard him before, but not on a news show. Then she realized it wasn't the newsman who was familiar. It was the victim. That was Charlie's voice.

Eric changed the station to *King Lear.* It was the storm scene. When the fool turned full-face to the camera, Irene screamed, "That's Charlie." But the camera angle changed before anyone else could corroborate her claim. No one believed her. It made no sense. They tried to calm her down.

The station was changed again and again, giving brief glimpses of half a dozen different programs. Charlie's voice or face appeared briefly, again and again. He used to enjoy watching violence on TV. Television made everything on it seem unreal. It mixed ads, news, cartoons, sit-coms, and adventure stories and reduced them to an electronic common denominator. Now, on TV instead of watching it, Charlie looked and sounded desperate.

The channel changed back to the PBS show. Irene insisted that they stay tuned to that show. And by this point, the others were willing to do anything to keep her quiet. The camera was now on the central figure.

The moderator was explaining how those whom we label *insane* are often logical and methodical. "Take this patient. If you grant him the initial premise of his hallucination, everything he says makes sense. If someone had told you this man was an author, you'd think he was telling you the plot of a science fiction story or an episode of *The Twilight Zone*. We could, of course, conclude that it's not the patient, but the world that is sick. And, indeed, our world is sick. Through the distorting mirror of his eyes, we see a caricature of ourselves, we see exaggerated the symptoms of our own madness—symptoms we have grown so used to that we have ceased to notice them."

As the credits for the show came on, the patient raised his head, and it was Charlie, as Irene and his other friends in the living room recognized.

After that movie, drunk and drowsy, Charlie then showed his most recent creation, *A Portrait of Irene*. He had shot some footage for this at Colonial Beach and the rest of it at his parents' house in Silver Spring. He had finished the editing after Irene left him.

The movie began with the camera scanning the bare skin of a young woman close up and below, so the body served as the horizon, with clear blue sky in the background.

The skin, lightly tanned, glistened with moisture clinging to tiny blond body hairs. The camera slowly moved to the right, following the curvature of the skin. It stopped and lingered, then turned back, then forward as the hip curved into the back, luxuriating, caressing.

Irene's face turned toward the camera, and the camera zoomed in until one of her eyes filled the entire screen.

Then a small version of that same face appeared in the foreground under the eye. That face smiled and winked at the camera.

The camera zoomed back to show Irene standing naked in front of a billboard-sized photo of herself lying naked on the beach.

Then another Irene appeared in the foreground, in a kitchen, washing dishes. She was wearing nothing but an apron. As she washed the dishes, cleaned the counter, and put everything away, her every motion was well-timed, as if, like a dancer, she carefully rehearsed her moves.

As she turned and reached to put a glass in a cabinet above, suddenly, she was clothed in a blue silk evening gown with bare shoulders, and her motion continued as if she were dancing with an unseen partner, and passing from that partner to another and another.

She stretched out her arm, as part of the dance, and that same arm emerged from the surface of water. She was swimming, doing the breaststroke, then backstroke. The camera focused on her breasts, and the ripples of the water as it flowed around them.

Those same breasts were now surrounded with soap suds. She was naked, luxuriating in a bubble bath.

Then hands reached across in front of the camera lens and pulled out a pan. The camera was focused on a sink full of dirty dishes, and once again Irene, clad only in an apron, was washing them.

Now she looked at the camera. She smiled. She winked. She put down the pan she was scrubbing, took off her yellow rubber gloves and the apron. She put her hands on her breasts and caressed them, making the nipples hard and displaying them for the camera.

Then she reached down and caressed her waist and hips, the inside of her thighs up to her crotch, where she took hold of the blond hair and pulled it to the side, opening her lips for full close-up view. A fast sequence of still photos followed, small rectangles in the middle on the screen, superimposed on Irene, then expanded to fill the screen. A baby, a toddler, a young girl, a teenager, a young woman, a mature woman, a middle-aged woman, an elderly woman.

Next, Irene was sitting, fully clothed, at a kitchen table. Her hands were folded on the table.

"Do you want to have children?" asked Charlie's voice, which came as a shock in what before been a silent movie.

"Never," she replied.

"Why?"

"You know very well why."

"But the camera doesn't know. Tell the camera."

"Is it the camera who wants to make me pregnant? No, it's you, nicht wahr? You, mein liebchen, you who I have told over and over that I will never have children. So if it's children you want, find yourself another woman."

In the background is heard the song "I can't get no, satisfaction."

"That's what you think, nicht wahr? Like the song says, you are frustrated, poor dear. Making love with me isn't enough for you. You must have children, too." She unbuttoned her blouse, unhooked her bra, and fondled her own breasts. "Forget babies," she coaxed him. "Think of me, only me."

Her smiling face filled the screen, then became smaller. The background once again was a beach. She was lying on her back, but only her face was visible. She arched her neck, and her face muscles became taut. She breathed heavily, then relaxed with a soft smile, then arched again and again, rhythmically, as if approaching orgasm.

The face of another woman filled the screen, getting tense then relaxing in a similar rhythm, then getting more frantic and less in control, with sweat running down her face. She started to moan, then to grit her teeth, as if holding back a scream. The camera shifted to her crotch, where rubber-gloved hands were taking hold of a baby's head and guiding it out of her vagina.

The focus switched to Irene seated in the foreground, watching this birth movie on a screen.

"You see what I mean," said Charlie's voice. "Birth is the ultimate female orgasm."

"You bastard," she replied, playfully. "You male chauvinist bastard."

"My, your English has improved."

"Being married to you is enough to drive me to learn every swear in the language."

"But seriously, fräulein, now is the time to begin —"

"Yes, *now*," Irene replied. "We must progress from *know* to *now*. From *I know you* to *I now you*. *Now* I believe in. This moment. Not yesterday. Not tomorrow. *Now*. The pleasure of the moment. For the moment is all we have, all anyone ever has."

Again, Irene was seated at a kitchen table. Her hair was shorter than before. Magnified close up, wrinkles appeared at the corners of her eyes and above the bridge of her nose.

"Do you hate your mother?" asked Charlie's voice.

"You joke."

"Did your mother neglect you or beat you?"

"On the contrary, my dear sir," she laughed, with a mock English accent. "My mother smothered me with love, just as she smothered my brothers."

"So that's it," he concluded. "She domineered with kindness, doing everything for her children and making sure they knew how much she sacrificed for them. She expected and demanded undying devotion. Her every kindness was an obligation that would have to be paid back later. She was a master of the guilt trip."

"No. She was a true saint. She devoted her life to her children. She expected nothing in return for her efforts except our well-being."

"You mean she was a model of motherhood."

"She thought of herself that way, I'm sure. But it was all a mistake."

"How could it have been a mistake?"

"If everyone sacrifices everything for the next generation, then all of humanity is on a treadmill, going nowhere. What about *now*? What's the point in everyone living for their children? Someone sometime should live for herself."

"And you think you're such a person?"

"I try to make myself one. I want to live for *now* and to remind others that they can and should do likewise."

"What if I were to tell you that you're pregnant?"

"I would tell you that you are a fool."

"But you're late."

"Yes, two weeks. That's not usual. The pills help make me regular. But it's not unheard of."

"You are pregnant."

She laughs. "I have not missed a pill."

"On the contrary, you haven't taken a pill."

"I know what I have and have not done."

"But you don't know what I've done."

"Und was ist das, mein Liebchen?"

"I have replaced your birth-control pills with harmless, useless pills. You haven't had a real birth-control pill for three months."

"Schweinhund," she screamed and swung at the camera with her fist. The film ended abruptly. The background music changed to "Goodnight, Irene; I'll see you in my dreams."

"You bastard," Frank shouted. "You really did that, didn't you? That's why she left you, isn't it?"

"Among other reasons, yes," Charlie replied with a self-satisfied smirk. "And that's why she'll come back. She needs me now, and our brat-to-be needs a father."

"I could—"

"You could what?" Charlie glared at him, with intimidating self-confidence.

The image of Irene's shocked face, and other sensuous images of her from the movie flashed through Frank's memory. For a drunken moment he remembered Irene as if he, not Charlie, had loved her for years. And now Charlie had made her pregnant, against her will, as good as raped her. Frank threw a half-empty beer bottle at Charlie's face and jumped at him, like a crazed cat attacking a huge dog.

Charlie pulled him off and threw him on the ground. But Frank got up and jumped on him again. Charlie grabbed his arms and legs, and heaved him onto his shoulders, and staggered drunkenly to the beach, where he dumped him in the cold muddy water.

Frank jumped up again, this time grabbing Charlie by the feet and tackling him so Charlie, too, toppled into the water.

Charlie flipped Frank over on his belly, pinned him with his face half in the water and took hold of his arms and bent them behind his back.

"Say uncle," Charlie insisted.

"Say shit, you bastard," Frank shouted in agony. "That's what you are—shit."

Charlie shoved Frank's head under water, then pulled it out by the hair. "Say uncle," he repeated.

"You've seen the last of her, you shit. She'll never come back to you. She'd have an abortion first."

Charlie, in a rage, shoved Frank's face into the mud.

"Say uncle. Say uncle. Say uncle," echoed in Frank's ears.

Frank gasped for breath and took in a mouthful of water and mud and vomited and had his face shoved down into the vomit.

"Say uncle, or I'll break your neck," warned Charlie, strangling him with both hands.

Frank wanted to quit. He'd had enough. He was sober and miserable now. He just wanted this to end. But he couldn't speak, couldn't breathe.

Images of Irene in the movie flashed through his mind again. Then he saw Marge in the same poses. Then, unaccountably, he saw his grandmother's face. She smiled at him and nodded. Frank smiled back. She shut her eyes.

At that moment Charlie let go and got off.

"Mom?" muttered Charlie in disbelief. "Are you sure you got that right, Max?"

"Yeah, Charlie," answered Max "That's what the lady next door said. Somebody called to tell you your mom's sick real bad. They want you to come home."

25 ~ The Lighthouse

Sarah had been admitted to the hospital complaining of severe and persistent abdominal pain. After a series of tests, they determined that she had breast cancer and that it had metastasized. They sent her home from the hospital as a hopeless case. Irene and Rachel were with her, performing the tedious and disgusting labor necessary to make her last days as comfortable as possible. It was Rachel who phoned Charlie at Colonial Beach, not knowing that her son Frank was there, too.

Charlie and Frank drove back in their separate cars. Sometimes Charlie would pick up his 16-mm camera and aim it out the window. And once they arrived, he carried the camera everywhere, as if only through the filter of the camera could he face the reality of his mother's impending death.

Afterwards, Charlie used the footage he shot then and the interviews he conducted in *The Lighthouse,* a movie that won a prize at the Montreal Film Festival.

The loose structure of the film echoed his silent movie *The Out House.* One by one, Charlie interviewed people before they walked through a doorway into an unseen room.

The film included shots of Uncle Harry, Carl, Fred, Rachel, Russ, Frank, and Irene. It began with handheld shots that Charlie took on the way there—the road, forests, traffic, and buildings racing by. The motion came to an abrupt halt at a closed door. Then Charlie spoke as narrator while the camera scanned the house, both outside and inside, upstairs and down.

"Sarah Daly was born in 1892," said Charlie, "in Plymouth, New Hampshire, a small town, whose greatest claim to fame was that Daniel Webster lost his first court case there. She lived at 4 Russell St., just a block from the Pemigiwasett House, where Nathaniel Hawthorne died and where she met her future husband.

"She was doing maid's work during summer vacation when she met Carl Uhland, her husband-to-be. He had come north for the mountain air, on his doctor's recommendation, because of allergies.

"Aside from those allergies, Carl was muscular and tough. He was the eldest son of a Pennsylvania Dutch farmer and grandson of a cabinetmaker. Carl wasn't interested in farming. From the day when his grandfather first showed him how to make elaborate sandcastles using boards for support, Carl dreamt of building houses. After finishing high school, rather than become a farmer, he ran away from home and hiked to Washington, where the building trade was flourishing. There he got a job as a construction hand and eventually became a successful builder.

"The house he built for Sarah and himself was in part his vision and in part hers. Hers were the stone fireplace, with the alcove in front of it, with hearthside seats and niches and shelves, and in the bedrooms the window seats that opened up as storage trunks. His was the exterior with its mixture of stucco and stone and wood. His, too, were the pear and apple trees, and the raspberry and blackberry bushes. Sarah would have preferred rose bushes, but Carl insisted, 'What's the point of a plant that doesn't bear fruit?'

"They had three sons—Fred, Frank, and Charlie—and a daughter, Sue, who died young."

The camera then scanned the living room, where the relatives had assembled.

"Charles Uhland, you turn that camera off this moment," bellowed Rachel, and the camera zoomed in on her angry face. "This is not the time or the place for such nonsense. It shows a lack of respect for your mother."

"This is the devoted daughter-in-law," Charlie chimed in.

"How could you?" said Rachel, turning away.

"We must apologize to the audience," added Charlie. "Rachel Uhland is the wife of Russell Uhland, oldest son of the almost deceased."

Rachel turned and glared at the camera. "How can you speak of your mother that way? With the Lord's help, she will recover and live many more happy years."

"Rachel Uhland enjoys watching soap operas and denouncing the morals of the characters and of the actors and actresses who play the parts," noted Charlie.

"You're impossible." She tried, unsuccessfully, to push away the camera.

"In all fairness, she's tired, having been up for forty-eight hours, working hand-in-hand with her dearly beloved sister-in-law Irene Uhland, caring for the nearly deceased."

"How can the rest of you let him do this?" Rachel exclaimed, looking around for help.

"Charlie needs to do this," Frank offered. "Just let him be. It's his way of coping."

"Coping? You call that coping?" Rachel went on. "His mother is fighting a battle against death and winning it, I believe, I sincerely believe, against all odds ... "

"*Do not go gentle into that dark night,*" Charlie quoted. "*Old age should burn and rage at close of day.*"

"For that much you're right, Charlie," agreed Rachel, "Indeed, *Rage, rage against the dying of the light.* All we can do is fight."

"Fight to the bitter end," added Charlie. "Fight despite all obstacles. Fight despite nature itself. *And death shall have no dominion.*"

"Indeed," Rachel agreed again. "What more do we have than life? Nothing is so precious as life."

"There we have it, folks," commented Charlie, like a moderator on television, shifting to commercial mode. "We have here the independent, unsolicited endorsement of an average housewife. Life, yes, folks, life itself—the finest product on the market today."

"You're absolutely impossible!" shouted Rachel, threatening the camera with her fists.

"Now setting aside for a moment this marvelous product named *life,* let's return to our topic for today, Mrs. Sarah Daly Uhland. What do you think of the old lady?" asked Charlie, putting the microphone in front of Rachel's lips.

"What do you mean?" asks Rachel, disconcerted by the microphone, suddenly self-conscious.

"Let's be honest, now. She can't hear you. We're all family here. You were an orphan, weren't you?"

"Yes, I suppose you could say that. Technically, yes. I was raised by my father's brother, my aunt and uncle, who now live in St. Louis."

"But you never spent much time with your mother-in-law, didn't speak to her much, never showed any particular affection toward her."

"It's not fair of you to judge. We were close the first few months after I married Russ, when we lived here with her. I have many fond memories of that time, especially of when she and I took you to your first movie, and later playing Monopoly with you and the Reverend Schumacher. Who are you to judge? I've always worked hard. Nobody ever got anywhere worth getting to without working hard. It takes drive to get anywhere in this world. If I've done nothing else for my children, I hope I've given them drive."

"And what does that have to do with the nearly deceased?"

"I've always been busy. There's never been time for idle chatter or indulging emotions. I went my way, raising my family, just as she went hers. It wasn't like we lived next-door to one another. There wasn't time for everything and everyone. I intended to stay close to her, to be like a daughter to her. But I never found time, except for at family gatherings, and then there was never an opportunity to really talk. We were always preparing a meal or cleaning up after one. There was always something else that needed to be done for Russ, for the kids, and, yes, for myself. Next thing I knew, twenty years had passed, and now here she's nearly gone."

"So here you are slaving for her in her final hours, acting the part of a devoted and loving daughter."

"I'm not acting a part. I do love her. She's a wonderful person. She needs me, and I help. It's as simple as that. I only wish she were at a hospital where there are people who can do these things better than I can. If it were up to me, she would be in a hospital."

"With needles and tubes?"

"If need be. Anything that might extend her life. As long as there's life, there's hope."

"And then what?"

"Why must you be so morbid?"

"Time for another commercial: Life. Love it or leave it. Life Eternal. Life Everlasting."

"Will someone shut him up?" yelled Rachel.

"Maybe you better check on Mother again," suggested Russ, taking her by the shoulders and guiding her toward the door. She opened the bedroom door and went in.

Irene started to follow her, but Charlie grabbed her by the arm and pulled her back.

"Ah, yes," says Charlie. "Here we have the charming Irene Uhland. Alias Irene Heinz. Alias Iris Heinz. Alias Helga Heinz."

"Take that hand off me."

He released her, but she stayed in front of the camera.

"You, too, seem devoted to the woman in the next room. Do you agree with your sister-in-law that the hospital is the best place for this patient?"

"Not at all, as you know, nicht wahr? Better that she die peacefully in her own home, among those who love her."

"Then, unlike your sister-in-law, you are convinced that she is dying?"

"Natürlich. The doctors say it's a matter of a few days. All they could do at the hospital is give her drugs for the pain."

"And that would be wrong?"

"No. If that is what she wants. But she said she wants to see her house and her sons and her husband. So, I insisted that they let her come here. And I do all I can to ease her mind, to make her ready, to help her find the strength to accept, with peace, the death that must come."

"A time to live and a time to die."

"So it is said."

"A stream flows into the ocean and becomes one with it and is no more."

"That, too, is true."

"God, heaven, and hell are all within us."

"That I do not know. But strength and peace can be found within."

"You and your sister-in-law must make a fine pair. She, raging for war against death, and you, preaching peace and acceptance."

"We get along fine, thank you. She cleans the sheets and the bed, and I clean the patient. She cooks the food, and I serve it. There is too much to do to argue. We both love her and wish the best for her. That is common ground."

"Perhaps the news that you are pregnant will give my mother joy in her final hours," suggested Charlie.

"No," she answered. "I will not lie to her. Let her leave, loving the world as it is, not as it might have been."

"What do you mean?"

"Abortion," she whispered softly, so only he and the camera could hear.

"What do you mean?"

"I don't feel good about it," she admitted, still in a whisper. "But I did what I knew was right for me. My body is mine. No one, not even a husband, has the right to force a baby on me." Charlie slapped her across the face, while continuing to hold the camera.

She turned abruptly and left through the door to the bedroom.

Russ rushed up, "How can you expect to win Irene back if you hit her? And in public, too. God, Charlie, when will you grow up?"

"Ah! That's big brother speaking. Welcome, big brother. Russell Uhland, renowned insurance executive."

"Actuary."

"Yes, indeed, an expert in all the statistics of mortality. How apt, considering the circumstances."

"Get off your high horse," Russ pushed him back with a sweep of his hand. "You're nothing but a ham, and never have been. Give you a microphone, and you act like you own the world."

"This is an historical narrative about a typical American family. Right now, we're focusing on the oldest son, who left college in a fit of patriotic ardor or academic failure to defend his country in World War II."

"You know very well that Fred and I wanted to join up but couldn't pass the physical—me with my flat feet and Fred with his dislocated shoulder. Then Uncle Harry let us know that people who were in far worse shape than us had gotten in. Mom was furious when she found out.

"Uncle Harry had stirred up the dream of a military career even before the war, with his tales about Paris and Istanbul and Cairo, his photos and picture postcards from World War I, the exotic coins and stamps he'd slip in our pockets whenever he saw us, and the books about war he gave us every Christmas and birthday. You'd think that war was the greatest thing that ever happened to a man—a chance to see the world and be a man among men. Personally, I didn't find the swamps of Georgia attractive."

"You did, however, find the girl of your dreams."

"I did?" he paused, staring off at the ceiling as if remembering.

"Your wife, of course, the charming Rachel Uhland."

"Yes, of course, Rachel, yes, Rachel," he repeated absent-mindedly. Then he, too, went through the door.

"And here is Uncle Harry himself, the debonair war-monger," Charlie continued.

"What was that, sonny?" asked Harry, coming close and leaning an ear toward Charlie. Harry was once nearly six feet tall but his back was now bent so badly that his head was no more than five feet above the ground.

"Had any more dreams, Uncle Harry? Any more war dreams to pass along to the kids? You know, you have to watch what you say, Uncle, because dreams are contagious. And Lord only knows what will happen once they get in someone's head."

"You have to speak up, son."

"Harry! Harry! Harry! Step right up and see your sister."

One after the other, each family member entered the room where Sarah lay. No one came out. And the camera never looked in.

Carl appeared, sitting in a rocking chair, telling Charlie about old times with his grandfather at the beach.

"Did you go there by horse and buggy?" asked Charlie.

"No, the Jersey beaches were a ways off. We'd go by train. The trains went everywhere. From Lancaster to Philadelphia and from Philadelphia to Ocean City. It was quite an excursion, and I was lucky to have a grandfather who went in for things like that. And he did, believe me. He probably enjoyed the beach more than I did."

"Was he a good swimmer?" asked Charlie.

"He couldn't swim a stroke, as far as I know. That's not what the beach was for. The beach was a place for castles and dreams, that's what grandfather loved."

"Sandcastles?"

"Not just your ordinary run-of-the-mill sandcastles. No, indeed. Grandfather could do anything with wood. He could take a stick that was six inches long and carve it into a chain of links that stretched to a foot. And he used wood to make his sandcastles."

"Driftwood?"

"No, he brought the wood along with him on the train—pieces he had cut and carved to just the right size and shape to meet his plans, based on real castles in Europe."

"He must have attracted crowds," Charlie comments.

"He didn't want crowds. He'd look for a stretch of beach where there was no one around."

"Those castles must have been sturdy, with all that wood to support them."

"No more than most. The tide would wash them away, just like any other."

"You mean he didn't build them high on the beach, sheltered from the tide?"

"Of course not. What would the point of that be? He liked to watch the power of the sea. Sure, we'd retrieve the wood. That was my job. Then we'd build again for the next tide. We could always build a new one, as long as we had our dreams and our drawings. And when the time was right, the sea would come again to take it away. I always loved the sea."

Carl went into the bedroom, and the door closed. Then the camera focused on the door, and behind the door came the sound of Sarah playing the piano, then Sarah's voice, reminiscing. The audio portion had been recorded a couple years before.

"'A mighty fortress is our God,'" she sang. "Come on, join in, Charles," she urged. "Surely, you know the words. You sang it in Sunday School. You always had such a deep voice for such a little boy. Surely, you haven't forgotten. It hasn't been that long. And the *Bible*. You must remember your *Bible*. Read a little every night. That will keep it fresh in your mind. 'A mighty fortress is our God,'" she began again, then stopped and laughed. "My mind wanders. It's blasphemous, I suppose, but who could blame an old woman for letting her mind wander. Age has its rights and privileges, you know. Like when I think of a fortress, I can't help but think of you and your father at the beach down on the Potomac, building sandcastles. Your father was always so careful about it, making drawings and gathering bits of wood and cardboard. And you'd just fill a bucket with sand and turn it over, building quick little ramshackle towers and with that smile, so proud that you could make so many castles so fast. And when your father built a beautiful and delicate castle, like the ones his grandfather had made, you'd jump on it and knock it to pieces before the sea could. You were a devilish little fellow, and still are.

"Russ and Fred were always respectful when he built one of those castles, like it was something religious. And they'd try to protect it from the tide, though your father always built it close enough to the water so nothing could save it. And when they were little, when the tide ruined a castle, they'd get upset. But not you, my little gremlin. You'd make short work of your father's fortress.

"'A mighty fortress ... ' Yes, there are many fortresses and houses in the *Bible*. In my father's house there are many rooms. You've never seen my father's house, have you? I mean Grandpa Daly's house up in New Hampshire. Of course not. My Dad had died by the time you were born, and strangers bought the house and were living there. But still I wanted to show you. It's far bigger than this house your father built.

"Maybe someday, on your own, you'll go up there and look for it—4 Russell Street, Plymouth, New Hampshire. I'm sure it's still standing, maybe with a different color of paint, and maybe they've turned part of the barn into a garage.

"It's one of those double kinds of houses where the barn and the house were joined so you didn't have to go out into the snow to get to your horse and buggy. There were only a few rooms with steam heat that you could use in the winter, but in the summer, you could play in the attic rooms, and the barn and the loft, with a cupola on top. Even what we kids called a *secret passage*—the crawlspace under the peak of the roof that led from the barn to the attic—was a place for play.

"I'd dearly love to go back to that house myself, and crawl through that passage once again. I've dreamt of it so often through the years that I'm not sure what was and what wasn't there. In my dreams there's this secret room where I stored my most precious things, things that had been lost for years: a rusty iron ring a boy gave me in grammar school, a notebook of poems I wrote, and photos of Sam, my brother who ran away. Only sometimes it's not just their pictures that are there, but they themselves. Sue, also, my daughter, Sue is there. They've all been playing a game of hide and seek. I just had to find the right room."

Now the door opened, but instead of the sick room, with Grandma in bed, a street sign appeared, Russell Street, and another door with the number four. Then that door opened, and half a dozen kids ran out.

***

Sarah exited quietly four months later, long after the family had returned to jobs and school. Irene was sitting in the bedroom with her, reading a paperback collection of movie scripts. It was her turn to watch in case Sarah needed anything. She didn't notice the moment of her passing. She thought Sarah was still sleeping. An hour or two later, Carl came in to give her pain-killing pills and found her stiffening form.

The family gathered once again. This time Marge came as well. She avoided Frank, talking to everyone but him. Once again, Charlie shot footage around the house to add to his *Lighthouse* film. At one point, he succeeded in getting Frank and Marge to stand in front of the door to the room where Sarah had died. He asked them to open the door and walk in. Frank signaled Marge to go first. Then she signaled Frank to go first. Then they both went at the same time and bumped into one another.

"I hate your guts!" she hissed at Frank.

Charlie laughed, "Perfect! You're in perfect sync."

The Reverend Schumacher conducted the funeral service for Sarah. "I knew Sarah for thirty years," he explained. "Over that time I've gotten a reputation for the eccentric interpretations I give to biblical passages in my sermons. I must confess that Sarah was my inspiration. She had a wonderful and naive faith in the power of language—of all languages. At Christmas she'd wish us all *Mary Christmas, and Joseph New Year*. She was intrigued by the echoes she'd hear—the meanings and associations that appeared as if by accident. She felt they were part and parcel of the mystery of God, and we would puzzle and rejoice over them together.

"When her daughter Sue died, we puzzled over the passage: *There are many mansions in my father's house.* I liked to think of the word *mansion* in the Latin sense of stages of a journey—the notion that this life is just one stage in a much longer journey. Sarah preferred the English sense of *mansion* as a huge house with many rooms and dying as moving from one room to another or from one *mansion* to another. I imagine her now, a little girl, standing in a vast *mansion*, lost and in awe, not frightened, just curious, as she always was.

"Today, when I was pondering what to say as a farewell, a hackneyed phrase came to mind: *And now Sarah is with God*. And I had a moment of recognition, an epiphany, like an electric shock. It was a typically *Sarah phrase*. She had puzzled over the echoes of *Mary was with child*, and *the Word was with God*. And now I cannot help but think, *Sarah was with child, and now she is with God*. And may the mystery of those words be revealed to her in everlasting joy."

Part Three ~ In Search of the Third Door

26 ~ Sarah Lives

Reading and rereading *Sandcastles*, Frank is interested in the characters and in how he portrayed himself. He's concerned about what others will think of his writing and also what they will think of him as a human being. He wants to censor some scenes that reflect badly on him. He wishes he could have edited and sanitized the book before Marge read it.

He wants it to be a good story, a publishable book that he can be proud of. It needs to flow and have internal consistency and emotional impact. He edits as he reads—finding typos, fixing dialogue that feels lame or out of character. He checks background documents and wonders if he should incorporate new information.

When the sun sets, Frank stands, stretches his legs, then sits on the recliner and hits the buttons on the arm of the chair to turn lights on and off, playing with them like a kid with a new toy.

"What do you think of the book?" he asks Marge.

"There are passages that are supposedly from my perspective that I find absurd and insulting. You have no idea what goes on inside my head. And I wouldn't want people to think that I think that way. You have no appreciation for multi-layered consciousness, where someone thinks one thing and says another or has several conflicting thoughts at the same time. You're missing the ambiguity when you don't know if someone is telling the truth. You don't have a clue how a woman thinks."

"I extrapolated from our common humanity."

"Nonsense."

"Then maybe this book could be of interest as showing how a man thinks a woman thinks."

"Like cross dressing. That's kinky."

"Well, thank you for your emotional response. That's far more helpful than bland compliments."

"Well, what do you think of it?" she asks him.

"Much of it rings true. It jives with what I remember. It didn't trigger new memories, but it did get me thinking about our situation."

"Okay. Tell me."

"That Bible passage Sarah asked about, *There are many mansions in my father's house,* and the idea that God's house is a mansion with many rooms, and that dying is like moving from one room to another. That got me thinking about videogames the way my grandson Barry described them. Maybe this world we are in is like an adventure game with many levels. Being born is like going through one door. Somehow, we went through a second door to get here. And now we might be able to find a third door that will take us to another world that will be better than this one."

"Or worse."

"Yes, or worse. That's the risk. Do we stay here and pretend to be natives, or do we take our chances looking for the third door and trying to open it."

"Frank, your mind works in weird ways."

"What about you? What are you thinking?"

"About your book? Or about us?"

"About us."

"Penny for my thoughts? Okay. Here goes. Imagine you're in a train and the landscape seen through the windows races by. You sleep, then you wake up, and you find yourself in a different place and a different time. Maybe in everyday life there are little gaps like that and our minds fill in the spaces, like when we watch a movie. The continuity we take for granted is an illusion. There are cracks in time and space, and by accident we slipped through."

"You consider that science?"

"We evolved to cope with the world around us, not to understand it. Illusions have survival value. Reality consists of force fields in empty space, not solid objects. But we see and react to solid objects because that illusion helps us stay alive."

"If that's your critique of reality, I can image what you think of my book."

"The story is flawed."

"Cracks or holes in the plot?

"Insofar as you want the story to reflect what actually happened, you started with a false premise. You depended on Irene as if she were a reliable source."

"Yes, I believe that a lot of what I wrote was based on what I heard from her. But why does that matter?"

"She lies."

"What do you mean *she lies*?"

"That's her shtik. You know that. Practical jokes and role play and lies just for the fun of seeing people's reactions."

"But where in the manuscript do you see that? Aside from when she was telling the tale of Saint Smith, which was an obvious fabrication, when did she lie?"

"Remember that scene on the beach when your mother Rachel came on to Charlie, right before he joined the Army? That wasn't just flirtation and temptation. He didn't restrain himself. He didn't resist temptation. They made love. He had good reason to go away quickly and far. Your brother Johnny may be Charlie's son."

"You don't know that. You couldn't know that."

"That's what Charlie told Irene, and Irene told me."

"She lied"

"Exactly. She lies."

"Well, if Irene told you that, that was a whopper of a lie. But I'd wager she didn't say that to other people. She certainly didn't say it to me. Telling it to you made no difference to anyone but you. Is there any lie of hers that matters?"

"Schumacher's son."

"What?"

"Irene told you that Reverend Schumacher's son wasn't really his son and that your grandmother tried to set me up with him."

"You mean he really was the preacher's son?"

"To the best of my knowledge, he wasn't. I heard that from your grandmother, and she had no reason to lie."

"Then Grandma didn't try to set you up with him?"

"She did."

"Then what's the lie?"

"Irene told you that I didn't go out with him. But I did. Half a dozen times. And we did it."

"Did it?"

"He, not Charlie, was my first. Thanks to Irene, you got it all wrong."

"What? You're joking. Tell me you're joking."

"Yes, I'm joking," she replies in a deadpan voice.

"You're not joking," Frank concludes.

She laughs. "Now I know why Irene does what she does. That was fun."

"Then you were joking, right?"

She laughs again but doesn't answer.

"And what else do you want to throw into question?"

"That kinky bondage scene you wrote about Charlie and me didn't happen."

"But Irene said she saw it."

"She wanted to know if I could be tempted to stray. She was trying to protect you. She asked Charlie to come on to me to see what my reaction would be. She gave him instructions like what you wrote, but he didn't go through with it. He told me about that, and we laughed about it. The next night, when I got back late from seeing Schumacher, I bumped into Charlie getting a snack in the kitchen. It was a warm night. I led him out to the back yard. We did it under the stars, on the lawn. No kinks. Very sweet."

"You're putting me on again."

She laughed again. "I could confess to anything, and you wouldn't believe me."

"Why are you doing this?"

"Because you lied to me so many times."

"I don't know what you mean."

"You can lie by omission as well as with words."

"What didn't I say?"

"Irene tested you, too, directly, herself. And you failed the test."

"She was lying. I never would—"

"You mean you never would try, or she never would let you? Did you not covet your uncle's wife?"

"Are you getting biblical now? Do you want to blame me for impure thoughts?"

"And impure deeds."

"Was that why you were and are so angry at me?"

"Remember your tale about Gillian, the hooker?"

"I should never have told you that. No, not just the telling. I should never have done it."

"And you didn't do it the way you said you did. That girl wasn't a hooker. She was a high school senior, a townie, barely legal. An innocent girl with a crush on you. And you seduced her. You satisfied your curiosity. You got your thrill. You boosted your wounded ego at her expense."

"Where did you hear that?"

"From Mary Jane, Brian's girl. She kept an eye on you. She talked to Gillian. And she talked to two of Gillian's friends who you came on to."

"We were talking about Irene and her lying," Frank switches the subject. "I admit she may have told some whoppers, and I may have been fooled. But in the case of Grandma, Irene's lying was a blessing, a creative blessing."

"I missed that. What chapter is that in?"

"It isn't in the novel. Maybe I should add it. In the background documents, I found a long letter from Irene that explained what she did and why. Irene told Grandpa that Grandma wasn't dying, she was only pretending to. Grandpa wanted to believe that was true. Reality was far too painful. Irene laid the groundwork. Grandma confirmed the story to him. She said she was going away for a while. Then she would come back, and they'd have a celebration. Irene had Grandma write a series of letters by hand during her final weeks. Then after the funeral, Irene delivered those letters, one by one, to Grandpa. Later, when he was in the Lutheran nursing home and his eyesight was failing, Irene forged new letters from Grandma and read them aloud to him. The Reverend Schumacher went along with the story. To the very end, Grandpa clung to the idea that Grandma was missing, presumed dead, but not really dead. Schumacher told him that he had tried to talk her out of pretending to die, but that she had a devilish streak like her sons Russ and Charlie, that she believed the temporary sorrow she was causing the family was nothing next to the joyous surprise of her return. In the meantime, she was on a fun trip with friends she hadn't seen in ages. She was taking a vacation from the cares of everyday life. At any moment, she might walk through the door and begin the celebration. As Grandma explained in her first letter to him, 'Imagine how happy everyone will be when I turn up alive.'"

27 ~ Size Doesn't Matter

Marge sits quietly reading documents on her computer. Sometimes she pauses and stares at her fingernails in boredom. Then she breaks out in laughter.

"What are you reading?" asks Frank.

"A story of Charlie's called *Size Matters*. This guy who is obsessed with breasts gives his girlfriend injections to make her breasts grow. They keep growing until they burst through the walls of the apartment and of the building and level the city. They become a force of nature and a symbol of the American economy. It's hilarious."

"And why do you find that so funny?"

"The irony, of course."

"What irony?"

"Come on. You can't tell me you didn't notice."

"Notice what."

"I'm not the same now. My body's not the same. Try to imagine this body in a bikini."

"We're fifty years older."

She laughs again. "You had a thing for tits. Did Gillian have big tits? Did her friends?"

"Enough of that. Let's move on from that."

"You really don't get it, do you? You think my bust would be as small as this? You think my breasts have shriveled so much from age that they can be stuffed into a bra this small? That's not what happened. I had breast reduction surgery. The back pain is gone, thank God. But, topside, this body is very different from what you knew and lusted for such a short while ago when we were both twenty.

"Go ahead and touch them," she offered, taking hold of his hands and putting them on her chest. "Give them a squeeze. What does it feel like? You used to delight in squeezing them. When we first met you had to struggle not to stare at them. What about now, sweetheart? I'm afraid to take my clothes off and see what I look like now. What about you? Do you dare look?"

He pulls his hands away, and she takes off her jacket and unbuttons her blouse, staring him straight in the eyes.

"Do you have any ones on you?" she asks.

"What?"

"Any one-dollar bills? Isn't that what you give to strippers? Have you ever seen a seventy-year-old stripper? Have you ever seen a grandmother's breasts? What a turn-on that must be. And your equipment—I wonder what it looks like at seventy. Does it still work? Do you even know if it works?"

She takes off her blouse. She unhooks her diminutive bra and holds it close to her body. Then with a dramatic gesture, she unveils herself.

"Well, don't just stare. Tell me. What do you see? What do you think?"

"Bite sized," he replies with a smile.

"Like Irene's?" she probes.

"Better," he confirms, and touches them, squeezes them, then hugs her tight.

He picks her up and carries her into the bedroom.

As they go through the doorway, she stretches to turn out the light.

He flips it back on. "Let me enjoy the look of you."

"You have quite an imagination."

"And you are one hot lady."

Out of their clothes and onto the bed, they stay above the covers and explore one another's bodies, with eyes and hands. Frank explores with his tongue as well. Then, to their mutual surprise and delight, his equipment works just fine.

28 ~ Two Lies Make a Truth

When Marge wakes up, the room is dark. It takes her a while to remember where she is and why. She scratches an itch on her neck. The skin is loose. This is the old body. That wasn't a dream. Or this is the same dream. Then she realizes that she's naked, and she isn't alone in bed. She remembers the man is Frank, so she doesn't pull away when he cuddles closer, and she doesn't push him away when he nuzzles one breast and squeezes the other. He takes an entire breast into his mouth and sucks. She had never felt such a sensation before. In the part of her life that she still remembers, the most a man ever sucked was a nipple and the surrounding areola. That was all that would fit in a man's mouth.

She had two children. She knows that as a fact from what she read about herself, but she has no memory of childbirth, no memory of breast-feeding. She wonders what it would have felt like to have a baby suck milk from her breast. But that, too, would have only involved the nipple and areola. Warmth extends down to her nether parts. She's aroused. She holds Frank's head and pulls him closer. He opens his mouth wider. She feels intimate, emotionally close to him. The scientific side of her remembers what she read about oxytocin. The sensations he is giving her with mouth and tongue are triggering the release of the *commitment hormone*. She is falling for this guy who caused her so much anguish on the other side of the fifty-year gap in her life. In another thread of thought, she is surprised at how good she feels, and not just the tactile sensations. There's a feeling of well-being, a welcome boost to her self-image, after the shock of finding herself in an old body with her breasts all but gone. She feels like a woman again, a young woman, a woman in love. It feels good to feel in love. In lust, as well. It feels good to know that she still wants and enjoys sex. She would have never imagined that she would have such urges in a seventy-year-old body. She never imagined her grandparents having sex. If this world she finds herself in is real and she can't go back or go anywhere else, it's good to know that here she can love and be loved. If her life is cut short by fifty years, at least what is left can be pleasurable, delightful, worth living.

"You like them?" she asks, confident and happy.

His only response is to suck deeper and caress more actively.

While her emotional side relaxes, enjoys, and pulls him closer, her rational side whispers in stream of consciousness, "It's good that you like them as they are. They'll never be any younger or larger than they are right now. But maybe there's a benefit to them being compact rather than shriveled and sagging."

He stops her monologue by switching from breast to lips.

"My memory is getting a bit rusty," he says.

"Mine, too."

"Maybe we need more therapy," he suggests.

After a round of exercise, Marge cuddles with her head on his shoulder.

"So, do you have a thing for older women?" she asks

"You're no older than I am."

"But I'm far older than I was a couple days ago."

"Carpe the diem. Carpe the nightem."

"You don't miss them?"

"Your mammaries? It feels linguistically appropriate, losing memories and mammaries at the same time."

"In this new life, you won't have regrets? You won't drool over pictures of big-breasted women and have wet dreams about them?"

"I'm not Charlie."

"Thank God you're not Charlie. He obsessed over my dear departed breasts. He loved Irene. I have no doubt of that. But he lusted for big breasts, like mine."

"You and he were a thing?"

"I didn't say that. But when he was trying to talk me into modeling for him, he showed me nude shots he had taken of models in California, and that was their common trait—big breasts. No wonder he wrote a story like that."

"And no wonder he came on to you. Tell me honestly. You said you did it with him in the backyard at my grandparents' house. Was that the only time? Or did he give you sex lessons?"

"Schumacher, remember?"

"Sure. And cows fly."

"You're jealous."

"You're evasive."

"Charlie's not the way you think he is."

"Or was."

"What?" she asks.

"He's missing, presumed dead. That's what I heard from my daughter. He and Irene disappeared five years ago. There's a lot of stuff by and about him on my laptop. I copied it to yours with the other background stuff for my novel."

"Dead?"

"Presumed dead."

"That's hard to believe. We saw them just a few days ago."

"Or so it seemed."

"Not *seemed*," she insists. "Those fifty missing years are nonsense. You know it and I know it, and the rest of the world be damned. We're sane, and the rest of the world is delusional."

"Well diagnosed, doctor."

"Well, you've read that stuff by and about Charlie."

"Some of it, yes, just now."

"Then tell me about him, the him we knew or thought we knew a few days ago."

"The California chapter was all wrong," Frank explains. "Irene lied about that to me, to you, to everyone. Charlie helped make three well-known movies, though he got no credit for them.

"Charlie and Irene met Woody Allen in a bar. Woody was depressed, having been given the assignment of doing English voice-overs for an awful Japanese movie. He would never get his chance. He would always be a Hollywood hack doing shit work in the background. Sitting there in the bar, Charlie and Irene came up with the idea for *What's Up Tiger Lily*—making a voice-over that had nothing to do with the original, telling an outlandish story, turning a boring and poorly acted action movie into a farce. Woody liked their pitch. Irene and Frank wrote the voice-overs. Studio voice actors recorded the soundtrack. Charlie worked with Woody on editing. It was a wild week of drunken all-nighters. Woody was sure he'd get fired for doing this, but he was delighted with the results. When he got praised and promoted, he didn't tell anyone about the input from Charlie and Irene. They had already headed back East." .

"It's funny you should mention Woody Allen," Marge adds. "Charlie's *Size Matters* story reminds me of the Woody Allen movie *Everything You Wanted to Know About Sex*. That movie has a scene where a giant breast created by a researcher rampages through the countryside."

"Well, that similarity wasn't a coincidence, at least not according to Irene in a letter of hers."

"Well if Irene said it, it must be true," Marge chuckles.

"When they were working on *Tiger Lily*, Irene read *Size Matters* to Woody. Woody dismissed the idea. Maybe he had forgotten about it by the time he did *Everything You Wanted to Know*, but to Irene and Charlie that scene looked very familiar."

"So, what's the third movie?"

"*Waiting for the Light*, with Shirley MacLaine and Teri Garr. Charlie and Irene had turned Irene's Saint Smith story into a screenplay. When they were in California, Charlie pitched that script repeatedly. Years later, this big budget movie came out. A review I see here says, 'a practical joke misinterpreted as a religious epiphany turns a Pacific Northwest backwater into a minor-league Lourdes.'"

"I'm not convinced."

"Well, if you saw the movie, you would be. The flashing light and everything."

"So what happened to them?" asks Marge.

"To Irene and Charlie?"

"Yes. Last I knew, Irene had an abortion and left Charlie. I thought they were getting divorced."

"No abortion. No divorce," says Frank.

"You're kidding. When your Grandmother was dying, Irene told Charlie she had had an abortion, and he was enraged."

"Well, she was lying, and she lied about having had an abortion in Germany, but that's another story."

"Well, what happened?"

"She left Charlie, had the baby, then returned to Charlie a couple years later. She told him that she felt so bad about having had the abortion that she adopted a baby. The kid looked like Charlie, but he believed that was a coincidence."

"Did she ever tell Charlie the truth?"

"Yes, but in such a way that he wasn't sure if she was joking."

"And the kid?"

"His name is Wolfgang. Wolf for short. As far as Wolf knows, he was adopted."

"But why would she do such a thing? That's cruel, never telling their son they were his real parents."

"She sent me a letter explaining her reasons."

"Do you believe her?"

"She told me this lie of hers was a gift to Wolf, a difficult gift to give. She wanted him to know that he was loved completely and unconditionally and that his parents weren't his parents just by the luck of biology. She told me that she fell in love with him the moment she saw him as a baby. When Wolf was college-age and looked just like Charlie at the same age, Charlie finally believed that Wolf was the child he thought had been aborted. But Charlie agreed with Irene that it was good for Wolf to think he was their son by love rather than by birth. Wolf still doesn't know."

"Irene treats people like they're characters in stories written by her."

"You have to admit she's creative."

"Life shouldn't be a practical joke."

"She meant well, and she got lots of people to believe her tales. It was fun to watch her in action."

"Whether she meant well or not, she changed people's lives. She knocked people off course with her lies. That's scary."

"You think that's scary? What if you couldn't remember anything that had happened for the last fifty years?"

"I'd say that calls for memory therapy. Lots of memory therapy."

"At your service, doctor."

***

Over breakfast, they continue their conversation about Irene and Charlie.

"Irene was complicated," insists Marge. "She built some of her stories with layer on layer of lies. First you think she's manipulative and controlling. Then you find out she was being generous in ways you wouldn't have imagined possible. Did any of those letters and notes tell you about Heinrich Schmidt, the sequel to the Saint Smith story and the sequel to that sequel?"

"That's new to me."

"Late one night when Irene and I were at your grandmother's house and Charlie was out with his buddies, Irene got to drinking and talking, and I think she let her guard down and told me the truth. You said you know that she didn't go through with the abortion in Germany. Remember the Saint Smith story she told so often? She played a prank on Heinrich, a fellow student, and he started acting like he was the Second Coming of Christ, and people believed he was. Then Irene confessed she had tricked him into that, and he went back to being like everybody else. Then he was depressed and hated himself and hated Irene, though he was content to sleep with her when the mood struck. And she was in love with him and hoped he'd turn holy again.

"Well, at that point, Heinrich met Ursula. He was working part-time as an orderly at a women's health clinic. Ursula was single and pregnant and wanted an abortion. After the procedure, the doctor told her that, because of complications, she would never be able to have children. She was devastated by that news. Heinrich found her sobbing, curled up on a bench in the hallway of the clinic. He comforted her, brought her home with him, and fell in love with her. For weeks, Irene slept in the living room while Heinrich and Ursula made out in the bedroom. Then Irene learned that she was pregnant and told Heinrich, hoping to win him back. No such luck. Irene moved out and soon after that, Heinrich and Ursula got engaged. Irene considered an abortion. Day after day, she walked to the clinic, then turned around and walked back to the rooming house where she was staying. Then, at the wedding, which she watched from a dark corner in the back of the church, she had a change of heart. When the newly-weds returned from their honeymoon in the Alps, she offered to carry her baby to term, and give the baby to them for adoption. Ursula was ecstatic and grateful. She and Irene became close friends during the course of the pregnancy, keeping careful watch on the development of the fetus. The baby was born, a healthy seven-pound girl. All the paperwork for the adoption was ready. But before the exchange could be made, while the newborn was still in the hospital's nursery, just an hour after Ursula had held her for the first time, the baby died. Sudden infant death syndrome. Ursula was inconsolable."

"God. What a way to end a story."

"The story isn't over. Despite the doctor's diagnosis, Ursula got pregnant soon after that and had a beautiful healthy baby girl, who they named Hilda. Heinrich and Ursula thought this birth was a miracle, and they credited Irene for it. Her loving generosity and the pain of the loss of the baby she had given them had somehow made this happen. They believed that Irene was godlike, that she shone with the light of God-within, as Heinrich once had at her prompting."

"Jesus!"

"To express their thanks, they told everyone, including the daughter herself, that Irene was her mother. They acted as if the original plan had gone through, that the first baby hadn't died, that Hilda was Irene's daughter and that they had adopted her."

"Impossible! How can you believe a word of this outlandish story? A story told you by Irene, of all people."

"Ursula confirmed it to me. I wrote to her, and she replied at great length. It's on my computer."

"And how did you get her address?"

"Charlie and Irene were still in touch with her. Irene had admitted to Charlie that she didn't abort Heinrich's child. She told him what had happened, and that Heinrich and Ursula told their daughter she was adopted, and that Irene was her birth mother. Charlie promised to keep up the pretense for the daughter as well as for the outside world. Over the course of twenty years, the two of them went to Germany for a week or two every year around the child's birthday."

"And the daughter still doesn't know?"

"As of five years ago, when Irene and Charlie disappeared, she still called Irene *Mom* and treated her with love and respect as her birth mother."

"My God."

"But that's not all."

"What more could there be?"

"You remember Wolf, the son of Irene and Charlie who was raised thinking that they had adopted him? Wolf and Hilda, having seen one another many times as they were growing up, fell in love with one another. At that point Irene felt she had to tell the truth that she was Wolf's birth mother and that Hilda was not her daughter. But Wolf didn't believe either of her confessions. He felt special being a child of nurture rather than nature. He understood that with Irene you never know what's truth and what's story. And that feature or flaw of her personality gave him the freedom to choose his own truth."

"This sounds like some eighteenth century novel, where siblings separated at birth fall in love and have incest."

"If you only heard or only believed half the story, that would be the case. Hilda and Wolf thought she was Irene's daughter and that Wolf was adopted. By that reasoning, they were off the hook. As it turns out, Wolf is Irene's son, but Hilda wasn't adopted. Hilda's actually the daughter of Ursula, not Irene. Both ways, it works. As Irene explained it to me in a letter, two lies make a truth."

"Well, what happened?"

"Wolf married Hilda. They live in the Colonial Beach house on the Potomac, with their two daughters—one natural born and the other adopted.

"As for Heinrich, he was a carpenter, then a Jungian psychologist, then a Lutheran minister. When he retired from that, he joined a dance band and played the trombone, like Charlie. Now he and Ursula live on a lake in Bavaria and in the summer, every day at sunset, he stands on his porch, overlooking the lake, and plays his trombone. The acoustics of the lake make it so the music can be heard for miles around. Neighbors look forward to the daily concert and call to make requests."

"Okay. This is making me dizzy. That's enough storytelling," Frank affirms. "The way I see this, we have two targets—we need to check my grandparents' old house. Our last memories were of Grandma's final days there. Then we need to go to Colonial Beach and talk to Wolf and Hilda and try to learn what happened to Charlie and Irene.

"We have nothing else on our plates. We're both retired, and we were each living alone. Money flows automatically into our bank accounts, and we can access it online from anywhere. We don't need to do a damn thing. I'll tell my kids that I decided to travel, open-ended, spontaneous and that I've been wanting to do that for years, and it's high time I give it a try. You can tell your kids that, too. Then they won't worry, and won't think that we too are missing, presumed dead."

"Are we dead? Are we really dead?"

"What would that mean, honey? What does it mean to be alive if it isn't this?" He kisses her and hugs her tight.

29 ~ Vanishing Point

The man at the ticket counter at Logan Airport presumes they are married, even though they have different last names and they aren't holding hands or giving any other overt sign of their connection. There's an aura about them, even when they aren't talking to one another or looking at one another. Their every move is reflected in a move of the other. Without consciously changing their behavior, they look and act like a couple.

At Baltimore-Washington, they rent a car. They'll need it to go to Silver Spring and from there to Colonial Beach. Frank drives, traffic is heavy, and Frank is tense. He freezes every time the GPS voice issues orders. They turn that off, and Marge acts as navigator, using an app on her iPhone to find back roads and avoid major highways. To ease Frank's tension, Marge sings,

"Over the river and through the woods,
to Grandmother's house we go.
The horse knows the way
to guide the sleigh
through the white and drifted snow."

Fortunately, there's no snow. It's a cloudless seventy-degree day, just like the previous two days. When Marge points that out, Frank replies without thinking, "It's unreal how good this weather is." Then he gets an uncomfortable feeling in his gut. "Maybe it is unreal," he admits.

Marge drops the subject, sings the song again, then focuses on the directions.

As Frank gets used to the car and the roads, he calms down, and they converse about this house they're heading toward and the special importance it has for both of them.

They know from Google World that the house in Silver Spring is still standing. In the online photo, the exterior is the same—Black Forest design, stucco with exposed beams and a roof that slopes this way and that, the kind of house you'd expect to chance upon if you were a character in *Grimm's Fairy Tales*. But the chimney is in the wrong place, which makes no sense. Who moves a chimney? Lots can change in fifty years with new owners, but not the chimney.

Their memories of the house were recently refreshed by reading *Sandcastles*. The stone fireplace. The spinning wheels on either side of it. The flintlock rifle displayed over the hearth. The grandfather clock with its Big-Ben gong. The living room where the family assembled to play music together: Grandma Sarah on the piano, Grandpa Carl and Fred on the violin, Russ on the clarinet, and Charlie on the trombone.

Marge notes, "Looking back, the vanishing point where our memories end is in that house—maybe at the fireplace or maybe in the bedroom, where your Grandmother died."

Frank adds, "Yes, if this were a videogame, those would be likely places to look for the door to the next level."

When the owner opens the door, Frank and Marge are shocked. The walls and doors are in different places, and the rooms are different shapes. There's no fireplace. Instead of antiques, the living room has plastic chairs, a large flat-screen TV, and a monstrous black sofa consisting of modules connected in a zigzag pattern.

Frank explains, "My grandfather designed and built this house back in 1927. My wife and I would like to see it again. May we take a look?"

"So you're back. I never expected to see you again."

"Back?"

"Yes, it must have been twenty years ago. But that was an experience I won't forget."

"Excuse me. I've been having some memory problems ... "

"Well, come on in. You're welcome to look around, same as before. I see you didn't bring your camera this time."

"Camera?"

"Yes, I'd expect a video camera this time around. Back then it was 35-mm film camera. Those things were bulky, not easy to haul around."

"That must have been my Uncle Charlie," Frank realized. "We look a bit alike. And Charlie wouldn't go anywhere without a camera."

"Yes, Charlie. Charlie Uhland was his name. He said he was a film maker. He said this house was his family's house when he was growing up. He needed shots of it for some project he was working on. He insisted on proving to me that he was a real film maker and not some con artist. He showed me an animated short he had done. That's why he was so memorable. It's not every day that a stranger comes to the door and insists on showing you a movie he made and gives you a copy. It was damn good work, too. I've watched it and showed it to friends dozens of times. Charlie Uhland, yes. For years when the nominations for the Academy Awards came out, I looked for his name. I figured sooner or later he'd make it. He had such determination. I never met anyone like him. Would you like to see the video?"

"You mean you've still got it?"

"Sure. Whenever I get a new computer, I copy that file from the old one. For me, it's a treasure."

***

The Mirror

A middle-aged man in a business suit is about to walk out of his apartment. He reaches for the doorknob, then halts abruptly. There's panic on his face. He tries again and again, but he can't bring himself to touch the doorknob.

He checks his pockets, his hair, his shoelaces, making sure everything is in order. Something is wrong. He doesn't know what, but he simply can't leave the room until he figures it out.

He turns around and starts checking and straightening everything in sight. But still something is wrong, something he can't identify.

Finally, he turns toward the mirror over his bureau. Once again, he checks pockets, hair, shoelaces. He checks his wallet, his zipper, his tie.

Once again, he halts abruptly. He feels the tie at his collar. Looking down, he sees the tie hanging in front of his shirt. But the image of himself in the mirror has no tie.

His eyes open wide as he looks from mirror to tie to mirror. It's a dull green tie, held in place by a silver-plated tie clasp. It goes well with his gray suit. But it simply doesn't appear in the mirror.

In the mirror, he looks the same as always. His height and build are the same. He'd recognize his face anywhere.

Everything in the mirror is the same as everything he sees on him and around him—the gray suit, the white shirt, the black shoes. Yes, that's certainly his face, with an expression of confusion and fear.

He shuts his eyes, turns around and looks again. Still the image in the mirror is not wearing a tie.

He goes to his bed and lies down again. Then he gets up and walks to the mirror and still no tie.

He undresses, climbs back into bed, gets out of bed again and dresses again, just as before. Then he walks to the mirror—still no tie.

He tests the image in the mirror as if it might not be real. He moves a hand quickly, then both hands, and his head, and hips, and a leg, faster, and faster. The image in the mirror falls at the same moment he falls.

He gets up, smooths his clothes, clenches, and unclenches his fists.

Then he checks his watch, takes a deep breath, and stares again at his image in the mirror.

Finally, he takes his tie off, hangs it with his other ties in the closet, calmly walks to the door, turns the doorknob, and enters the world.

***

"Do you remember anything else about Charlie?" asks Frank.

"He was proud that he had never been to college and had never worked for a major studio. To him, that was a badge of authenticity. He wasn't doing things the way professors and critics said to. He was finding his own way. "

"Did you hear from him after that?"

"I googled him a few times. Once I saw a newspaper article about him as a street artist, in Denver, I think. Chalk on the sidewalk. Performance art. He was quoted as saying that the act of creation was what mattered, not the finished product. He deliberately left his work unfinished. He used a chess clock. When the time he had allotted himself was up, he would stop and walk away. And he liked working in the rain, so his work would be washed away.

"And I found other videos of his online. Silent animation on the early web was a throwback to the days of silent films when the technical limitations of the medium forced you to be creative. Charlie and others used clay for animation—Claymation they called it. There was no money in it. It was art for art's sake. Then computers got faster, and bandwidth improved. One day they were on the cutting edge of technology, and the next they were obsolete."

***

That night in their motel room, Marge joked, "Do you think I'll get pregnant?"

"In this world, who knows. Maybe we'll wake up tomorrow, forty years old, with half a dozen kids."

"That would be sweet."

"Indeed, it would. Any of a hundred alternate lives would be sweet, so long as they were with you."

"How gallant of you."

"I am your knight. And this is your good knight kiss." He flips her over and kisses her from head to toe and up again, lingering at her bellybutton, where he tickles her repeatedly with his tongue.

"What am I going to do with you?" she asks.

"For better or for worse, for richer and for poorer, in sickness and in health, for life after life."

"So we're like cats, then?"

"No, we're not limited to nine lives. There are many rooms in our father's mansion."

"Then we'll have to make love in each and every one of them."

"It's a deal, babe. I'm all in."

30 ~ Life is a Many-Layered Cake

On the four-hour drive to Colonial Beach, Marge took out her laptop, opened the Charlie folder, and took notes. She learns that Irene stayed home to raise their son Wolf, then did volunteer work for social causes and charities. Charlie became the sole supporter of the household, working for corporations—making films for training, recruitment, and trade shows. When videotape came into its own, he started his own business, taping weddings and parties and converting home movies from super-8 to video, and Beta to VHS. Then, when the Internet went public, he launched a few startup companies, none of which took off.

His Old Mill Stream company did custom editing of home-made videos and streamed the finished products over the Internet. Customers paid for his editing and conversion services, and as part of his deal with them he bought the right to include clips from their footage in video creations of his own, telling stories by collage.

Later, his Hear Say company used snatches of random dialogue recorded on city streets to make audio stories.

He also tried a language learning site, Beginning German for Lovers, focusing on the specialized vocabulary of dating and flirting, and using Irene's sexy voice.

Taking notes on her laptop, Marge was frequently annoyed by changes made by the spell checker. She couldn't figure out how to shut it off. She complained to Frank, "Mistakes used to mean something—a misspelling could be a window to the workings of your unconscious. Now mistakes aren't yours anymore. They're random glitches of spell checkers and signify nothing."

Frank joked, "Imagine if God used an automatic correction program on Judgment Day."

When they reach the Potomac, heavy rain falls, and the two of them break out in laughter at how silly they were to worry that the weather was too good to be true.

Wolf and Hilda and their two daughters now live in the family summer house in Colonial Beach. Wolf has a part time job as lighthouse keeper. He and Hilda freelance as web designers. When Frank and Marge arrived, the family was at the beach, building sandcastles.

Many of the old furnishings and antiques from the house in Silver Spring were there, including the mirror from the grandparents' bedroom, the flintlock rifle from above the fireplace, the grandfather clock, the picture of Christ standing behind a young ship's pilot, the photo of Uncle Harry in his World War I uniform on a camel near the pyramids, the three spinning wheels, and the horse's skull and the sketch of it. A snippet of wisdom, in calligraphy and framed, hangs over the front door, "You can't take your time and have it, too."

According to Wolf, Charlie often talked about the cracks in space and time. He experimented with animation and with software that can take photos of two different people and show the one image gradually changing into the other or can show what someone is likely to look like at different ages.

Charlie enjoyed running photo slideshows so fast that the different images blurred into one continuous image. He was fascinated by the cracks and discontinuities in time and space and the illusions by which the mind patches them over.

When they disappeared Charlie and Irene stood on the end of the dock while, following orders, Wolf and Hilda turned on the massive light in the lighthouse and set it spinning so it illuminated Charlie and Irene, then left them in darkness, over and over, faster and faster, until they weren't there anymore.

Irene had said she had terminal breast cancer. Wolf thinks they made a suicide pact. Maybe the current carried their bodies downstream.

***

That night, sitting on rocking chairs on the elevated porch, across from the lighthouse, Frank and Marge tried to make sense of what happened to Charlie and Irene and tried to figure out what they can and should do next. It was a cloudy moonless night and swarms of fireflies provide the only light, flickering on and off in sync with one another, like a strobe light at a high school dance.

"Are we dead?" Marge asks again. "Or are we stuck here in seventy-year-old bodies that are getting older every day? Fifty years of our lives disappeared, and we can't do anything about it. Case closed. Maybe we should move to an old folk's condo in Florida, play cards and golf, and wait to die."

"Whatever happened to us was random," Frank speculates. "We didn't do anything to make it happen. But Charlie and Irene did what they did on purpose. They knew what they were doing."

"Unless Wolf's right, and they killed themselves."

"Look, Marge. You and I know that something weird happened to us. I'm not going to presume that what happened to Charlie and Irene has a simple explanation, or that it has only one explanation."

"Do you think we can get our fifty years back?"

"That's too much to hope for. I doubt that we can go back. But maybe we can go forward. I think that's what Charlie and Irene did."

"And get even older?" asks Marge.

"That's one of many risks. But I'm guessing that there's another level and maybe a level after that, and so on. Maybe there are many rooms in the mansion. I think that Charlie and Irene found a way to get there. Maybe it has something to do with cracks in time and space, like you said. That was Charlie's shtik, with animation and film."

"Maybe. And maybe there's more than one answer. Maybe life's like a multi-layered cake," she speculates.

"You mean life's crumby?"

"Seriously, I mean layers of truth, layers of reality existing at the same time."

"Are you talking allegory? Looking for secret meanings behind everyday events? That sounds lame."

"I mean like the view from the courtyard in the Boston Public Library—he nineteenth century stone edifice around you, and beyond the roof you see the Prudential Center and the John Hancock Tower. The past and the present are both there at once. Or walking around this cottage, littered with relics from three or four generations. Or seeing Wolf and Hilda's girls playing dress-up with clothes their great-grandmother wore. Or like a palimpsest—"

"A what?" asks Frank.

"A manuscript that was written on and then erased and written on again, maybe several times. And traces of the earlier documents remain and can be recovered. Memory is probably like that—earlier memories that are erased to clear space for new ones are never completely erased, and what happens now is perceived and remembered in the context of those earlier layers. Maybe in some sense there are layers of reality, like the river they found a couple miles under the Amazon. Two or more streams running in parallel but at different speeds like streaming video."

"You've lost me."

"I was never comfortable with that old rule of science that the simplest answer is the best answer."

"Occam's Razor?" asks Frank.

"Yes. That doesn't make sense to me. Just because you've found a simple answer doesn't mean that that is the only answer. I believe that sometimes there are layers of truth."

"That sounds like Irene."

"Or Iris," Marge affirms. "Truth may be a rainbow. Many colors in parallel, and all true."

31 ~ The Choice

Frank woke up in the middle of the night and wrote another story, automatically, the words coming to him and he racing to put them on paper before he forgets them. He explains to Marge, "It must have been your talk about allegories and layers of meaning that triggered this. That and Irene's idea that God is in us."

They read it together.

***

The Choice

Frank is in a long winding corridor of a building that looks like a hospital. The man beside him, who is acting as his guide, keeps referring to him as *my lord*. That feels good and comforting. But there is something about this place that reminds him of a recurring nightmare.

He explains to his guide, "I remember the blazing heat, the smell of sweat and excrement. I remember the pain—sharp, like nails pounded through flesh."

"And this place reminds you of that, my lord?"

"In my dream, I was given a choice. I could be born into that world where life was brutal and short, where I would die in nail-sharp pain. Or I could live in another age and another place—this one."

"Well it's hard to imagine that that could be a serious choice, my lord. Who wouldn't want to live in this world, where life is sweet, where many find a vocation that suits their talents and their interests and work that they can take pride in. And through their combined efforts, all benefit from an abundance of goods and pleasures."

"My memory must be failing me. What you say rings true. But I feel disoriented. I feel uncertain of things I should know as well as my name. This world feels less real to me than that other one I dreamt of. In that world most people died by age of forty from accident or war or disease. But I've forgotten, what is the average life span here and now?"

"Over eighty, my lord. Healthcare has eliminated many diseases that used to be fatal. And our world is far safer and more peaceful than that other horrid place and time you dreamt of."

"And forgive me for asking, what do people do with that extended lifetime? How do they spend their golden years?"

"It's interesting that you should ask that, my lord, in this very place."

"What is this place?"

"It's a home for the elderly, my lord."

"A special home for them? They don't live in their own homes or with their families?"

"Here they get special care, my lord. Their meals are made for them, and all the tedious chores of life are taken care of. They benefit from controlled diet and exercise and the very best geriatric healthcare to extend their lives even more. And trained staff are ready to take care of any contingency twenty-four hours a day, seven days a week."

"But what do they do for themselves? What do they do with their time?"

"They watch television. They play bingo and scrabble and canasta and Mahjong and double solitaire. Some read."

"I imagine with their advanced age their bodies must be frail. They must be limited in what they can do."

"Indeed, my lord. many are confined to wheelchairs."

"Like this one?"

"Indeed, my lord."

"It's so nice of you to take me for a stroll like this while I recover from the pain in my feet and hands, the aftermath of that terrible dream. And you are so kind and patient to explain all this to me—facts I should know as well as my name."

"It's no problem, my lord. It's always a delight to talk with you."

"And these people, these elderly in this happy world, while their bodies may be weak and their activities limited, they have their memories to enjoy over and over again, right? That's the reward of a long virtuous life—to remember all the good times and the good friends. Am I right?"

"Yes, my lord, more or less."

"And where does this long winding corridor end?"

"What, my lord?"

"That door we're headed to. All the others we've come to have been double doors that swung open as we approach. But that one is a single door with a handle. And as we get closer now, I see there's a keypad next to it, like a telephone keypad. Yes, my memory is getting clearer now. I remember telephones, now, with touchtone keypads."

"Excellent, my lord, you'll be back to yourself in no time."

"But what's beyond that door? I don't remember."

"Don't trouble yourself about that, my lord. No need to trouble yourself about anything. We'll be in there in a moment. I just need to enter the code."

"The code? You mean that's some kind of lock?"

"Exactly, my lord. You are your old self again."

"Then this is—"

"The Alzheimer's Wing, my lord."

"And I live here?"

"Yes, my lord."

"And I have no memory?"

"It comes and goes, my lord. On a good day, you can remember my name, and your own, as well, my lord."

"But this is a mistake, a terrible mistake. I fell and hurt my feet and hands. I'm in rehab until they get better and I can get out of this wheelchair and go home to ... to ... where did you say I live?"

"You live here, my lord."

"But this is a mistake. I didn't choose this life."

"None of us does, my lord. None of us has a choice."

"But I did. I did have a choice. I was special. I was chosen. I was the son of God."

"We are all God's children, my lord."

"But it was real. The sun was blazing. I was coughing with dust in my throat. I would have done anything for a taste of water. Then I was lying on my back on the ground. My arms and legs were tied to boards. They drove nails through my hands and feet. And when they raised the cross and planted it in the ground, my weight pulled me down, tearing my flesh against the nails. The pain. The pain. And I begged for water. The thirst was almost worse than the nails."

"Here's some nice cold apple juice, my lord. That should make you feel better."

"But there's been a mistake. Take me back. Take me back! Nail me to the cross! Please, God, nail me to the cross instead of this."

***

"I get it," said Marge.

"Get what?"

"You're afraid that if we leave this level of reality, we'll wind up older than we are now, in wheelchairs, with Alzheimer's. I'm scared of that, too. Sometimes I'm scared that that might have happened to us already. All that talk about gaps in time, that reality may be like a scene lit by strobe lights, on and off, over and over again. That makes me think of what it must be like to have Alzheimer's. Clarity, then darkness, alternating, with the times of clarity getting shorter, and the mind having a harder time trying to patch together the pieces of consciousness and give it rational sense."

"We have to get out of here," Frank insists. "The weirdness of this world is getting to both of us."

"And how are we going to do that?"

"Follow Charlie and Irene."

"They didn't leave instructions. And we have no idea what the mechanism is or how it works. Think of the story of the mirror. There are two realities—the reality in the room and the reality in the mirror. The main character is stuck as long as the two are out of sync. To leave the room, to go through the door, he needs to mimic what he sees in the mirror. We have no way of knowing what they saw on the night they disappeared, what they may have been mimicking. But, of course, we should try."

That night they do what Charlie and Irene did. They go to the end of the pier. They launch three ghost bags. Then they signal for Wolf and Hilda to turn on the light in the lighthouse at its brightest setting and to start it spinning, with the beam swinging at them on the pier and past them and spinning faster with every revolution.

They vanish.

Part Four ~ In Search of the Fourth Door

32 ~ Welcome to the Mansion

Complete darkness. A light flashes in the distance. A strobe light. Then multiple strobe lights. The floor tremors. There's a loud crackling noise and the smell of ozone. Flickering lights turn on, and Frank and Marge find themselves in a long corridor. Frank is in a wheelchair. Marge is leaning on a walker. They are old and frail. They hear music that they have never heard before. As the music gets clearer, the flickering stops.

Marge tries to speak. Her tongue is dry and the muscles of her throat and tongue don't respond as they should. She manages to say, "Christ."

Frank replies, "Yes. Christ almighty."

"I mean you. Do you feel like Christ now? Is this your dream come true?" she asks with bitter irony. "Where do you think we'll end up when we die from here? I doubt we can age any more than this."

"Okay, I blew it," he admits. "We should have left well enough alone."

A soldier wearing a World War I helmet comes marching down the corridor, shouting cadence calls, "Give me a left, a left, a left, right, left." He's heavyset, with a handlebar mustache. He looks like Teddy Roosevelt.

He halts abruptly, marches in place, and asks, "You two look lost. Can I help you?"

"Are we dead?" Marge asks back. "Is this the Underworld?"

"That's one theory. Everybody has a theory. I call this the Overworld. I presume you're newcomers."

Frank explains, "First we woke up having lost fifty years of our lives, suddenly older and with no memory of what had happened in those years."

"Did you take drugs?"

"No. That just happened to us out of the blue, randomly. To the two of us, separately. Then we left that world from the end of a pier in the Potomac. We think we went through a crack in time and space."

"That's funny."

"I'd call it freaky."

"I know where you're coming from. I just don't know how it happened that way. I had an experience like yours in Middletown. That's what I call that realm you just came from. Most people come straight to here from Everyday, the place you get to by being born. And they come here by dying. But I woke up in a place that looked like Everyday, only I was thirty years older and I had no memory of the missing years. That was scary, being all alone, figuring out how to cope, without letting people know what I was going through and getting treated like a lunatic."

"And how did you get from there to here?" Frank asks.

"I died. And, as far as I know, the other people who came here by way of Middletown all died, too. Anyway, I'm glad to meet you, very glad. There's a bond I feel with the others who had that same experience—the gap of lost years and the craziness we had to live through after that."

"How long were you in Middletown?" asks Frank

"Nearly forty years. I was twenty in Everyday, then woke up fifty years old in Middletown. Then forty years later, I died and landed here."

"For us, Middletown lasted just five days."

"Both of you?"

"Yes."

"You must have died together in an accident."

"We didn't die. Like I said, we slipped through a crack."

"That's creepy, seriously creepy."

"You haven't heard of experiences like that?"

"Never. Like I said, not many people come here by way of Middletown and, as far as I know, they died to get here. That's a joke we have among us—you can only die twice."

"Then what happens next? What happens when you die here?"

"We don't know."

"What?"

"As far as I know, this is it. End of the line."

"You're sure of that? People don't leave some other way?"

"Nobody disappears, if that's what you mean. The population just keeps growing and so does the Mansion."

"Mansion?"

"This place where we live. The building you're in now. We call it the Mansion because it's so big, with so many rooms and new rooms being added every day to take care of the newcomers, like you."

"Why are we so old?"

"That's random, and it can change without warning. That adds an element of unpredictability to life. Your perspective on yourself and those around you changes all the time. Lots of variety. You'll never get bored here."

"Are there people here from ancient times?"

"Not in this Mansion. The folks here are all from America around the twentieth and twenty-first centuries. And people who knew one another wind up close to one another here, otherwise they wouldn't be able to find one another. This place is huge."

"You mean there's more than one mansion?"

"Of course. There are many mansions in what I call the Big House, and every mansion has many rooms."

"And this age changing happens to everybody?"

"Almost everybody. Some people get stuck in defective bodies and can't move on. And a few find their true selves and stay in one body, like my nephew Charlie Uhland."

"Charlie?"

"He's legendary here. He looks even older than you two. And the right side of his body is paralyzed. And he can't speak."

"Then you are ...?"

"His Uncle Harry."

"Then you're my Great-Uncle."

"Which one are you?"

"Russ's son Frank. And this is my friend Marge."

"Welcome, Frank and Marge. Welcome. Glad to meet you, and hope to meet you again soon. I've got to continue on my constitutional. I've got to keep this body in shape, or I might get stuck in it for another cycle or two. "

33 ~ Tomorrow and Tomorrow and Tomorrow

A young woman in a nurse's uniform comes toward them from the corridor to the right, whistling the same tune as piano music that's playing in the background.

"She looks familiar," says Marge. "Can you make out who she is?"

"All I see is a blur. I must need glasses."

"You're wearing glasses."

"Oh, yes. But they don't help much. I guess I'm beyond help. The Great Beyond isn't what it's cracked up to be."

"Irene?" asks Marge, in surprise.

"Jawohl, Irene."

"But you're young," says Marge "younger than when I met you."

"And who are you? I don't recognize you in that body."

"Marge. Marge Callahan, and this is Charlie's nephew Frank."

"Oh! Marge, dear Marge. I'm so glad to see you."

"We just got here, wherever *here* is. It doesn't feel like heaven. This isn't my idea of heaven—getting old, and weak. I can barely stand using a walker."

"This isn't heaven, Marge," Irene insists. "You aren't dead."

"But we were just talking to Frank's Uncle Harry, and he said—"

"Don't believe a word that man says. He enjoys spinning wild tales."

Frank complains, "This damned wheelchair doesn't have a power button. It's manual. I have to push these wheels by hand to get anywhere."

"That's good exercise," insists Irene. "It helps keep your muscles in shape. Otherwise they'd atrophy, and you'd have problems when you get younger again.

"Younger?" asks Marge.

"Like you said, Marge. I was thirty, about ten years older than you when we first met."

"And now you're what? Mid-twenties?"

"That's about right."

The lights dimmed.

"What the hell is going on?" asks Frank.

"The change. We just had one, and I sense another one's coming soon. It's that kind of day."

"The change? What kind of change?" asks Marge

"Change of life, of course."

"Menopause? I'm afraid that in this body I'm well beyond that," says Marge

"Here it comes again," she says. "The lights are dimming. That's the first sign. Think of it like a thunderstorm, without the rain. It will be over fast."

Complete darkness. Bright lights flash in the distance. The floor tremors. A loud noise crackles. The lights flicker back on. They smell ozone.

"Good God!" exclaims Frank. "I ... we're ... we're all different."

"Yes," replies Irene. "You look about forty now. That's a good age, a good body. You should take advantage of it while you have it."

"Let me get this straight, time moves backwards as well as forwards?"

"No. Not time. Imagine somebody shot film of you at all ages, then randomly spliced the pieces together. Now you're in a young body, now in an old one, now in a young one again. It's still you. Nothing to worry about. You get used to it. But do take advantage when you get a good one like this. I have to go now. There are people waiting for me."

Frank does jumping jacks, then bends down and touches his toes. He hasn't been able to do that since he was a teenager. Marge checks out her shapely full-breasted self in a full-length mirror hanging on the wall. Frank takes hold of her around her waist and lifts her high.

"Russ. Russ!" a woman calls. "Come on over here and say hello."

"My name isn't Russ. I'm Frank. Maybe you mean my father. Who are you? And how do you know Dad?"

"I'm your mother, of course. I mean your grandmother. Grandma Sarah."

"Sarah," exclaims Marge. "But you died."

"So you were fooled, just like the rest of them. I told Carl I was going to pretend to die, but he didn't believe me for the longest time, until he joined me here. You should have seen his surprise. We had such a party with my brother Sam, my daughter Susan. And now you're here, we should celebrate again."

"But I don't understand," Marge insists. "When I saw you last, at your funeral, you were nearly eighty and now you look no more than thirty."

"Yes, that was part of the surprise. Not only am I alive. I'm a young woman again, at least some of the time. And who are you, dear?"

"Marge, Frank's girlfriend."

"Ah, yes, Margaret, dear Margaret. It's so good to see you, and to see you with Frankie, together, really together. And don't worry about the age thing, Margaret. It comes and goes, but you are who you are whatever body you wake up in.

"Have the two of you seen Grandpa Carl? He's building with toy blocks now. Wherever you put him, he ends up building something. That's how his mind works, imagining all the ways things can be put together. An architect by nature. That was his calling, not just a builder. He drew the plans for our house in Silver Spring, you know. The same plans that Fred used for his house in Missouri. He's always shaping the world with his thoughts, giving order to matter, like the Great Architect Himself. And whatever time or tide tears down, he can build back up again following his plans. Yes, the Great Architect. No wonder He wanted His Son to be a carpenter. The two work so well together. The Word and the Word made Flesh. Yes, Carl, dear Carl is down the hall to the left. He's playing with Gwena."

"Gwena?" asks Frank. "Who's Gwena?"

"Your great-granddaughter, of course. Her mother Denise is there, too. She's pregnant again. It'll be a boy this time, they say."

"Just a minute now," Frank began.

"Oh, you're confused. That's only natural for newcomers. Your daughter Brenda's down there, too."

"What you're saying makes no sense."

"Yes, isn't that wonderful? I love the way things get jumbled here. I find it inspiring, in a son-is-the-father-of-the-man sort of way. Go talk to Carl. He and Brenda and Denise need help making castles with building blocks. You could help by distracting Gwena. She's great at knocking them down, but sometimes she doesn't give the grownups time to finish building."

Richard Seltzer

Frank and Marge go to see his twenty-something grandfather, their fifty-something daughter, their thirty-something granddaughter, and their toddler great-granddaughter.

Marge gets down on the floor with Gwena and makes stacks of block two and three high that Gwena can delight in knocking over, while the others build full-scale castles.

"Hello, Brenda, is your mother here?" asks Frank.

"Which one? Evelyn is playing bridge with friends. And Marge is right here. You came with her, right? Are you okay?"

"I just got here, and I'm a bit lightheaded and confused by the change. I'm not used to being a father, much less a great-grandfather. These past few days, I've gone from being young to old and half-way back again. I don't know if I've been dreaming or dying from one world to another. I don't know what's real and what's not."

Brenda laughs. "I know what you mean. Before I figured things out, my head was spinning."

"You mean you understand this madness?"

"In my own way. There's no single gospel truth. Grandpa Carl here gave me the first clue with his designs for castles—sandcastles, block castles, castles made out of anything. Then Grandma Sarah got to talking about God being an architect, not a creator, not making the universe out of nothing, but giving shape and purpose to matter and space. That got me thinking about the architecture of the mind."

"Do you mean like in diagrams showing what part of the brain is for sight and what part for hearing?"

"No. That's the brain, not the mind. The brain is the hardware, the machine that does the thinking. The mind is the pattern of our ideas and memories and how we make associations. I think of it as the operating system, the software that other software is built on. It's the structure of how we think."

"And what does that have to do with this strange world?"

"Everything," she insists. "And it's true of all the worlds, not just this one. Imagine God wrote the basic software of the mind that enables us to think and establishes the ways in which we can think. That's the only reality we can understand because the very concept of understanding depends on it.

258

"Your mind changes over time as you learn and remember and make fresh associations and come up with new ways of thinking. Your body changes, too, as you age and as you youth. But changes in your software are independent of the changes to your body, except in extreme cases, like brain injury."

Marge joins in, "So your mind, all that you remember and how you remember it and how you think, can run on different hardware, in different bodies?"

"We know that much. The body you have now is very different from your body as a child and your body when you are old, and yet you have no doubt that you're the same person."

"So to you, the mind is like what others call the soul. It isn't attached to any particular body. It could move from one body to another?"

"I think that's what happens during the change. Each of us has a set of possible bodies, and our mind moves randomly from one to another."

"Like a kaleidoscope?"

"No. The changes are constrained to a limited number of possibilities. More like a slot machine."

"And this world?" asks Frank.

"I wouldn't call it a world. It's a different mode of being, a different level of understanding within the mind."

"A different layer of the cake," adds Marge.

As they laugh, the background music gets louder.

"It's time for Charlie's performance," says Grandpa Carl. "We'd better get going so we won't be late. Hurry up, Gwena, give these castles a good whack. We'll put the pieces away when we get back."

"Performance?" asks Frank.

"Irene can explain. Here she comes. She knows Charlie's story better than any of us."

Mobs surge forward from all sides, all moving toward the auditorium. Frank takes Marge's hand so they won't be separated, and they keep an eye on Irene and maneuver to get seats near her.

Before the show starts, Frank asks, "What happened to Charlie?"

"He had a stroke," Irene explains. "It left him both helpless and godlike. It brought out the god-in-him. He found a way to connect to others. That connection gives him joy as he gives joy to others. To him, others are him, an extension of himself. He loves others as himself because they are him."

"I don't understand," says Marge. "He can't talk. He can't walk. How can he connect to anyone?"

"Between arthritis and the effects of the stroke, he can't unwrap a piece of candy, but he plays the piano beautifully, not other people's music, but his own, spontaneously, improvising."

"But Charlie didn't play the piano," insists Frank. "The trombone was his instrument."

"Most but not all of us go through the change from one body to another. In some cases, a defect in one body prevents moving on to another. And the trauma of the change sometimes triggers a stroke. A therapist here was interested in using music for stroke recovery and for boosting the quality of life of stroke victims. She sat Charlie down at the piano, and with his left hand he tinkled the keys, getting used to what keys make what sounds, and enjoying the sound of each key. Then he experimented with chords, getting used to which notes harmonize with which others. Then he added his right hand, despite the damage from the stroke. He improvised, savoring the sounds, in a dreamlike state, surprised by the sounds his fingers were creating, making music on the fly, as surprised and pleased by the music as the people who heard him. The therapist started recording his performances and posted them as podcasts. Then online radio stations asked for the privilege of streaming his music live whenever the mood strikes him to perform.

"I help as best I can, stringing together pieces that seem to belong together and sometimes overlaying two pieces that work well in harmony. This way, we make new composite creations, like we used to do with cellphone videos and random bits of sound, film, and video that Charlie collected over the years. Charlie lets me know when it's right and when it's not and has me try different combinations. His face is very expressive.

"Now Charlie thinks music. Music is his natural language. He has devoted followers. Billions listen to his music. I believe it helps them feel at peace with themselves, to reconcile the different selves they have been over the course of all their multiple lives."

34 ~ Getting It Right

After the performance, Irene leads Marge and Frank to Grandma Sarah's room, where she's sitting at an electronic piano, playing, and singing the Bob Dylan song *The Times They are a Changing*. From that she glides into a tune or her own and the words:

"The change is coming
I can feel the change
Big change
And small change
Monnaie
Monet
Monai
My father's house has many mansions
It goes through many changes.
Such is life
And after life
And after birth
What on earth?
How you have changed."

"When she sees Frank and Marge, Sarah calls, "Susan! Where are you, Susan? Come meet your nephew and his bride-to-be.

"I'm afraid you just missed her," she continues. "Susan doesn't have a room of her own, after all this time. She says she doesn't want one. She's so social, visiting here and there and everywhere. Everyone's her friend. Everyone welcomes her. But that means you never know where she might be, and she's often out of ear shot. She was here a little while ago. It's a shame you missed her. It's a shame you missed her, too, before, in your other lives.

"Now she's off again. It's something in her nature, I suppose. But it does bother me to lose her like this, and there's no telling where she's gone this time. But I have faith we'll be together again, eventually. It's happened before. I'll happen again. Only it's such a shame you missed her. You never had a chance to get to know her. She has such a way about her, like Irene and like Charlie now. She brings out the best in you. She helps you find your true self. Maybe that's why I miss her so, aside from loving her so much. When I'm with her, I feel at peace with myself and with the world.

"Never mind," Sarah continues. "We'll all be together some day. Savor the moments you have while you have them.

"I love this part of the Mansion. The chandeliers." A chandelier appears above her and lights up brightly. "The magnolias just outside the window." A window appears and opens, and the scent of magnolia blossoms fills the room. "I love having a room of my own, where I can do everything I ever wanted to do.

"Things are so easy here. People are not so easy. You can't expect people to pop up out of nowhere whenever you want them. Maybe the person you want to see wants something else just then or even wants something else forever. Do you believe in four-ever? Four is such a lovely number, like the number of the house I grew up in back in Plymouth, New Hampshire. Some say there's a fourth door and the rooms on the other side are to die for, so to speak.

"Welcome to 1234. I loved it when Carl gave our house in Silver Spring that number. It was visionary doing that. Ours was the only house on the street when he built it. But that number helped me to see the street as it would be, filled with houses and the houses filled with people, and the people filled with love and joy.

"One, two, buckle my shoe.

Three four, open the door."

A door opens beside her. Frank and Marge walk through, and it closes behind them.

They find themselves in Grandma Sarah and Grandpa Carl's bedroom in the house in Silver Spring. In the full-length free-standing mirror, they see family pictures on the bureau and on the walls and on all surfaces. They see the fading funeral photo of Susan, the aunt who died before Frank was born, the horse's skull from Russ and Fred's legendary prank, still shots from *The Pictures of Charlie's Wedding*, and words of wisdom in ornate calligraphy, "You can't take your time and have it, too."

The bed is made as Grandma Sarah always made it, with a dozen pillows in bright-colored pillowcases stacked by the headboard on top of a Pennsylvania Dutch quilt. A spinning wheel is standing by the door of the closet. It's a real spinning wheel, not a reproduction, but it had never been used as intended. It was made at the time when store-bought thread was becoming cheap and readily available. It gathered dust unsold in a carpenter's workshop for decades. It was bought as a quaint decoration. Later it was varnished and cherished as an antique. Of all their antiques, Grandma was most proud of the spinning wheels—this one in their bedroom and the two others near the fireplace in the living room. Sarah jokingly told visitors that the spinning wheels once belonged to the three Fates. When the choices of what people could do with their lives expanded, when people could meet and marry who they liked, rather than just who their parents chose, when they could make their own decisions about careers and the places they would live, the Fates became as obsolete as matchmakers and buggy whips. They retired and now live in an old folks home, playing canasta and sharing the gossip of the ages with other residents.

When Frank and Marge look in the mirror, they see the room as it was when last they were there. But when they look around them, the room is nearly empty.

That the room exists is a shock to them. They know that the house was gutted, and all the furnishings were removed, including the spinning wheels, which went to the three sons.

They look at each other, then they look again in the mirror.

The only furniture in the room itself is the mirror and an end table that used to be by the bed, when there was a bed. On the table lies Grandma Sarah's engagement ring.

"God," Frank mutters softly as if he doesn't want to wake a sleeping dragon. "Where are we?"

"And when are we?" asks Marge.

"I mean where are we in the mirror? I don't see us in the mirror."

He takes hold of her left hand.

She breaks from his grip, and says loudly, "I hate your guts!"

"I love you, too," he says and takes her hand again.

Their image begins to form in the mirror—first their outlines, then their bodies, then their faces.

In the mirror, they are twenty years old.

In the mirror, they see themselves hugging, then kissing, and Frank picks up the engagement ring, goes down on one knee, and puts the ring on her finger.

In the room outside the mirror, they mimic what they see in the mirror: Frank takes the ring, goes down on his knees, puts the ring on her finger, and asks, "Will you marry me?"

"Maybe we can get it right this time," she says with a smile.

Suddenly, the room itself has all the furnishings that before had appeared only in the mirror, everything in its proper position. And, as in the mirror, they are both twenty years old.

They hear children running and laughing in the hall, and Rachel imploring them to settle down and show respect for the dead. Charlie tells the kids to run and laugh again and tells Rachel to reprimand them again so he can capture the scene on film.

Hand in hand, Frank and Marge open the door and walk out into a familiar world, ready to lead a new life.

About the Author

Richard now lives in Milford, CT, where he writes fiction full-time. He worked for DEC, the minicomputer company, as writer and Internet Evangelist. He graduated from Yale, with a major in English, went to Yale grad school in Comparative Literature, and earned an MA in Comparative Literature from the U. of Mass. at Amherst. At Yale, he had creative writing courses with Robert Penn Warren and Joseph Heller.

His published works include: *Parallel Lives* (published by All Things That Matter Press), *The Name of Hero* (historical novel), *Ethiopia Through Russian Eyes* (translation from Russian), *The Lizard of Oz* (satiric fantasy), and pioneering books about Internet business. His web site is seltzerbooks.com

Made in the USA
Monee, IL
02 August 2020